SMUGGLERS'
SUMMER

SMUGGLERS' SUMMER

Carola Dunn

Walker and Company
New York

First published in the United States of America in 1987 by the Walker Publishing Company, Inc.

Published simultaneously in Canada by Thomas Allen & Son Canada, Limited, Markham, Ontario.

Library of Congress Cataloging-in-Publication Data

Dunn, Carola.
    Smugglers' summer / Carola Dunn.
        p.   cm.
    ISBN 0-8027-0976-1: $16.95 (est.)
    I. Title.
PR6054.U537S68   1987   823'.914—dc19   87-18348

Printed in the United States of America

10 9 8 7 6 5 4 3 2 1

SMUGGLERS' SUMMER

=1=

SIR TRISTRAM YAWNED.

Undoubtedly it was highly gratifying to be permitted to escort the season's most eligible Beauty about the town, with no other chaperone than her package-laden maid. However, the Honourable Julia Langston seemed to be on the friendliest terms with half the Ton. Their progress up Bond Street was interrupted constantly as she stopped to greet acquaintances, a large proportion of them admiring gentlemen of all ages.

Sir Tristram, though he was twenty-seven, equally admiring and generally envied, longed for the peace of his quiet library at Dean Park.

A glance at the cloudless sky disappointed his hope of an April shower to persuade his beloved to seek shelter in his carriage. When they were married, he vowed, he would keep her all to himself in Gloucestershire.

"Do you not think so, Sir Tristram?" enquired the matron with whom she was presently exchanging civilities.

"By all means, ma'am," he said hurriedly, wondering to what he was assenting.

Miss Langston, her pale gold ringlets dancing beneath her bonnet, looked up at him with the enchanting smile which had made him decide that if he must marry, this was the wife for him.

"Pray excuse us, ma'am," she said. "I have still one errand and must not try Sir Tristram's patience."

"Too late, child, I fear. But he will certainly forgive

1

anything for the sake of your pretty face. My compliments to your mama." She acknowledged Sir Tristram's apologetic bow with a stately nod and sailed on.

"What did she say," he demanded.

"That the new fashion for fuller skirts and quantities of ornament vastly become my figure," replied Miss Langston primly, her lips twitching. "I daresay that she expected you to enlarge upon the compliment, not to pass it off with 'by all means, ma'am.' "

Sir Tristram flushed. "I beg your pardon. I fear I was woolgathering."

"No matter. I assure you I do not mean to tease. Why, here we are at Hookham's already. Now, what was the name of the book Mama desired me to borrow for her? I have it here somewhere."

Miss Langston paused before the bow window of the library to search her reticule. Sir Tristram watched her. The elaborate walking dress of cerulean blue Circassian cloth, trimmed with two rows of darker blue flounces about the hem, did indeed set off her tall, willowy form. He ought to have remarked upon it. He wondered momentarily whether some wool from his own sheep might have gone into the making of it, and whether he might turn a phrase upon the possibility.

A volume in the window behind her caught his eye.

"A new edition of the *Georgics!*" he exclaimed. "Shall we go in?"

As the baronet opened the door, the pale spring sunlight flooded past shelf after shelf of books to illuminate the farthest corners of the room. Half hidden in an alcove, a plump young woman, dark-haired, in a gown of plain grey stuff, raised her head from the book in her hands and blinked brown eyes at the new arrivals.

Cousin Julia! she thought. *With one of her beaux. I hope she will not see me, or I shall scarce have time to finish the chapter before I must go.*

She watched as a pair of assistants vied for the honour of

2

serving her cousin, then returned to her book. Engrossed in the adventures of Rob Roy, she did not look up again until she heard a clear soprano voice close beside her.

"Octavia, how delightful to meet you here!"

"Hello, Julia." Looking past her slim, elegant cousin, she saw that the young gentleman who had entered with her was deep in discussion at the counter. "Has your escort abandoned you?"

"In favour of Virgil! Alas for my vanity!"

"He is handsome enough to have more regard for his own vanity than for yours. We are agreed, are we not, in preferring dark hair in a man, and those artful curls set off his broad forehead to admiration."

"Not artful, I think. Look at his dress. It is perfectly proper but without any of the latest quirks of fashion."

Octavia studied the young man's well-cut brown coat and buckskin breeches, boots gleaming but without white tops, and neat but plain neckcloth. "True. No dandy he. I noticed particularly when he entered that he is some inches taller than you."

"Is it not gratifying? Do you recall Lord Aldridge?" Julia giggled.

"Was he one of the gentlemen who offered for you last season?"

"No, no, my dear. It is my belief he was never able to forget that when I danced with him I could not but see how his hair was growing thin on top."

"I remember now. We thought in kindness to revive the fashion for wigs! Has this gentleman yet made so bold as to ask for your hand?"

"Not yet. But I am certain that if he comes up to scratch, Mama and Papa will favour his suit. He is rich enough to buy an abbey."

"Do you like him?"

"Well enough, I daresay, to marry him. Papa was so indulgent as to let me reject several unexceptionable offers last year, but I am turned nineteen, remember. Last year I was known as an Incomparable. This season I am merely an acknowledged Beauty. I cannot wait forever to fall in love."

"No, indeed! As an elderly lady of twenty I can only commend your resolve. How shocking it would be to come unmarried to a third London season!"

"You are a great tease, Tavy, but I promise you I should not consider him as a husband were there anything about him to give me a disgust of him. There is not, which is more than I can say for most of my beaux. It is only that . . ."

"Hush, he is coming. Pray do not feel that you must introduce us." Octavia was suddenlly aware that the stain on her skirt was still faintly visible in spite of all her scrubbing, and that her bonnet was so unfashionable as to be positively dowdy.

"Of course I shall. Allow me to make known to you Sir Tristram Deanbridge. Sir, my cousin, Octavia Gray."

"Your servant, Miss Gray." Sir Tristram bowed politely. With a glance at the volume in her hand, he added, "I see you are a lover of books. May I beg you to plead with Miss Langston to forgive me for my disgraceful neglect?"

"I will not, sir, for I can think of nothing to say in mitigation of so heinous a crime. And besides, I must be on my way." Regretfully she returned Rob Roy to his shelf and picked up her basket.

"You do not take your book with you? If it is too heavy a burden, pray allow me to take you up in my carriage. It is close by."

To her annoyance, Octavia felt her cheeks grow pink. "Thank you, sir, but I do not care to take the book today, nor to put you out of your way to carry me home." She knew she was being ungracious, but to acknowledge her poverty to Julia's rich suitor was more than she could bear.

"I shall see you on Thursday as usual?" asked Julia.

"Yes, cousin, if you are not otherwise engaged." She

bobbed a curtsey to Sir Tristram and hurried past him towards the door.

A group of fashionable ladies was entering at that moment and she was forced to wait. She glanced back and saw Sir Tristram, head bowed, listening gravely to something Julia was whispering to him. Julia waved to her, and she flushed again as she realised her good-natured but sometimes indiscreet cousin was explaining her behaviour. She looked away quickly, dreading to catch the gentleman's eye.

The doorway was clear; she stepped outside into the bustle of Bond Street.

"Miss Gray!"

Octavia turned at the hail. A lanky young man, carelessly dressed, with yellow handkerchief knotted about his throat, was half running to catch up with her.

"Mr Wynn!" She smiled as he came up to her and bowed, removing his hat to reveal an unruly bush of reddish hair.

"Are you on your way home? May I accompany you? I am going to see your father about Brougham's speech."

"Have you written another? I understand your last was a great success. Papa said he had never heard a better in all his years in the House."

"Thanks to Brougham's delivery. What a speaker! I am proud to work with him."

"I am sure he values you as he ought. Have you not been promised a safe seat at the next election? There is certainly a great future ahead of you and I daresay we shall see you Prime Minister if ever the Whigs return to power."

"You are too kind, Miss Gray."

They were still standing outside Hookham's as they spoke. Octavia was about to suggest that they move on when the door of the library opened and Julia emerged with her suitor. They were too close to be ignored, and indeed Julia came straight up to her. Mr Wynn stepped back politely.

Octavia hesitated. Her father's colleague, though a gentleman, was by no means a member of the fashionable world. Moreover, he was not merely a Whig but a Radical Reformer, while Lord Langston, Julia's papa, had sat firm on the Tory bench since inheriting his viscountcy. It would not do, she decided, to introduce them.

Her cousin had other notions.

"Who is your friend?" she asked, regarding with interest his almost Bohemian dress and thin, clever face. "Will you not make us acquainted?"

Reluctantly, Octavia performed the introduction. Sir Tristram bowed slightly, looking thoughtful.

"James Wynn?" he murmured. "The name sounds familiar." He turned to Octavia. "Miss Gray, I beg you will not be offended if I offer you a small token of my regard for you as Miss Langston's favourite cousin, which she assures me you are." He pressed a piece of paper into her hand.

Octavia looked at it in surprise. It was a receipt for the payment of a year's subscription to Hookham's Lending Library. Choked with embarrassment, she thrust it back at him, muttering, "I cannot accept this, sir!"

"You are not to consider it as a personal gift, if you please." His strong fingers closed her trembling ones about it. "If you cannot accept it as a result of my admiration for Miss Langston, take it as a small contribution towards the Encouragement of Literacy. Surely there must be a society for such an excellent purpose!"

"More likely, for the Suppression of Illiteracy, sir, for I have frequently noticed that the vast majority of charitable societies are more concerned with suppressing the bad than encouraging the good!"

"Come, that's better," Sir Tristram said with a laugh. "You will keep it then? Believe me, you do me a favour. It will be a source of satisfaction to me whenever I sit down to read, to think that through my agency you are able to do likewise."

"You are very kind, sir." She raised her eyes to his face, but he had already turned back to Julia, who was by now engaged in animated conversation with Mr Wynn. A wave of envy swept through her. Not only beautiful, wealthy, wellborn, her cousin was also blessed with an effortless charm, an instinctive interest in people which made all those she met her friends. The bemused look on the young politician's face made it plain that here was yet another conquest.

"James Wynn—I have it!" exclaimed Sir Tristram. "Did you not write an article lately in the *Edinburgh Review?* And that not your first, I think."

"I had that honour, sir."

"Brilliant, but inflammatory! Miss Langston, I have kept you long enough from your mama. My carriage awaits on the next corner. Your servant, Miss Gray."

Wistfully, Octavia watched them walk up the street. The maid followed a pace or two behind with her neatly wrapped parcels, doubtless containing kid gloves and silk stockings, perhaps French lace and velvet ribbons.

She shifted the heavy basket on her arm, and tucked the precious subscription into one corner, between the beetroot and the saddle of mutton. It was too late now to go back into Hookham's.

"Do you dine with us today, sir?" she asked Mr. Wynn. "I have been to market myself this morning, since Betsy has leave to visit her sick mother."

James Wynn's eyes lost their glazed look as he returned to the present.

"Mr Gray was kind enough to invite me," he confirmed. "If it does not inconvenience you, with your maid away?"

"Not in the least. You know that I am always prepared for a multitude of guests." She sighed. "If it is not Papa's political acquaintances, it is Mama's charity committees. Or simply family. You must know that I have seven brothers and sisters, most of them married and with families of their own."

"Let me carry your basket," offered Mr Wynn, abashed. "It looks to be heavy."

On the way to Holborn, he interrogated her about her cousin. By the time they arrived at the narrow terrace house he was despondent.

"She is too far above me in every way," he said moodily. "Even if her father were not the greatest reactionary alive. I must put her out of my mind."

"I own I should think it wise." Octavia's voice was gentle. "It was wrong in me to have made you known to her, when I am aware of the effect she has on gentlemen."

"She mentioned that you take tea with her on Thursday afternoons, and walk in Hyde Park if it is fine?"

"I do. But for your own sake, Mr Wynn, I trust you will not lurk in the park on the next fine Thursday in hopes of encountering us. Julia is incapable of snubbing you, as I am afraid my aunt would think she ought, and another meeting could only add to your distress." She opened the front door, stepped into the dark hallway, and turned to relieve him of her basket. "Will you go up to Papa? I must take this to the kitchen."

He caught her hand and raised it to his lips in a gesture unusually graceful for him.

"You are right, Miss Gray, and kind withal. Yet I see her bewitching face still as though she stood before me. I shall go up."

Octavia repaired to the kitchen, buttered and ate a couple of slices of bread, and started peeling potatoes.

A few minutes later the doorbell rang. Wiping her hands on her apron, she admitted two Members of Parliament and a political agent.

It was very amiable of Julia's baronet to give her a library subscription, she thought, but what she really needed was time to read!

=== 2 ===

TWO DAYS LATER, shortly after noon, Octavia set off for Chapel Street. It had rained in the morning, so though the sun now shone she wore a light cloak over her best dress of lavender silk, and pattens on her feet.

The streets were muddy but the air was fresh and clear after the showers. On an impulse, she spent a penny of the shilling in her pocket on a posy of violets from a hawker. As she walked, sniffing now and then at their sweet scent, she tried to imagine spring in the country, with flowers blooming in the hedgerows instead of lying in squashed bunches in an old woman's basket. Waiting to cross Oxford Street, watching the endless stream of carts and carriages, she pictured green fields spreading into the distance, inhabited only by placid cows.

The noisy crowd on the corner rushed forward, hustling her across between a phaeton and a lumbering stagecoach with twelve passengers packed onto its roof.

The streets of Mayfair were somewhat quieter and cleaner. The clicking of her pattens echoed between the elegant façades of the town houses of the wealthy. Turning into Chapel Street, she saw ahead the still-bare trees of Hyde Park and glanced up at the sky. There were a few high, puffy clouds, but with luck the sun would shine until she had persuaded Julia out for a stroll.

The Langstons' stout, dignified butler, who could wither an encroaching mushroom with a glance, beamed at her benevolently.

"Fine day, miss," he offered, taking her cloak and bonnet and beckoning a powdered footman in olive green livery to help her remove the pattens. Miss Gray was a prime favourite with him, ever since she had shared her lessons with Miss Julia. Nothing to look at, he admitted to himself, but always polite and considerate to the servants, though she knew how to keep her distance. Miss Julia, otherwise a paragon of perfection, was apt to be a tad too familiar. Of course it was only her friendly heart, God bless her.

"Miss Julia's in the blue drawing room, miss, and her ladyship with her."

"Thank you, Raeburn. You need not show me up." Octavia shook out her skirts and trod up the wide marble staircase.

Her aunt greeted her fondly but languidly.

"Come in, my dear," she murmured. "How does my sister go on, pray?"

Octavia always found it hard to believe that Aunt Millicent and her mother were sisters. Lady Langston seemed to have been permanently exhausted by the effort of bearing her single child, while Mrs Gray had produced eight offspring and gone on to make a career of founding and managing charities for every purpose under the sun.

Julia had been brought up by nannies and governesses, Octavia by her older siblings. Sharing the last of the governesses, they had grown as close as possible for two girls leading such different lives.

"My mother is very well, I thank you, Aunt."

"Tavy, do come and look at this pelisse in *Ackermann's*." Julia was sitting by the window, studying a magazine. "It is trimmed with ruby velvet, with a bonnet of the same; is that not a charming conceit?"

Lady Langston sighed faintly. "I must call on Mrs Burrell," she said, rising with Octavia's assistance. "She was kind enough to say last night at Almack's that you was a pretty-behaved female, Julia. A pity that you do not practise your manners on your family. I shall see you at dinner, or do we dine out this evening?

"At the Overtons, Mama, and then to the play. Papa goes with us."

Her ladyship sighed again, and made her way out of the room.

"Don't talk to me of clothes, Ju," begged Octavia. "This gown is montsrous tight about the waist and cannot be let out further, I vow."

"You are growing excessively plump," said her cousin, regarding her critically.

"I know! But when I spend the greater part of my time organising meals and entertaining my parents' acquaintances, it is horridly difficult not to eat too much."

"You ought to dine on biscuits and vinegar, as Byron did. Never mind, I have a hundred dresses you are welcome to, as I have told you time and again."

"And all by far too fine."

"But Tavy, you have worn that lavender silk every Thursday and Sunday these two years! Surely my aunt realises that you need a new one!"

"Mama thinks the money better spent on clothing the South Sea Islanders, and Papa mutters ominously about giving up politics and returning to the law. It is all I can do to wheedle a new stuff gown for daily wear now and then. And you know that I was unable to go to parties with you last year because they would not allow me to accept any of your 'frivolous garments,' as well as because of their dislike of the Haut Ton. It is a matter of principle with them."

"I shall find you something sufficiently sober in my wardrobe. Let us go and look at once."

"I am so much fatter than you that I doubt it would take a month to alter anything to fit," Octavia replied gloomily, following Julia out.

"Nonsense." Julia turned as she reached the landing and regarded her plump cousin. "I appear slimmer because I am taller. I'll wager we need only turn up the hem."

"Later perhaps. I should like to go to the park while the sun is shining."

Julia acquiesced. In a few minutes, cloaked and bonneted, they were sauntering down a gravel path, attended by a footman. There were a number of strollers about, and even one or two carriages, but it was not yet the hour of the fashionable promenade and they met no one they knew.

On oak and elm leaf buds were swelling. Soon the park would be fresh and green for a few brief weeks, before the city's dust and soot cast their dingy pall.

"Is the country like this?" asked Octavia. "Only more of it?"

"Not really. It is . . . oh, it is just different. Though of course I only see it in the summer; I have not been at the Priory in the spring since I was a child. It must be very dull, because all one's friends are in town. I wish your mama will allow you to come with us this summer, so that you might satisfy your curiosity. We always have lots of guests and it is the greatest fun."

"I am very sure she will not. You always have such grand company at the Priory that I know I should need as much finery there as here in London, to go about with you."

"But my aunt need not see it. I have plenty for both; they need be at no expense. I must and will ask again for your company."

"I fear your pains will be for nothing, as they were last year and the year before. I am reconciled to remaining a dowdy city dweller, so let us not speak of it further, if you please, Ju dear. How delightfully the daffodils spread beneath those trees! Now tell me, we were discussing your latest suitor when we were interrupted. You had just reached 'It is only that . . .' when our subject appeared to silence you."

Julia grimaced. "It is only that . . ." she repeated. "You will think me quite puffed up, Tavy, but he does not seem to me quite so devoted as I have been wont to find my suitors. You saw him detached from my side by a new edition of Virgil. That has not been the only instance of a mind easily distracted from the contemplation of my perfections!"

"How very shocking! But surely this is a sign that he is a serious gentleman. How often have I heard you castigate as mere fribbles the majority of those who court you! To have attached a gentleman who has more in his mind than the latest fashion in waistcoats or which horse is to win at Newmarket, is certainly no mean triumph."

"I am far from sure that I have attached him. And besides, I have a horrid feeling that when he says he prefers to spend his time in the country he not only means it, but does not include large house-parties of congenial acquaintances among the pleasures of country living. However, I daresay I shall have him, always supposing he should come up to scratch."

"He will scarce offer for you if he is not in love, and being in love, how can he deny his bride a house in town and as many guests in the country as she should care to invite? Only lack of means could excuse that and you say he is well-to-do."

"Rich as Croesus."

"He seemed both amiable and generous. I daresay you might come to love him, would you but try."

"Do not you start to sing his praises! I hear nothing else from Mama, I vow. Let us turn down this walk beside the Serpentine. I love to see the swans. Oh, look, Tavy, is that not your friend Mr Wynn?"

James Wynn's lean figure was indeed rapidly bearing down upon them. Octavia was dismayed to see that he had on a new coat and a snowy white cravat, neatly if not exquisitely tied. She could only put it down to a desire to impress her cousin.

He doffed his well-brushed hat and bowed bashfully as he came up, but would have passed on without speaking had not Julia addressed him.

"Mr Wynn! What a charming surprise!" She cast a

mischievous glance at Octavia. "We were saying but a moment past that we were sadly in need of male company. It is beyond anything fatiguing to walk without a gentleman's arm to lean on."

"Pray take my arm, Miss Langston!" he offered with incredulous delight. "I am happy to be of use. Miss Gray, my other arm is at your service."

"Thank you, sir, I am made of stronger stuff than my cousin." Octavia was annoyed with both of them. She felt herself responsible for their meeting and knew very well how strongly her aunt and uncle must disapprove. Still, it seemed highly unlikely that the ardent reform politician and the indulged, frivolous daughter of a Tory peer should have a great deal to say to one another.

She listened in growing consternation as Julia questioned the young man about his articles in the *Edinburgh Review*. She sounded positively fascinated! And when they went on to catalogue mutual acquaintances, it was alarming how many they found. Not all her father's colleagues despised the fashionable world, apparently. Mr Wynn and Miss Langston might be sure of meeting at balls and routs and breakfasts if they only made the effort.

Left out of the conversation, Octavia was the first to notice that the sky was no longer a benevolent blue. A sudden breeze shook the branches of the nearby trees and a few heavy drops fell, splashing in rippling circles into the Serpentine. The cloud blew over but there were others, darker, behind it.

"Julia, it's going to rain. We must hurry back."

The footman, who had been following several paces behind, stepped up and offered a huge black umbrella. Mr Wynn unfurled and raised it, and they retraced their steps towards Park Lane.

By the time they reached that grand thoroughfare, the rain had abandoned all attempts to disguise itself as an April shower and was coming down in torrents. A gusty, chilly wind make it difficult to keep the umbrella upright, and blew the moisture in beneath it. When they reached Lord Langston's house in Chapel Street, the footman was soaked and the other three all decidedly damp.

Mr Wynn cursed himself for not turning back sooner, and vowed never to forgive himself if Miss Langston should catch cold. He took his leave at the foot of the steps, refusing, to Octavia's relief, Julia's pressing invitation to come in and dry himself.

Raeburn swung the door open before they reached the top of the steps.

"Miss Julia, you'll catch your death," he cried. "Come in, come in quick, Miss Gray. Henry, whatever were you about to let the young ladies get so wet?"

The footman, dripping miserably on the marble floor, muttered an indistinguishable excuse.

"You must not blame Henry," said Octavia quickly. "It was entirely our own fault."

"See that he changes his clothes at once, if you please, Raeburn," added Julia, "and has something hot to drink."

Henry's expression lightened to something approaching worship as he gazed at his young mistress.

The butler hurried him off to the servants' quarters. "I'll see to it at once, miss," he assured them, "and I'll send the tweeny up to light the fire for your chamber, for you'll want to get into something dry right away, and Cook shall send hot soup up as soon as she can have it ready."

"Thank you, Raeburn, and pray do not tell her ladyship that we received a wetting. She will be quite sure I shall develop an inflammation of the lungs."

"My lips are sealed, Miss Julia," he promised.

"You see," said Julia with considerable satisfaction as they mounted the stairs, "you will have to accept one of my gowns, and a nice warm pelisse too, for yours will never dry before you must leave. I'll call up every maid in the house that can wield a needle. It will be done in a trice. Only come and choose what you will have."

She ran lightly up the second flight.

Octavia could not repress feelings of envy as the entire wardrobe of a fashionable young lady was opened before her. Walking dresses of Circassian cloth and mull muslin, trimmed with blond lace and embroidery; satin slips with overskirts of spangled gauze or *crêpe lisse* in pink and pale blue and primrose; in pride of place hung the *grande toilette*, white silk sewn with seed pearls and tiny silver roses, which Queen Charlotte's death the year before had rendered useless before it was ever worn.

"Here is the very thing!" exclaimed Julia, pulling out a promenade dress of canary yellow jaconet ornamented with pale green ribbons. "There is a matching bonnet somewhere, too. Ada will find it."

"Aye, put away in the attic, I doubt," said her abigail severely. "You never did wear that outfit, Miss Julia, for it's quite the wrong shade, but 'twill suit Miss Gray's colouring to perfection."

Octavia gazed at it wistfully but shook her head. "That hue is by far too gay for my needs," she said. "It will grow dingy in no time. Have you nothing darker that you can spare?"

Ada, a red-cheeked, middle-aged woman whose grim face hid her absolute devotion to her mistress, riffled through the row of gowns.

"There's the dark blue," she offered, "though with your dark hair and brown eyes, miss, 'tis not the best colour. Or this grey figured silk that Miss Julia wore when her great-uncle died and left her all that money. There's a pelisse goes to it, of lutestring as I call to mind, grey and white striped. Aye, here it is."

"It is certainly more practical. But can you spare it, Ju?"

"Certainly. I have no more rich great-uncles waiting in the wings."

"Let me take your measure, miss. 'Twill be done in two shakes of a lamb's tail."

In her petticoats, a large, warm shawl wrapped about her shoulders, Octavia watched the abigail bear the gown and pelisse off to the sewing room, and with them a grey velvet bonnet with white ostrich feathers which needed new ribbons. She joined her cousin by the fire.

"It is very smart," she said with a sigh, "but at least the colour is unobjectionable. Mama would have accused me of setting up for a Bird of Paradise in that yellow. She has worn black as long as I can remember."

"Enough to give you the megrims. Octavia, is Mr Wynn often at your house?"

"Often enough for Papa to wonder whether he might take his last daughter off his hands."

"Oh, no, cousin, has he indeed shown a decided preference for you?" Julia was horrified.

"Not in the least. Nothing beyond common courtesy. He knows how to make himself pleasant in company, and as he is younger than most of Papa's friends we have seen a deal of each other. I do not consider him as a suitor, I assure you. Nor ought you, my dear, for he has certainly no more than a modest competence which must be quite unacceptable to the family of an heiress."

"Fustian! I did not look to hear *you* talk so. I have enough for two to live on in perfect comfort, so why I should marry a fortune I cannot understand. I suppose you will not call Mr Wynn a fortune hunter?"

Octavia laughed. "No, no. I acquit him of that. He has less interest in money even than Papa, who you know gave up a lucrative legal practice to enter politics because he thought it his duty to fight for the oppressed."

"That is just how Mr Wynn feels. I had never considered, but he says most gentlemen in politics are looking out chiefly for their own interests, or at least those of their class. He instanced Papa's support of the Corn Laws."

"Certainly Lord Langston, with his vast acreage of arable land, must benefit largely from the Corn Laws. On the other hand, why should not Mr Wynn oppose them if he does not?"

"You are too cynical, Tavy. I am convinced Mr Wynn acts only from principle."

"Let us not quarrel. Tell me who danced with you at Almack's last night."

Julia allowed herself to be distracted and regaled her cousin with descriptions of her partners and with the latest gossip. Octavia listened with interest, but was on the whole glad never to have been displayed at the Marriage Mart like a prize heifer at an auction. Not that it would have been of the least use, for even if she had paraded before the cream of the Ton dressed in cloth of gold, none of the gentlemen would have given her a second glance.

Just as she was reaching this lowering conclusion, not for the first time, Ada returned with the grey silk over her arm.

" 'Tis all tacked up, miss," she announced. "If you will try it on, I can check the fit."

Octavia cast aside her shawl and stood obediently still while the maid slipped the gown over her head and buttoned it up. It was a little tight about the bust, though less so than her old dress. When she mentioned it, Ada assured her that the seams were wide enough to let out.

"Stand straight now, miss, while I check the hem." There was a knock on the door. "Ah, there's the pelisse. Bring it in then, girl. Hold still, Miss Gray, while I stick a pin here, and another here. Now the pelisse. Turn around, if you please. No, don't look in the looking glass till we're all done. Off with it all, now. I've five girls working on it, Miss Julia. Give me another half an hour."

"You can stay half an hour, can you not, Tavy? You must. Since clothes are our subject, tell me why Mr Wynn dresses so oddly? Has he not enough income even to dress with propriety?"

"I should be surprised if he even notices what he is wearing, in general. His mind is on matters of greater import."

"He admired my gown most particularly."

"Oh, dear, he must be more smitten than I'd have thought possible after only two meetings. Pray do not encourage him, Ju. He is not the sort to take a flirtation lightly, and there can be no hope of anything more."

Julia fell silent, gazing into the flames. Octavia lounged back in her chair and enjoyed the unaccustomed sensation of doing nothing. Rain still beat against the window panes. She would have to take a hackney home, and that would save enough time to allow her to go by Hookham's and borrow a volume of *Rob Roy*. On Thursdays, being the day she visited Julia, she was not expected to help at home, so there would even be time this evening to read a little, if she could escape early from her parents' inevitable guests.

All too soon, Ada returned with the altered garments.

"I took the liberty, Miss Julia, of adding this goffered lace down the front," she said, draping the skirts to fall gracefully over Octavia's petticoats. "Very slimming, I think, and I'm sure we have a hundred yards of it about the place."

Julia laughed. "True. I cannot resist lace and cannot use half I buy. How do you like it, cousin?"

Octavia was gazing at herself in the mirror. "It's beautiful," she breathed. "I don't know if it's the lace, or just that it is well cut, but I do look a little thinner. Do you not think so?"

"Definitely. Now only think what the yellow would do for you! I wish you will take it."

"I must not. Let me try the pelisse."

The grey and white stripes were still more flattering, and the plumes on the hat added an impression of height. Octavia twisted and turned in front of the glass, studying her reflection from every angle.

"It might almost be worth going on a diet of biscuits and vinegar," she said at last. "I never thought I could look so elegant. Bless you, Ada." She dropped a kiss on the surprised abigail's cheek. "Will you ask Raeburn to call me a hackney? I shall go home in style today."

=3=

THE NEXT TWO Thursday mornings brought notes from Julia with apologies for being otherwise engaged in the afternoon. Octavia was not surprised. The exigencies of fashionable life not infrequently interrupted their long-standing arrangement.

She seized the opportunity to visit Hookham's, retiring with her spoils to the chamber she had once shared with two sisters but which was now all her own. *Rob Roy* finished, she started on *The Heart of Mid-Lothian*, and discovered the novels of Miss Jane Austen.

Absorbed in her books, and thinking about them when she was not reading them, she found the constant coming and going in the little house in Holborn less irritating than usual. It was easier to resist the temptation to nibble, and though she did not go so far as to try drinking vinegar, she managed to eat less at the endless dinners her parents provided for their acquaintance.

She took in the seams of her new dress where Ada had let them out.

By the third week, the first Thursday in May, she was anxious to see her cousin. She wanted to discuss what she had read with her only intimate friend, and she had missed their walks in the park.

She donned the grey silk, so far worn only to church. Her mother had not even noticed the addition to her wardrobe. It was a sunny day, the sky a clear, pale blue,

20

but the breeze was cool enough to make the pelisse welcome.

Before putting on the bonnet she tidied her hair before the mirror. What would she look like, she wondered, if she had the dark masses, so heavy and difficult to manage, cut short in one of the new styles? Her cheeks were a little thinner, but too pale, almost sallow. She pinched them to give them some colour. Brown eyes gazed into deep brown eyes and she shook her head at herself. No use dreaming of being as beautiful as Julia, but it was amazing what a difference a pretty dress and a few lost pounds made.

Julia was distrait. She listened with half an ear, could not decide whether she wanted to walk in the park, and made no comment on Octavia's appearance.

Octavia decided sadly that the improvement she had detected must have been imaginary. She could not make out whether Julia was in a pet, in the mopes, or in alt. Sometimes a dreamy smile crossed her lips, sometimes her eyes filled inexplicably with tears, and once or twice a frown creased her smooth forehead.

"Are you unwell?" Octavia asked at last. "I have never known you behave so oddly. Perhaps you have a fever."

"Am I behaving oddly?" Julia blushed. "I beg your pardon, dear cousin. My thoughts are wandering, but I will call them to order and attend to what you are saying, I promise. You are reading *Sense and Sensibility*? A delightful book. I quite dote on Jane Austen."

"I told you that at least half an hour ago. Will you not tell me why you are so agitated?"

"I am so happy, Tavy! And so miserable. No, do not press me. I cannot, indeed I cannot talk of it now. I know what your advice must be and I do not want to hear it! Forgive me. Pray say that you forgive me, and let us go to Hyde Park at once. You will not tell Mama?"

"Of course I forgive you," said Octavia, adding reluctantly, "and I will not tell Aunt Millicent if you swear that you are not ill."

"Not in the least."

"But, Ju, whatever you suppose my advice would be, you know that if you are in the briars I will do everything in my power to help you."

Julia hugged her. "I know. I'm not in trouble, not yet. Is it cold out? Wait here a moment while I put on my cloak."

Puzzled and alarmed, Octavia was forced to be satisfied with that meagre reassurance.

The following week, their meeting was again cancelled. Octavia had hoped to persuade her cousin to confide in her; she wrote to her, pleading for an explanation.

Six days passed before she received any response. A footman in the familiar olive-green Langston livery brought a sealed package, and announced that he had orders to wait for an answer. He condescended to grace the kitchen with his presence, an honour which set the Grays' cook-maid "all of a flutter."

Octavia was in something of a flutter too, as she ran up to her chamber. The package was both larger and heavier than a mere letter might explain. With trembling fingers she opened it.

There was an almost indecipherable note from Lady Langston, begging her to come at once. She could not make out where she was to come to.

There was a line from Lord Langston, enclosing thirty guineas to pay the fare of herself and her abigail to Plymouth.

But she had no abigail, and why was she to go to Plymouth?

And lastly there were several pages in Julia's hand, liberally sprinkled with blots which, she decided as she read, must be caused by tears.

"Dearest Octavia,
   "Your unhappy cousin has been Banished to the dreary wilds of Cornwall. Oh say you will come to lighten my Exile! You are the only Com-

panion my unrelenting father will allow. Little does he know how closely concerned you are in my Downfall, for I have not told him, and Never shall, that it was you who introduced me to my beloved James!"

Octavia paused to admire the style. She had never guessed that Julia had such a turn for the melodramatic. So James Wynn was at the bottom of the mystery. No wonder her advice had not been wanted: it had already been given. She read on.

The rest of the first sheet detailed the growth of Julia's attachment to Mr Wynn. Remembering the waiting footman, Octavia skimmed over the list of supposedly chance encounters, followed by clandestine meetings attended only by Ada.

"All this time," the letter continued, "Sir Tristram Deanbridge grew ever more particular in his Attentions until, the evening before I saw you last, he asked Papa's permission to address me. I told Papa I must have time to consider. He strongly urged Sir Tristram's suit, and but for James I believe I had accepted him without ado. He is everything one might look for in a Husband, but I do not Love him!

"Papa gave me a week to make my decision. James was Eager to approach Papa in his own behalf but I Dreaded the event and persuaded him to wait. The day came; I told Papa I did not wish to marry Sir Tristram. He asked, did I hold him in aversion? No, said I, but I cannot love him! What is that to do? he asked. You will come to love him after you are married. You do not whistle such an offer down the wind for so feeble a reason!

"Alas, I Weakened! I confessed that I loved Another! How he Stormed when he learned the Object of my Affections! He called my Beloved a

Fortune-hunting Scribbler, a Revolutionary, a Penniless Coxcomb, and many other Names, while your Unhappy cousin was an Ungrateful girl who would bring her father's grey hairs to the Grave.

"I will not weary you with all the Ranting and Tears. Suffice it to say that I am sent down to Cotehele, in Cornwall, an ancient and isolated house belonging to Papa's relation, the Earl of Mount Edgcumbe. There is no Road hither but the river; I have no companion but Mama, who is laid down upon her bed with the Palpitations since we arrived yesterday; my Beloved I have not seen since that Dreadful Day and he knows not where I am.

"It is given out that I am on a repairing lease in the country, being worn down with the gaieties of the Season. I promised Papa that if he permitted me to write to you, I would not ask you to pass any Message to James, but oh! it breaks my Heart to think that he may suppose I have Cast him Off!

"Dearest cousin, do not leave me to fall into a Decline alone in this Dreadful place. There is no Society here that my aunt might object to. Pray come, Tavy, if you love your Unfortunate

Julia."

There was one more missive, a twice-folded sheet addressed to "My Sister Gray" in Lady Langston's hand. Octavia sat tapping it against her hand as she thought.

Her immediate impulse was to go, if her mother should permit. However desolate Julia's prison, it was in the country, buried in it apparently, and she longed to escape from London. She did not believe that her cousin would go into a decline. Her character was too sensible and sanguine to indulge in such foolishness. But she was certainly unhappy, and with only a lachrymose and indolent parent present she would have nothing to do but dwell on memories of Mr Wynn.

It was the outside of enough that James Wynn had pursued Julia, being perfectly aware that he could never be an acceptable son-in-law to Lord Langston! She had no sympathy with him. Nor did she see how Julia could prefer him to Sir Tristram Deanbridge. It was all excessively unfair to poor Sir Tristram. If she went down to Cornwall she might succeed in persuading her cousin to regard with favour the baronet's manifest advantages of manner, person, and estate.

She took her aunt's billet to her mother.

"I am sure I cannot make head or tail of Millicent's writing," was Mrs Gray's first, acid response. A tall, heavy woman with a commanding countenance, she gave an impression of overflowing energy even while seated at her escritoire.

"She wishes me to keep my cousin company in the country, Mama. My uncle has sent thirty guineas for my fare."

"Thirty guineas! One might decently clothe half the natives of Senegal with thirty guineas! Where are you to travel to with such a sum? Paris?"

"Only into Cornwall, Mama. His lordship supposed I should take a maid. It will certainly not cost half so much, but I cannot think I am at liberty to donate the excess to the natives of Senegal."

"Hoity-toity, miss! These gentlemen born hosed and shod have no notion of the value of money, the way they squander it."

"May I go, Mama? I have never been into the country, and I so long to see it. I am assured that they will not be receiving visitors. It will be quite different from the summer house-parties at the Priory."

Mrs Gray peered at her sister's letter, then gave up. "As you wish, child," she said indifferently. "You are old enough now not to have your head turned by catching a glimpse of society, and I daresay you will come to no harm travelling alone on the stage. Betsy can certainly not be spared to go with you, you know."

"I know. Thank you, Mama. I shall manage very well on my own."

"It will take four days, I suppose. You will not wish to travel on the Sabbath, so you will wait until Monday."

"Very well, Mama, but I must go and write my acceptance at once." Octavia curtsied, kissed her mother's offered cheek, and almost skipped out of the room.

Apart from such practical matters as what to pack and where and when to catch the stage to Plymouth, the only problem remaining was whether she ought to get a message to Mr Wynn, and if so, what it should be.

There was no difficulty in reaching Mr Wynn: he came to dinner the next night, looking thoroughly blue-devilled and scarcely opening his mouth, either to speak or to eat. Octavia could not bear to see him so despondent. She had no wish to encourage his pretensions, but she went so far as to say that Julia's absence was not voluntary. He brightened at once, only to sink again in gloom when Octavia would not provide her cousin's direction.

He spent the rest of the evening expatiating upon Julia's perfections, so that by the time Octavia retired to bed she was altogether out of patience with him.

Unearthing a small trunk in the attic, she discovered that every garment she possessed fitted into it, making choice unnecessary. She packed on Sunday, keeping out only the drab stuff gown and heavy cloak she would wear for travelling. With mounting anticipation she called Betsy to help her close and rope the box. A hackney had been ordered for five o'clock the next morning, and there was nothing left to do but try to sleep in spite of her excitement.

The great day dawned bright and clear. The hackney arrived on time and the driver carried down the trunk. Mr and Mrs Gray arose betimes to wish their daughter a safe journey, and Mr Gray went so far as to press a guinea into her hand "for any little necessaries you do not care to be beholden for to his lordship."

Octavia arrived in good time at the Belle Sauvage Inn on Ludgate Hill. Her name was on the waybill, so she had no difficulty obtaining a seat inside the coach, but to her disappointment she was not next to the window. As the huge vehicle rumbled out of the yard, the coachman crying "Mind your hats!" to his twelve outside passengers, her view was almost completely blocked by the stout farmer on her left and the positively enormous woman on her right.

She deeply regretted not being able to see the country-side, but at least for once in her life she felt positively slim.

It soon became apparent that this mode of travel did not agree with her. Her companions all talked ceaselessly in loud voices, and as none of them cared for fresh air, the atmosphere inside the coach soon grew stale. At the frequent halts, there was no time to descend to stretch her legs. When at last they stopped at an inn for luncheon, her soft voice was lost in the hubbub of the coffee room and she managed only a sip of scalding tea and a bite of bread and butter before the coachman herded everyone back aboard.

As the long spring day wore on, she found she was developing a headache, a rare occurrence with her. By the time dusk fell and the stage rattled under an archway, to new shouts of "Mind your hats!" followed by "Everybody off!," she was so relieved she could not have cared less what town she was in.

A bowl of soup and a comfortable feather bed sent her off in good spirits the next morning. She had the window this time, and for a full hour enjoyed the sight of the bare, rolling hills of Salisbury Plain, their short grass scattered with grazing sheep. Then it began to rain. The glass misted over and she was once again confined to a jolting box.

At nine o'clock in the evening of the fourth day, the coach rolled into yet another rain-washed inn yard. Octavia was helped down by a stalwart young Customs lieutenant who had been entertaining her, or so he believed, with tales of the sea since Exeter.

"Well, here we are in Plymouth," he said, suddenly bashful. "I've to report to my ship, but I shall be free tomorrow. I'd be honoured, miss, if you'd allow me to show you round the town and the dockyards."

"Thank you, Mr Cardin, but I shall not stay here longer than I must." Octavia passed a weary hand across her forehead. "The sooner I reach my friends, the happier I shall be. I suppose you cannot tell me how to get to Cotehele?"

"Cotehele? Lord Edgcumbe's house? Your friends reside at Cotehele?" His voice was incredulous as he took in her travel-worn appearance.

"Yes," she said with some irritation. "If you cannot help me, I expect the innkeeper will know." She turned away to watch the coachman unloading her trunk from the roof.

"I beg your pardon, miss," stammered Lieutenant Cardin. "Of course I know how you may reach Cotehele, only I do not precisely know the tides at the present. You there!" He hailed an ostler. "When does the tide turn?"

The man looked at his uniform and grinned. "Tides is your business, Mr Revenooer. Hosses is mine."

"There's not an inn servant in the town couldn't tell you precisely when the next cargo of run brandy is due," muttered the lieutenant, looking harassed. "But you are tired, miss. Pray come inside and sit down while I make further enquiries."

He offered his arm. Octavia took it gratefully and he ushered her into the inn. He saw her seated on a wooden settle in a quiet corner of the coffee room and went to find the landlord. She leaned back, closed her eyes, and relished the feeling of being stationary.

Mr Cardin returned in a few moments.

"The innkeeper was more cooperative," he said with satisfaction. "They like to keep on the right side of the Customs. The tide has just begun to ebb, so low tide will be in six hours or so, say three o'clock in the morning. There's a barge, the *River Queen*, leaving Phoenix Wharf, heading upriver. It'll carry limestone but mine host says Captain Pilway's not averse to taking on passengers. Unless you care to hire a boat?" Again he looked doubtfully at her shabby dress.

Octavia touched her purse, where twenty-three guineas of the thirty still remained. "How soon could I get there if I hired a boat?" she asked.

"No sooner. Nothing goes up the Tamar without a flood tide. But it would be more comfortable for you."

"I shall do very well with the limestone." She was after all her mother's frugal daughter, she thought with a sigh. "I'll send a message to Captain Pilway. Thank you, sir, for your help. I believe I shall take a room here and rest until it is time to go."

He flushed. "I took the liberty of ordering a pot of tea," he confessed. "I believe you are burned to the socket and my mother says there is nothing better than tea to perk you up. And if you will not think me encroaching, I shall return at half past two to show you the way to the Phoenix Wharf."

For the first time she noticed that he had nice eyes, dark blue with a rather sad, doglike expression.

"Thank you, sir. You are very kind, and at that horrid hour it will be reassuring to have a friend present." She smiled at him.

He bowed awkwardly over her hand, and strode out.

The tea was vastly welcome, still more so the small but neat chamber where she sank into a troubled sleep without undressing. She was called at two, tidied herself as best she could with the aid of a single candle and a small square of mirror, and went down to the silent, half-dark coffee room. The drowsy maid who had woken her offered to fetch bread and cheese or cold meat, but she settled for another pot of tea and some biscuits.

These last she nibbled at and then slipped into her

pocket. She was cold with the chill of the small hours of the morning. The tea was reheated, black as pitch and bitter as aloes, but it warmed her hands and she swallowed some with an effort.

"Summon's coom for thy trunk," the maid announced, covering a yawn with her hand.

Octavia went out into the passage and found a skinny, wrinkled little man carrying her trunk out to a two-wheeled barrow. An oil lantern burned smokily above the door, but more light came from the full moon, sailing in the starry night sky. It had stopped raining at last.

Quick footsteps sounded in the street and Lieutenant Cardin turned into the yard. He had doffed his uniform, and without its anonymity he seemed more of a real person, if anything was real in this strange, pale world. Wordlessly, Octavia took his arm and they set off, followed by the rumbling of the iron-wheeled barrow.

"This is the Barbican," he said in a low voice as they entered a maze of narrow streets. "It is the oldest part of the town, and rather picturesque. I wish I could show it to you by daylight."

She murmured a response. They were walking downhill now, and the damp air smelled of seaweed, fish, and tar. They turned a corner and were on the quay.

A burly man stepped out of the shadows.

"Miss Gray?" he queried in a voice so deep it might have been Neptune's. "Cap'n Pilway at your sarvice. Take care wi' thet chest now, Joey. This way, if you please, ma'am."

Mr Cardin pressed her hand warmly. "Let me know that you are arrived safely," he whispered. "A note to the New Customs House will find me. Good-bye!"

"Good-bye. And thank you."

She followed Joey down a long, slippery flight of steps, open to nothingness on her right. Captain Pilway's hand on her elbow steadied her. The plink and gurgle of water grew closer until she could see a long shadow lying alongside, moving gently up and down. A two-foot-wide abyss, inky black and crossed by a single plank, separated the steps from the restless barge.

"Tom?"

"Aye, cap'n. All's well."

The captain picked her up with two hands about her waist and lifted her across as if she weighed no more than a feather.

=4=

BEYOND THE SHADOW of the quay the moon shone bright on Plymouth Sound, silvering the ripples and whitening the swirling wake as the sailing barge took the breeze. The Barbican, the Citadel, and the Hoe loomed as dark masses and the opposite shore of the estuary was a black line between sea and sky.

Seated on a neat coil of rope, Octavia leaned back against her trunk and wondered if she was dreaming. The creak of the wheel, manned by the silhouette of Captain Pilway; the slap of bare feet on wood as Joey and Tom moved to adjust the square sails; the rush of water against the hull: all these were as foreign to her as the salty tang of the air blowing in her face.

"Warrum enow, miss?" queried Tom, materialising beside her.

She pulled her cloak closer about her and nodded; then, not sure if he had seen, said, "Yes, thank you. How long will it take to Cotehele?"

"Ah," he said, and slipped away again like a shadow.

To judge by the gleaming path of the setting moon, they were headed south of west. Octavia thought back to her geography lessons. Surely the Tamar flowed into the Channel from the north? For a moment she was alarmed: had she fallen among white slavers, or ruffians of some other ilk? But Lieutenant Cardin would not have handed her over so calmly had he anticipated danger, and Captain Pilway had been perfectly polite.

There must be all sorts of navigational hazards to be avoided, she realised with relief. The island they were passing on their right, for instance, was probably surrounded by rocky reefs. The Eddystone Lighthouse was somewhere near Plymouth, she thought, and the coast of Cornwall was noted for shipwrecks.

As they rounded the island, she saw a larger ship rocking on the water a few hundred feet off, its single mast bare. The barge approached it, slowing as the sails were furled. A dinghy put off from the stern of the sloop.

"Ahoy there, *River Queen!*" came a low hail.

"Ahoy, *Seamew!*" Captain Pilway called back, his deep voice hushed.

The dinghy drew alongside, the rowers shipping their oars; a giant of a man stood up in it and gripped the rail of the barge. Captain Pilway went to him and they held a whispered consultation. Octavia thought he turned his face in her direction for a moment, but in the moonlight she could be sure of nothing.

The giant said something to his men, passed up several small packages to the captain, and then heaved himself aboard. He dwarfed Captain Pilway, himself by no means a small man. The two retired to the stern to talk, while the rowers lifted several barrels over the side into the barge. Joey and Tom rolled them aft, and Joey started lashing them together with rope.

"Right, boys!" called the big man. The dinghy cast off and headed back towards the sloop.

Sails raised, the *River Queen* turned north.

The new passenger made his way forward and stopped beside Octavia. Squatting down so that his face was nearer her level, he saluted her.

"How do you do, ma'am," he said in an educated voice, removing his cap and running his fingers through his thick hair. "Captain Day's the name, Red Jack Day. You're bound for Cotehele, I hear."

"Yes," stammered Octavia. "I—I am going to stay there with friends."

"I'm heading that way myself. You're no Edgcumbe, though, are you?"

"No. My friends are related to the Edgcumbes. Are—are you a smuggler, sir?"

"Best not ask, little lady," he said grinning, his teeth white in the moonlight. "Those who don't know, can't tell. You've seen some interesting goings-on tonight, eh?"

His tone was friendly, not in the least threatening.

"Are you not afraid I shall tell someone?" Octavia ventured.

"There's nothing the Revenuers can do unless they catch us with the goods and by the time you found someone to tell, those'll be long gone. Suspicions don't hurt us; there's not a captain nor a ship doesn't run goods now and then. Were you planning on turning us in?"

"No, I suppose not. My father says the duty and excise tax laws make very little sense."

"Then your father is a sensible man. You're not from these parts?"

"No, from London."

"Ah." He settled back more comfortably on his haunches, swaying slightly with the roll of the boat. "Then allow me to point out the sights. Sun'll be up soon."

The eastern sky paled over Plymouth even as the moon set behind rolling hills in the west. On the slope overlooking the Sound stood a mansion, barely visible in the near darkness. That was Mount Edgcumbe, said Red Jack Day, seat of the second Earl of Mount Edgcumbe and home of the Edgcumbe family since the house was completed in 1553. There was an odd pride in his voice, as if he shared in the reflected dignity of the ancient line.

On the other side was St Nicholas's Island, sometimes known as Drake's Island. As they cleared it and the light grew, Octavia saw a bewildering swarm of shipping, from dinghies to men-o'-war, sailing in various directions or anchored in the maze of inlets which led off the sound. Red Jack pointed to a particularly busy area: Devonport, the Royal Navy docks.

Somehow Captain Pilway chose among the various waterways, and soon the river narrowed. There were low hills on either side, a patchwork of fields and woods, with occasional villages and quays. The sun rose in a sky streaked with pink and crimson clouds, turning the water the colour of blood. They passed Spanish Steps, then the river divided again and narrowed still further.

Steep, wooded cliffs alternated with wide beds of reeds, yellow tipped with green, as they followed the twisting Tamar upstream, the rising tide fighting and overcoming the opposing current.

"Nothing much to see till we reach Halton Quay," grunted Captain Day. He rose to his feet and stretched. His hair caught the sun's low rays and Octavia saw that it was flame-red, fading to straw at the temples. "I'll try for a couple of hours of sleep before we arrive."

Warm in the sun, Octavia drowsed.

She was roused by a shout. There was a tiny chapel on the left bank, a few cottages, and some extraordinary stone structures, square and solid-looking, with huge half arches at the base.

Tom was pointing at a washing line hung with clothes. It looked quite unremarkable except, perhaps, for a scarlet petticoat at one end.

Red Jack yawned, rubbed his eyes, and sat up. He made his way forward and sat down beside Octavia.

"Halton Quay," he said. "That spectacular garment is a sign. According to whereabouts on the line it hangs, it even tells who is watching and where. That's a Riding Officer, I believe, at Cotehele Quay. I don't work this way myself, so I'm not certain of the code.

"A Riding Officer?" she asked.

"That is what the Customs call their inland excisemen."

"So the petticoat is a warning! What are those extraordinary arches?"

"Limekilns. We're carry limestone now, in the hold there." In the well amidships huge baskets of broken rock were neatly stacked. "Throw limestone and coal in the kiln, fire it, and out comes quicklime. It's used as a fertiliser. Excuse me, ma'am, I'd best go lend a hand."

The crew of the *River Queen* had pulled a pile of sails off the mysterious barrels from the *Seamew*. With Red Jack's assistance, they slung them from the bulwarks then, at a sign from Captain Pilway, pulled on a couple of knots and let the whole string of a dozen or more slide into the river.

Brandy, thought Octavia. They must be sorry to lose so much.

Captain Day returned to her side, grinning.

"They'll pull 'em up with grapples some day when the red flag's not flying," he explained. "The rest of the stuff's small enough to hide where no Riding Officer will find it. But I've a little something here for a pretty young lady, if you've somewhere about yourself to conceal it."

She blushed as he handed her a small, flat package, wrapped in oilcloth.

"There is an inside pocket in my cloak," she said. "Will that do?"

"Aye, they'll not search a guest of the Edgcumbes. Another bend or two of this confounded snaky river and we'll be there. Give me the open sea any day."

He lent her a huge paw as she struggled to stand. Stiff from her awkward position, she still ached in every joint after four jolting days on the stage. She stowed the package in her pocket, and felt for the comb she kept there.

It was gone. It had probably fallen out when Captain Pilway had lifted her aboard, but at least her heavy purse was still there. Tiredly she pushed a few loose curls behind her ears. She would not have been able to do much without a mirror anyway.

Red Jack was standing in the bow, gazing upstream. She picked her way forward to join him. They were passing a tributary stream on the left, half hidden in·reeds. Beyond it, dead ahead as the river curved right, was a flat stretch of bank with three stone quays and a number of buildings, including more huge limekilns with smoke rising from their tops.

"Cotehele!" announced the smuggler with satisfaction as the barge swung wide to head directly into the small dock. "Will there be someone to meet you, miss?"

"No. They have no idea when to expect me."

"It's not far up to the house but it's a steep walk. If you care to wait below I can send someone to fetch you."

"If you are walking up the house, I shall go with you. It will be good to stretch my legs. Will you think me impertinent if I ask what business a smuggler has at Cotehele?"

Red Jack flushed. "I'm courting the housekeeper," he muttered, suddenly shy. "Ever since she was parlour maid at Mount Edgcumbe. She won't have me till I change my profession and I won't quit free-trading till I've a fortune to support her with. It's been a long time, but it won't be much longer."

"I beg your pardon, I *was* impertinent!" cried Octavia penitently. "It was none of my business."

"The whole world knows," he said wryly. "Well, here we are. Let me help you ashore."

Several men had appeared from one of the buildings, an inn bearing the sign of the Edgcumbe Arms. There was much shouting and bustle as the *River Queen* was tied up and they prepared to unload with the aid of a hand winch on board and a derrick on the quay.

Suddenly a tall, thin, elderly man in uniform pushed through the crowd, followed by a pair of beefy troopers.

"In the King's name!" he shouted in a high, rather squeaky voice. "Every basket is to be inspected as it comes ashore. Slowly, now."

"I've a cargo of fruit on the Lower Quay that's waited for in Plymouth," said Captain Pilway angrily. "Ye may inspect what ye please when 'tis all off my ship."

They stood face to face, arguing loudly. Red Jack quietly directed a couple of men to carry off Octavia's trunk, and swung her lightly over the side, following her onto the quay.

"The Riding Officer," he explained. "He'll have a hard time inspecting tons of limestone. We'll be off."

He waved to the men with the trunk to come after them, and they edged round the jeering crowd. They were a few feet beyond it when the Riding Officer noticed them.

"Halt, in the King's name!" he cried. "I know you, Red Jack Day, and I'll see the contents of that trunk, if you please."

The men parted to let him through and he came strutting forward to face Octavia. She drew herself up, her chin raised.

"The trunk is mine," she said icily. "I am Miss Octavia Gray, a guest of the Earl of Mount Edgcumbe."

He looked somewhat disconcerted, but a glance at her appearance revived his officiousness. "You expect me to believe that?" he said with scorn. "Unlock the chest at once!"

"You may apply to his lordship for my credentials." Octavia quaked inside. "I do not think my lord will be best pleased if you strew my undergarments about in public. Come, Captain Day."

The crowd roared with laughter as she stalked off, Red Jack at her heels. The two men picked up the trunk and followed, leaving the Riding Officer purple-faced and gaping like a fish.

"Well done, ma'am," said Red Jack. "You could not have carried that off more coolly had the box actually been filled with contraband."

"Do you know," confessed Octavia, "for the moment I was quite convinced that it was!"

They passed a grey stone lodge and started up the hill. Long before they reached the top Octavia was glad to lean on the captain's arm. She walked in a blur of fatigue, unable to appreciate her surroundings in the least, aware only of the effort to be made to put one foot in front of the next again and again and again.

The ground levelled off at last, and Octavia revived enough to notice a horseman coming towards them.

"Jack Day!" the rider hailed her companion from a little distance, in a vaguely familiar voice. "Come to visit the fair Martha, are you? Who is this you have brought with you?"

"It's Miss Gray, sir. She's a guest here. I ought to have left her below though, to wait for the carriage. The poor lass is worn to the bone, I fear me."

"Miss Gray? Good God, so it is! You look fagged to death, ma'am, and in no fit state to walk farther. Jack, raise her up to me and I'll carry her in."

Too tired to protest, Octavia allowed herself to be lifted into Sir Tristram Deanbridge's arms and sank back against his shoulder.

=5=

WHEN OCTAVIA AWOKE, she had not the least idea where she was. She lay in a four-poster bed with golden silk draperies. The room was tiny, hung with faded tapestries and furnished only with a pair of chairs, besides the wide bed. There was a large window, where a shaft of rosy light from the setting sun slid between closed curtains.

Suddenly ravenous, she hoped she had not slept through dinner.

She sat up, feeling a little light-headed. Doubtless a meal would solve that. She could not remember when she had last eaten properly. Her dressing gown, a depressingly shapeless object of dun-coloured cloth, lay on one of the chairs, but she decided to stay where she was for the moment and see what would happen if she pulled the bell-rope by the bed.

Lying back, she tried to remember her arrival at Cote-hele. A smile curved her lips as she recalled the scene at the river and her saucy but successful rebuff of the Riding Officer. After that, everything was blurred. Had she dreamed that Julia's suitor, Sir Tristram, was there? An unknown woman's voice had said in worried tones that the ladies were yet abed, then she had been set down gently outside a door and Ada had helped her into a room. Yes, Ada, Julia's abigail, and Julia had been in the room, sitting up in a vast bed.

She had caught sight of herself in a mirror; that she remembered clearly. A horrid sight, dirty-faced and hollow-cheeked, her hair escaping from its braids in all directions, her cloak and gown grimy and torn. And she had been ashamed at her first meeting with Sir.Tristram to have a small stain on her skirt! He must think Julia's cousin was little better than a ragamuffin. He *had* been there, she was sure of it.

Of undressing and changing into the lawn nightgown she now wore, she had no recollection.

There was a tap on the door and Ada came in.

"You're awake at last, miss," she said with satisfaction. "Plumb wore out you was, when Mrs Pengarth's young man brought you in this morning. How do you feel now?"

"Glad to see you, Ada. And very hungry. Am I too late for dinner?"

"Her ladyship dines at seven in the country, miss, and 'tis past eight now. Shall I ask Mrs Pengarth to send a tray up?"

"Yes, please do. I believe I shan't go down this evening. Convey my compliments and apologies to Lady Langston, if you please. Is Mrs Pengarth the housekeeper here?"

"Yes, miss."

Octavia giggled at the thought of Captain Red Jack Day being referred to as "Mrs Pengarth's young man." She hoped the "Mrs" was a courtesy title.

Ada looked puzzled at her mirth, so she said quickly, "I should like a bath, too, if possible."

"Of course, miss. I've done my best by your travelling dress, miss, but it won't ever be the same again, I fear. I found these in the pocket of your cloak." She handed over the clinking purse and the oilcloth-wrapped package. "If there's nothing else, I'll order your dinner and bath now, miss."

"Thank you, Ada. Oh, if you could find me a pair of scissors?"

"There's some in Miss Julia's room, miss, right next door. I'll fetch them to you."

Provided with a neat little pair of gold-handled embroidery scissors, Octavia tackled Red Jack's gift. The wrappings unfolded to reveal half a dozen pairs of silk stockings and several yards of French lace.

"I'll never wear cotton stockings again!" Octavia promised herself. "At least not in the evenings."

She inspected her purse: twenty-one guineas and a handful of silver and copper. There was a slip of paper on which she had detailed her expenditures as she made them. Studying it, she decided there was nothing on it she need hesitate to set to Lord Langston's account, so she need only return twenty guineas and the change to her aunt. Her father's guinea was still intact.

She felt rich.

A tray laden with asparagus soup, poached salmon, and strawberries smothered in thick Cornish cream did nothing to dispel her feeling of affluence. And an hour later, sitting before a dancing fire in Julia's chamber while Ada combed her long, damp hair, she thought she had never been so comfortable in her life.

Scarce had a pair of bustling maids drained the copper hip-bath and borne it away, when the door was flung open. Julia swept in dramatically, flung her arms about her towel-draped cousin and burst into tears.

"Tavy, I've never been so miserable in my life!" she wept.

"Hush, love, hush." Octavia stroked her hair. "Your nerves are quite overset! Pray compose yourself and tell me all about it."

"Come now, Miss Julia," said Ada, gently but firmly. "Come and sit down. Miss Gray's had a long, weary journey for your sake and there's no call to go acting a Cheltenham tragedy soon as she arrives."

Julia sank to the floor, leaned against Octavia's chair and hid her face in a lace handkerchief.

"I'm sorry, Tavy," she sniffed. "When you came in this morning I was so disappointed not to be able to talk to you. I've been waiting all day for you to wake up. Are you quite recovered?"

"Yes, indeed. I was only tired. But tell me, Ju, what is Sir Tristram doing here?"

"Papa was not able to leave London so Sir Tristram offered to escort us into Cornwall. It seems Lord Edgcumbe is his godfather and he spent a great deal of time here in his youth. But tell me, have you seen James?"

"He dined with us the night before I left. How kind of Sir Tristram, when you had refused him!"

"How was James? Did you tell him where I am?"

"He seemed unhappy. Does Sir Tristram continue to pursue you?"

"He has not withdrawn his offer, but does not pester me with his attentions. Tavy, does James know where I am? Does he know I did not willingly abandon him?"

"Sir Tristram is all that is gentlemanly! Does he stay here long?"

"I don't know and I do not care to know," said Julia reproachfully. "Tell me about James!"

"Mr Wynn knows that you did not leave town by choice. I did not inform him of your direction, but he knows that I am come to you, and if he has only the initiative to enquire of my parents, he may find out where I am. I told you Papa thought of a match between us. They know nothing of his infatuation with you and will certainly enlighten him."

"Infatuation! Do not say so! He has vowed eternal love and we are promised to each other. And if you dare suggest that he cares only for my fortune . . ."

"No, no, I will not say that. His income may be small but he has no expensive vices that I know of, and he is always willing to contribute to Mama's causes. But an adequate income for a single man with no pretensions to fashion will not do for a family, and even with the interest on your fortune you would not have more than three thousand a year, I daresay. You are used to spending that on your clothes, Ju!"

"The wife of a politician does not need the wardrobe of

a debutante. Only think how little my aunt spends on her attire."

"You will not dress always in bombazine like Mama! You yourself said it was enough to give you the megrims. If you married Sir Tristram you would always have elegant clothes and everything else of the best."

Ada interrupted. "Your hair is nearly dry, miss. Did you want it braided up again?"

"No!" cried Julia. "Since my cousin has so great a regard for the elegancies of life, you shall cut it and curl it as you do mine. And to show how little I care for dress, you shall alter to fit her everything I have that will suit her. Indeed, Tavy, you misjudge me if you think me so frivolous. I had rather live in a hovel with James than in Carlton House with anyone else."

Octavia clutched at her hair. It had never been cut, her mother considering it sufficient adornment to make up for every deficiency of attire. It fell like a dark cloak past her waist and her one vanity was to stand brushing it before the mirror. Then she thought of the hours spent braiding it, the heavy weight of the braids and how little they became her round face. She lowered her hands.

"Yes," she said. "Cut it, Ada, if you please."

"I didn't mean it!" Julia was horrified. "Your beautiful hair! And what would my aunt say!"

"It is beautiful when it is loose," Octavia said dispassionately, "but I cannot wear it loose. It is thoroughly impractical. In town it would pick up the dirt, and in the country I daresay it would get caught in brambles or something. Cut it, Ada."

For all her brave words, she sat with her eyes screwed closed as the scissors snipped and long tresses fell to the floor. Her neck felt strangely chilly and her head so light she could hardly believe she had any hair left.

"Well now," said Ada in a pleased voice, "there's a natural curl to it. But I don't think it's ringlets you want, miss. More sort of curly all over."

"Like Lady Caroline Lamb?" asked Julia.

"I don't believe as I ever saw her ladyship, but I saw a picture, in *Ackermann's* I think it was, as would suit miss to perfection. Not too short but kind of bouncy."

"In for a penny, in for a pound," said Octavia, eyes still shut. "Go ahead, Ada."

There was silence but for the click of the scissors, until Julia said thoughtfully, "Yes, I see what you mean. It's perfect. And with that natural curl you will never have to sleep in papers, you lucky creature."

Ada removed the towel from her shoulders and brushed the back of her neck.

"Come and look in the looking glass, miss," she suggested.

The reflection in the ancient mirror of burnished steel was so unexpected that Octavia half turned to see if someone was standing behind her. She had not realised how much thinner her face had grown, and surmounted by a fluffy cloud of feathery curls it was unrecognisable, belonging to some elegant stranger.

"Ada, you are a genius!" she cried. "I never thought I could look half so pretty!"

"Just wait till I've altered that canary yellow to fit, miss! If you meant it, that is, Miss Julia?"

"I meant it. I'm sure I do not care if I go dressed in rags so long as James is not here."

"Aye, and mighty careful you was what you wore to meet Mr Wynn in the park!" Ada shook her head.

"I'd not place the least dependence on his having noticed what you had on," said Octavia. "Ada, do you think you could finish that walking dress by tomorrow? Otherwise it will be the lavender silk, and let alone that I am heartily tired of it, I think silk is not appropriate to the country."

"No one will see you," Julia said gloomily. "There is not a soul for miles.

"I daresay you are missing society in general as well as your James. Whereas I am looking forward excessively to not having to entertain for a few weeks. Oh Ju, are you sure you can spare that gown?"

Ada had produced the canary yellow jaconet promenade dress with its pale green ribbons. She looked at Octavia measuringly, then nodded in approval.

"It's my belief, miss, as we won't have to do much but turn it up, and maybe take in the seams a bit which is a sight easier nor letting out. You've fined down a tolerable bit since I did the grey. Stand still a minute while I take your measure, if you please, miss."

"You *are* thinner," said Julia approvingly. "I had not noticed it before but Ada is right. Tomorrow we must find some more gowns for you."

Ada bore off the dress, promising to have it done by morning if she had to persuade Martha Pengarth herself to take up her needle. As soon as she was gone, Octavia turned to her cousin with a question.

"You said Ada went with you when you met Mr Wynn clandestinely. How is it your parents have not turned her off?"

"Papa was going to. He was in a great rage. But Mama said that she could not possibly find me another maid at such short notice and if he insisted on sending me away the very next day I must take Ada with me. In any case, he said I could not possibly be up to any mischief here at Cotehele. And he was right. Even if James should come after me, this horrid place can only be reached by water and there is nowhere within miles for him to stay."

Octavia was beginning to think that Lord Langston had gone quite the wrong way about detaching his daughter from her unsuitable suitor. Here in the wilderness there was nothing to distract her from dwelling on his merits, his devotion and her own inclination. Removed as she was from the Fashionable World, worldly considerations held little sway. Even Sir Tristram's presence might be a mistake, acting as an irritant rather than a counterbalance.

Poor, faithful Sir Tristram! His absence might do his

cause more good than his presence for the moment. Left for a while to the society of her cousin and her mother, Julia could not but regret the loss of his company and his admiration.

"How long did you say Sir Tristram is fixed here?" Octavia enquired, interrupting a description of the impassable lanes, treacherous river, and uninhabited desolation surrounding Cotehele.

"Mama has invited him to stay indefinitely. She prefers to have a gentleman in the house, and she thinks I shall give up and marry him if I see no one else. If Papa were not intransigent, I believe she would let me marry James."

"Not because she considers it a respectable alliance, but for the sake of peace! I know my aunt. But I know also how Lord Langston dotes upon you. It is for your sake he does not want so unequal a match, I am certain. The very thought of seeing you reduced to uncomfortable circumstances must distress him beyond bearing."

"Fustian! If he would but continue my present allowance we should have everything necessary to comfort if not elegance. The truth is he does not care for James's political views; indeed he holds them in abhorrence!"

"Even my father, who is a Reformer, considers Mr Wynn's rhetoric extreme. He hopes that he will mellow with age, for he is a brilliant man and could do the cause no end of good would he but learn to compromise a little."

"He is brilliant, isn't he?" asked Julia eagerly. "I am certain there is a great future ahead of him." She fell silent, contemplating, no doubt, the stimulating life of a Prime Minister's wife.

It crossed Octavia's mind that, with her love of company, Julia might make an excellent political hostess, on a par with Lady Holland or Lady Melbourne.

"Tavy," her cousin said suddenly, in a tortured voice, "have you noticed the tapestries in here? They are of Hero and Leander. You remember the story: he swam the Hellespont every night to see her until at last he drowned. I keep having a nightmare—no, not really a nightmare, for I am awake. You know how dreadful everything appears when you wake in the early hours of the morning? I see James swimming across the Tamar to reach me and I watch him drown and can do nothing to help."

"You had best move to another chamber," suggested Octavia practically.

"It is too late. The idea is in my head now and I cannot be rid of it so easily."

"Well, now I am here and in the next bedchamber, next time such horrid thoughts enter your mind you must come to me and we will talk until you are ready to sleep. You must not give way to such morbid fancies. I can think of few things less likely than that Mr Wynn should attempt to swim the river."

"I know. Tavy, you are such a comfort to me. I am excessively glad that you came."

"Poor Ju. It will all come right in the end."

Ada came in.

"Mr Raeburn just took in the tea tray, Miss Julia. Her ladyship is calling for you to pour. And it's bed for you, Miss Gray, for I can see you're still not in very plump current."

As Julia went down to pour the tea for her mother and her unwanted admirer, Octavia wandered back to the steel mirror. The stranger looked back at her again, still too unfamiliar for her to be sure if she liked her appearance.

"Your dress will be ready this evening, miss. I'll hang it at the end of your bed so you can see it first thing."

"Thank you, Ada. Thank you very much."

She would get up early in the morning and put on her new gown and go walking in the garden. How things had changed already from her London life! Octavia felt herself turning into a different person, and she just could not wait to see who she was going to be.

=6=

SIR TRISTRAM TOOK a bite of ham and spread his fourth muffin with marmalade. A drip fell on the letter he was reading, which had just been carried up from the quay. It was from his bailiff in Gloucestershire, and the marmalade neatly obscured a vital figure.

"Damnation!" he swore, just as the door opened and Raeburn ushered into the dining room a pretty, elegant young lady he had never seen before in his life.

"Good morning, sir," she said composedly, her lips twitching as he sprang to his feet with an apology. She watched his expression change from mild embarrassment to puzzlement to astonishment.

"Miss Gray? No, I must be mistaken. I beg your pardon, ma'am, won't you join me?" He shook his head as if to clear it. "Miss Gray?"

Octavia giggled.

"I've had my hair cut, and this is one of my cousin's gowns," she said frankly, taking the seat the butler held for her. "A cup of tea, if you please, Raeburn, and a muffin. I am sorry if my appearance was the cause of your imprecation, Sir Tristram."

"Not at all, ma'am. I had just spilled maramalade on a letter of some importance. I was cursing my own clumsiness and your arrival at that precise moment was an unfortunate coincidence."

"Allow me, sir," murmured Raeburn, and carefully removed the offending piece of orange peel.

"I expect you are not used to ladies at the breakfast table. Julia and my aunt are not early risers."

"It is a delightful improvement. I hope you mean to make a habit of it."

She smiled and her brown eyes sparkled. "I am longing to explore. This is my first day in the country, for you cannot count sitting in a stagecoach with rain pouring down outside, and I slept all day yesterday. I have never been in the country before."

"Never!" Sir Tristram looked stunned. "You are a Londoner, I collect, but have you never been even to Richmond or Hampstead?"

"Hyde Park is the closest I have come to rural England. I have always been too busy to go further afield."

"You must allow me to show you around the gardens, Miss Gray. They are particularly fine at this time of year."

"You know them well? Julia mentioned that you are Lord Edgcumbe's godson."

"And his heir William, the Viscount Valletort, was my intimate friend. I spent the greater part of my school holidays at Mount Edgcumbe and we came often to Cotehele."

Octavia wanted to know why he had not spent his holidays at home and whether Lord Valletort was not still a friend, but she managed to hold her tongue. She felt as if she had known him forever, but this was only their third meeting and she had no right to ask such personal questions. She sipped her tea thoughtfully.

"Tell me about the house," she said. "It is very ancient, is it not?"

"It is essentially fifteenth century, though there are the remains of an older manor house. The tower is more recent—early seventeenth century. The Edgcumbes have owned it since 1353, but two hundred years later they built the great house at Mount Edgcumbe and since then Cotehele has been used as a dower house and summer retreat."

"Some rainy day I should like to explore the house, but

now I am ready for the gardens. Oh, I forgot your letter. I daresay you wish to finish reading it, now it is de-marmaladed, and perhaps to answer it."

"It can wait." Sir Tristram folded it and put it in his pocket, ruthlessly ignoring his bailiff's pleas for prompt advice and the fact that his reply would miss the tide. "We must go while the sun shines."

Octavia looked about her curiously as they passed through the Great Hall, with its high timbered roof and grey stone walls hung with arms and armour. They crossed a courtyard, then through a passage beneath a battlemented gatehouse. Looking back at the façade, with its narrow, defensive windows, she was tempted to investigate the house first.

A large figure emerging from a nearby gateway distracted her.

"Captain Day!" she called.

The huge smuggler approached, his eyes widening.

"Miss Gray?" he asked uncertainly, doffing his cap.

Sir Tristram laughed heartily.

"A transformation, is it not, Jack?" he said. "Miss Gray is no longer the waif you delivered yesterday."

"I'm happy to see you recovered, miss."

"I must thank you for taking care of me. I was too exhausted yesterday to express my gratitude."

"It was nothing, miss. A fine earful I'd have had from Martha if I'd done anything else."

"And thank you for the package. I hope you brought another such for your Martha."

"I did indeed." He grinned. "I must be on my way now, or the *River Queen* will leave without me."

"Take care, Jack," said Sir Tristram meaningfully.

"Aye, sir. Good day, miss." Red Jack saluted and strode off down the drive.

Octavia took the baronet's offered arm and they turned in the opposite direction.

"How is it you know Captain Day?" she asked cautiously.

"He is well known locally. William and I used to go out on his sloop when we were boys."

She thought his answer evasive but did not press him. After a moment's silence she burst out, "How Mrs Pengarth must worry about him!"

"You know his occupation, then?"

"If I may trust the evidence of my own eyes!" She was going to tell him of the moonlight meeting between the *River Queen* and the *Seamew*, but at that moment they rounded the corner of the house. The view took away her breath.

A lawn, a hedge, a wooded valley framed by two flowering magnolias and leading down to the river, which glinted between the trees. Rounding a hidden bend, the river stretched into the distance; the mists drawn from its surface by the morning sun made a mystery of the hills on its other side.

Octavia became aware that Sir Tristram was watching her face, his own satisfied and slightly amused.

"This is the country," he said. "Does it meet your expectations?"

"It is magnificent! I never imagined anything half so impressive."

"Magnificent? That adjective is usually reserved for scenery such as the Alps. We have here a pleasant panorama, charming if you will."

"You are laughing at me, sir, but indeed, having never seen the Alps, I consider it magnificent."

"It is worth going out of one's way for," he conceded. "The river adds a felicitous touch worthy of Capability Brown, in spite of being entirely natural! Should you like to sit on this bench and admire it or shall we go down into the gardens?"

"Let us go down. I shall save my admiration for when I

am tired of walking, and when you are not by to roast me for my choice of adjectives!"

Crossing the lawn, they passed through a gap in the yew hedge and down a flight of steps. Turning left at the bottom, Octavia found herself entering a long, dark stone tunnel. It had a sinister air, even though she could see daylight at the other end. She stopped and looked back at Sir Tristram.

"It runs under a lane," he explained. "The way is quite smooth, but take my arm if you are uneasy."

She could not really claim to be nervous, but took his arm anyway, then hoped that he did not think her so gooseish as to fear a gloomy passage.

When they emerged into sunlight, she could not repress a cry of delight. The valley was filled to the brim with flowering bushes. There were rhododendrons in every shade of pink and purple, scarlet and orange azaleas, yellow laburnam, all set off by the different greens of their own foliage and the taller trees scattered among them.

"Glorious!" exclaimed Sir Tristram. "It is years since I saw it at this season and I had forgot . . ."

"Glorious?" said Octavia. "Surely that word is better applied to a conquering hero returning in triumph . . ."

"Wretch! I am hoist by my own petard. We will take this path and I shall see if I cannot impress you with my knowledge of botany."

"That will be easy, for I am shockingly ignorant. I am willing to believe anything you tell me!"

They wandered down a twisting gravel path. Between the bushes and trees were banks of wildflowers and he pointed out red and white campion, tall foxgloves and tiny, deep blue speedwell. There was a fish pond, edged with yellow flags, overlooked by a thatched arbour, and a stone dovecote shaped like a huge beehive and half buried in greenery. Somewhere an invisible stream gurgled and chattered, rivalling the cooing of the white fantail pigeons.

The garden turned gradually into woodland, and soon

they could again see the Tamar through the trees. Sir Tristram pointed out a path leading along the river to the quay.

"It goes by Sir Richard's chapel," he said. "Shall we go that way?"

"Is it far? I ought to go back to the house soon. I have not seen my aunt since I arrived and she must surely have risen by now. What is Sir Richard's chapel?"

As they walked on through the wood, he told her the story. Sir Richard, the great-grandson of the first Edgcumbe of Cotehele, had supported Henry Tudor against King Richard III in the Wars of the Roses. The King's supporters followed him to Cotehele and surrounded the house, but he managed to slip past them. He headed for the Tamar with his enemies in hot pursuit.

Hiding in the bushes on the high bank of the river, he filled his cap with stones and threw it down into the water. King Richard's men heard the splash; they looked over the cliff and saw the floating cap. There was no sign of Sir Richard, so they assumed he had drowned and went off.

In due time, Sir Richard emerged from the bushes and fled to France. When Henry beat his enemy at Bosworth and became king in his place, Sir Richard returned to Cotehele. In gratitude for his escape he built on the cliff above the river a tiny chapel, dedicated to Saint George and Thomas à Becket.

They reached the chapel as the tale ended. It was a little stone building, whitewashed inside. Octavia gazed down the cliff and saw that the ebb tide had exposed mud flats along both sides of the river.

"It must have been high tide when it happened," she said. "How very fortunate for Sir Richard! If his enemies had seen his cap lying on the mud, they would not have stopped searching."

They took a different path up the hill, crossing a flat stone bridge over the tiny rill she had heard, which tumbled and scurried in its hurry to join the river. When they reached the arbour by the pond, Octavia was ready to rest for a few minutes. It was nearly a week since she had had any exercise worthy of the name, and her legs were weary. Sitting on the wooden bench, she relished the peaceful scene. Huge carp swam lazily in the pool; pigeons strutted and bowed on the roof of the dovecote; a climbing rose scented air filled with the chirp and twitter of bird-song.

A flutter of wings and a scolding sound made her look up. A tiny brown bird with cheekily tiptilted tail perched on a crossbar, regarding her with bright-eyed disapproval. Its long, sharp bill held an insect.

"Hush, don't move," said Sir Tristram in a low voice. "It's a wren, and I'll wager it has a nest nearby."

Octavia held her breath. After another moment of close scrutiny, the wren decided they were harmless. It flew up into the thatch atop the dovecote, returned a moment later with emptied beak, and darted off in search of further prey.

Letting her breath out in a sigh, Octavia said simply, "I like the country."

"Just wait until it rains, and there is mud everywhere."

"A very good excuse for staying home with a book!"

"I must show you the bookroom up at the house. Miss Gray, you are in your cousin's confidence, I think. Tell me, have I any hope of winning her?"

Startled, she looked at him. His gaze was fixed on his clasped hands and his cheeks were flushed.

"I—I hardly like to say, sir. I have known you such a short time. To be giving you advice seems scarcely proper, even if I knew the answer."

He turned to her. "A short time! Yet I feel as if we have been friends forever. You may say what you think without fear of offending. How should I hold you responsible for Julia's coldness! What am I to do?"

"Do not despair, I beg of you. Only let me observe her behaviour to you before I venture to say anything more." She wondered if he knew he had a rival.

"Forgive me. I do not mean to oppress you with my demands. I fear I have spoiled your morning."

"Oh, no. I have enjoyed it immensely. And I *will* help you, if I can, but give me time. I must go now. My aunt must be wondering where I am."

"Of course." He rose at once.

To her relief he did not begin a catalogue of Julia's virtues, another point in his favour against Mr Wynn. Instead, he showed her the little well, with its moss-grown lintel, which sheltered the cold, clear, bluish spring that fed the streamlet and pond.

"When we were boys," he said, "we used to throw in pennies and make a wish. I do not remember whether any of them came true." He sighed, and they went on in silence through the tunnel and into the house.

Crossing the Great Hall, they met a tall, slim, dignified woman with greying hair, whose dress proclaimed her an upper servant. Sir Tristram introduced her as Mrs Pengarth. Her curtsey was as stately as that of a dowager meeting a queen.

Octavia looked with interest at the housekeeper. It was difficult to imagine the lively Red Jack wooing this respectable matron, though she thought they might suit very well if the smuggler ever decided to settle down.

"Her ladyship and Miss Langston are in the drawing room," said Mrs Pengarth in response to the baronet's query. "You know the way, sir."

As they negotiated stairs and landings, which seemed to crop up in the oddest places, Sir Tristram explained that the housekeeper was in sole charge of the house for many months of the year. The earl was rarely there, and though he had an agent to look after the estate and gardens he did not consider it necessary to employ a butler or steward especially for Cotehele.

"No wonder my aunt brought Raeburn, then," said Octavia. "I cannot conceive how she would go on without a butler. With Raeburn and her dresser here she must feel completely at home, and without the fatigue of having to welcome callers or pay visits. Poor Julia is the only one to feel the lack of society!"

=7=

THE ENTRANCE TO the drawing room was a strange sort of interior porch of carved wood. Beyond it was a light, airy room, comprising the entire second storey of the tower of which the top floor was the girls' chambers. The inevitable tapestries, faded to a yellowish grey, depicted the History of Man, perhaps a more edifying tale than that of Hero and Leander, or the Trojan Wars in Octavia's own room.

Lady Langston reclined upon a carved ebony settee, apparently exhausted from the effort of rising from her bed. An embroidery frame lay in her ample lap, but the needle sticking into it was unthreaded.

Julia knelt on a seat in an alcove in the far wall, gazing listlessly out of a small window which faced east, across the river and eventually to London, some two hundred miles beyond.

After bowing to the viscountess, Sir Tristram went to join her.

Octavia curtseyed to her aunt and kissed her cheek.

"Dear child," murmured her ladyship. "How good of you to join us in our exile. I hope you are quite recovered from the journey?"

"Yes, aunt, perfectly. I have some money left from what Lord Langston gave me. I will fetch it down to you."

"No, no, keep it, my dear. Langston undoubtedly intended that you should travel post, but since you came on the common stage you shall certainly keep your savings.

When I think of your discomfort, I declare I grow quite agitated. How came you to do such an imprudent thing?"

"Why, to tell the truth, ma'am, it never crossed my mind to hire a chaise. How Mama would have stared at such an unnecessary expenditure."

"Ah, sister, sister!" The thought of Mrs Gray seemed to drain Lady Langston's last drop of energy. She closed her eyes and remained inert until Octavia could only suppose she was dismissed.

Twenty guineas! Even if she set aside a tithe for Mama's Africans, she had never in her life owned so much at one time. Her thoughts turned at once to clothes. She had been conscious all morning that the glory of her new dress was spoiled by her old, shabby shoes, and if she ever went beyond the gardens she would need gloves, a bonnet, even a parasol. If only Plymouth were not so inaccessible.

Pondering the problem of reaching the shops, she wandered over to an ornate cabinet and stared at it blankly. The only person she knew who went regularly from Cotehele to Plymouth was Captain Pilway. However obliging, he could hardly be trusted to choose a bonnet for a young lady.

"An extraordinary piece of furniture, is it not?" asked an amused voice behind her.

She glanced back at Sir Tristram, then focused on the cabinet. To her dismay, it was lavishly decorated with naked figures.

"I must write some letters," she stammered, knowing her cheeks were crimson. "I wondered if there might be paper and pen within."

"I expect so, if we can but find them. It is full of secret drawers and boxes, and one can never be sure what one will come across." He let down the front to form a writing surface. "Have you investigated this desk, Miss Langston?"

Julia had moved to a chair and picked up a magazine. She looked up, then languidly joined them.

"No. Why should I investigate a desk?"

"Sir Tristram says it is full of secret compartments. Perhaps we may find a map showing the way to buried treasure."

In spite of herself, Julia was interested. She opened a little door, revealing an inkstand and several quills. Octavia took possession of them.

Sir Tristram pulled open a drawer and presented her with several sheets of paper. Then he slid it all the way out. Behind it was a tiny cubbyhole containing several agate marbles.

"That is one of the simplest," he said. "We used to hide our treasures in it. Now watch this."

Julia was fascinated. Nobly, Octavia retreated with her writing materials to a small table, leaving Sir Tristram to impress his inamorata without distraction. It was difficult to ignore the oohs and ahs, but she managed to concentrate sufficiently to inform her parents that she was arrived safely and would write again soon with a description of her surroundings.

Lieutenant Cardin was next. He had probably forgotten her existence by now but she had promised to write. A quick note thanked him for his assistance and assured him that her river journey had been without mishap.

She folded the paper and was about to address it to the Customs House when it dawned on her that the only way for letters to reach the post was by way of the Tamar. According to no less an authority than Captain Day, most if not all of the sailors on the river were engaged in smuggling, or free trading as they preferred to call it. It seemed tactless, if not downright dangerous, to expect them to deliver a letter to the stronghold of their adversaries.

She set it aside for the moment and, unable to restrain her curiosity any longer, joined the pair at the cabinet.

Julia's cupped hands contained, besides the agate marbles, a pale blue, speckled bird's egg, a champagne cork, a jay's feather, a cartridge, and a horse-brass depicting a Cornish piskie and the motto "Trelawney shall not die."

"A veritable treasure trove!" exclaimed Octavia, laughing. "I trust the cartridge is empty."

"That was William's. The first time he ever bagged a pheasant. We were ten or twelve, I suppose. The gamekeeper was teaching us to shoot and I cannot say whether he or William was more astonished when he hit the bird. Out of season, I may say."

"You mean Lord Valletort?" asked Julia. "He died last year, did he not? I met him only once or twice, though he was some sort of distant cousin." She noticed the sadness on Sir Tristram's face. "I beg your pardon. I did not mean to grieve you, sir. I spoke without thinking."

"We grew up together." The baronet basked in her pity but had the good manners not to push his advantage. He turned the subject. "Miss Gray, there is a sort of box in there—you see it?—which we were never able to open. Perhaps you can fathom the trick."

Octavia inserted her hand in the space he indicated and felt around. There was a knob, which she pulled on without effect.

"It seems to be stuck," she said, just as her fingers found an edge of paper. "Wait a minute. There is something here, if I can only grasp it." Trying to slide it out, she touched some hidden catch. There was a click, the box came loose, and she pulled both it and the paper out of the interior of the cabinet.

The box was small but surprisingly heavy. There was a leather bag in it which clinked when Sir Tristram lifted it out. He thrust his hand in and pulled out a couple of gold coins.

"*Louis d'or!* From the reign of Louis XV." He emptied the bag on the desk. "A Venetian ducat, and some Roman pieces. Nothing later than 1750."

"This paper fell out of the bag," said Octavia, bending

to pick up a scrap which had fallen to the floor. "Do you think I ought to read it?"

"Yes, do!" cried Julia eagerly.

"Perhaps it should be given to Lord Edgcumbe unread." She looked at Sir Tristram and thought he agreed with her but in the face of Julia's enthusiasm he said nothing. "Very well. There are some numbers on the back. Inside, an old-fashioned hand, a gentleman's I would guess but somewhat shaky. 'For my son,' it says, 'lest I gamble away all that is not entailed.' It is signed, 'Richard, Second Baron Edgcumbe.'"

"The bad baron," said Sir Tristram. "Losing money at cards or dice, probably foxed to judge by the uncertain writing, suddenly struck by maudlin repentance and setting aside the relics of his Grand Tour: I can picture the scene clearly."

"The coins are no pirate's hoard, then, but merely belong to Lord Edgcumbe," said Julia, losing interest.

Sir Tristram shook his head. "No, not to Lord Edgcumbe. I hope you ladies will trust me to pass it to its rightful owner."

"Who is that?" asked Octavia. "You are being very mysterious, sir. Surely the earl must be the baron's heir."

"His heir, but not his son. I cannot say more. It is not my story to tell. Will you entrust the gold to me?"

Julia shrugged and turned away.

"Of course," her cousin said quickly. "Wait, Ju, we have not yet looked at the other paper I found."

"Have you not read *Northanger Abbey?* I thought Jane Austen was a favourite of yours. It is probably a laundry list."

"You know how little opportunity I have had to read." Octavia's hurt sounded in her voice and Julia was immediately contrite.

"I'm sorry, love." She hugged her. "That was beastly of me, forgive me. What is on the paper, Sir Tristram?"

He had unfolded the sheet and stepped to the window to examine it in a better light.

"It is a map of the house and grounds, with certain vastly interesting additions. It seems a number of hiding places were built at various times and this gives instructions on how to find them!"

"It looks very ancient," said Julia, trying to appear interested.

"At least two hundred years old, for this tower is not shown."

"If I am not mistaken," Octavia added, studying the map, "the tower was built right on top of the only secret place in the house itself. How very provoking!"

"There is a tradition that Sir Thomas Cotehele, who built the tower, buried treasure chests somewhere about the place. He was a Dutchman whose daughter married one of the Sir Richards and he lived here for many years. I'll wager he used the old priests' hole, or whatever it was, to hide his wealth!"

"Mama's chamber is on the ground floor of the tower," said Julia, her indifference forgotten. "Mama, may we search your chamber for an entrance to the treasure room? Mama!"

Lady Langston sat up, looking flustered. "I was not asleep," she protested. "You should take a turn about the shrubbery this afternoon, Julia. It is not at all healthy to be cooped up in the house all day."

"I shall, Mama, but we have found an old treasure map and we need to look about your chamber. May we?"

"There is no treasure in my chamber, child, for I brought scarcely any jewels since we do not entertain."

"Not in it, Aunt, under it. But if you will permit us to look about for an entrance, we promise not to disturb your belongings."

"Oh, dear." Her ladyship looked to Sir Tristram for guidance.

"It will do no harm, ma'am," he said, smiling over the girls' heads as one adult to another.

It dawned on the viscountess that her daughter was for once in charity with her highly eligible suitor and willing to accept his company, however dubious their enterprise.

"Very well," she agreed with a sigh. "But Julia, before you go, pray thread this needle for me. The silk seems to be lost."

"Let me do it, ma'am," offered Octavia. "You two go ahead; I shall join you in a moment."

Sir Tristram's look of gratitude almost repaid her for the possibility that they might find the treasure without her.

It took several minutes to sort out her aunt's silks and find the right one to match the pink rose she thought she had been working on. More time was lost in trying to find her way amid the confusion of stairs and landings. In the end she had to ask a maid.

"You mean the White Bedroom, miss? 'Tis just through the Punch Room, under the arch and up them stone steps. Careful, miss, they're right steep."

She reached the top of the granite staircase in time to hear her cousin say pettishly, "The map is perfectly useless. It shows nothing in the least resembling this room."

"No luck?" she asked. "What a shocking disappointment! I quite thought to find you both dripping with emeralds and pearls and running your hands through chests of Spanish doubloons."

"Not a single emerald," said Sir Tristram. He spoke cheerfully but it was plain he was mortified.

Octavia doubted it was because of the lack of treasure. She was sure that he had taken up the hunt with such enthusiasm because of Julia's interest. Her cousin was behaving like a spoiled child, her usual sunny temper and friendliness changed to irritability.

If that was the result of falling in love, Octavia was glad she had never succumbed.

"I should like to see if we can discover some of the other

hidey-holes," she said, "but not immediately. It seems a very long time since I breakfasted and if my aunt does not have luncheon served I shall repair to the kitchens and see what I can find.

"I should be happy to join you, Miss Gray, but I am even happier to be able to assure you that Mrs Pengarth provides a more than adequate luncheon in the dining room at about this hour."

"Come, Ju. I expect you are hungry, for I remember you never eat in the morning. A cup of chocolate will not sustain you for very long."

Sir Tristram looked relieved, and Octavia hoped he set down Julia's disagreeable remarks as the effect of a lack of proper nourishment.

Lady Langston joined them as they entered the dining room. The table in the center was laden with cold meats, a side of salmon, bread still warm from the oven, huge bowls of fresh fruit.

"Mmm, strawberries," said Octavia. "Oh, and cherries! I do not know which I like best."

"Then have some of each," suggested Sir Tristram. "And this is a gooseberry fool, if I am not mistaken. My lady, if you care to be seated I shall serve you."

The viscountess sank into a chair near the window. "A morsel of salmon and just the tiniest bit of the fool," she murmured. He served her with generous portions of both, and a couple of slices of bread and butter, setting the plates on a small table at her elbow. "Thank you, Sir Tristram. Has Raeburn brought in the tea? He knows I like a dish of tea at noon."

"Here it is, Aunt," said Octavia, pouring a cup and taking it to her. She returned to the table, selected a deep red cherry and popped it in her mouth. "What is in the jugs?"

"Cider," answered Sir Tristram, helping Julia to clotted cream on her strawberries. "Made at the mill in the valley.

There are two kinds, and I must advise you not to take the darker one if you do not want to sleep all afternoon."

"Is it so strong? I had better stick to tea, perhaps. Julia, shall I pour a cup for you?"

"Some salmon, Miss Langston?"

"A little, thank you. It is good but we have had it every day since we arrived."

"It is caught in the Tamar at this season. In the last century, in fact, it was so plentiful that a law was passed in a local village that apprentices should not be given it more than twice a week."

"I shall have some," decided Octavia, as Julia retired to a settee with her luncheon. "I am not yet grown tired of such a treat." Resisting with difficulty the fragrance of new-baked bread, she took her bowl of cherries and went to sit by her aunt.

Sir Tristram, with a loaded plate, joined Julia on the sofa. They made a charming picture, her golden ringlets contrasting with his carelessly arranged dark locks, his strongly built form complementing her slender figure. Lady Langston looked at them and sighed.

"Such a desirable *parti*," she whispered. "He is every-thing that is amiable, too. Yet my silly girl will whistle him down the wind, for one cannot expect a gentleman to put up with the sullens forever."

"She is conversing with him perfectly amicably at pres-ent, ma'am. It is natural to her to be friendly with every-one, and he has so much to recommend him that I am sure she cannot continue to reject him."

"It is so very unfortunate that she should have conceived a *tendre* for that other young man. I do not recall his name, and I believe I have never met him but Langston says he is shockingly ineligible. A revolutionary, my dear, who would murder us all in our own beds like the Jacobites in France. Or do I mean Jacobins? I could never keep the two of them straight."

66

"The Jacobites were the Stuart supporters, Aunt. The rebellions of '15 and '45? Bonny Prince Charlie?" Octavia seized the opportunity of taking her ladyship's mind off her vexing offspring. The effort was wasted.

"I can see you know a great deal of history, Octavia, but I am sure such an education must be a mistake if it leads to Julia refusing to obey her papa and wanting to marry a murderer instead of a perfect gentleman like Sir Tristram, with fifty thousand pounds a year."

"Julia's suitor is no murderer, ma'am. Indeed you malign him."

"He is not? I must say that is a great relief to me. But how can you be certain? Can it be that you are acquainted with him?"

"He often visits my father." Octavia was sure her aunt would guess that she had introduced the unhappy pair, but if so she gave no sign of her suspicions. "He is a political writer and expresses himself with extreme vigour in print. In person, he would not hurt a fly. He is greatly concerned with the plight of the unfortunate. Papa believes he will mature into a fine politician."

"Well, my love, I do not mean to speak disrespectfully of politicians, for I am sure my sister goes on very well with Mr Gray. But it *cannot* be thought an unexceptionable match for Julia, the daughter of a viscount and with her own fortune besides."

Octavia was glad to have relieved her aunt's mind of at least one of its apprehensions. She had no desire, however, to persuade her that James Wynn was a suitable husband, since she was herself convinced that Sir Tristram was by far the better man to make her cousin happy.

"I am going to get some more cherries," she said. "Can I bring you anything, ma'am?"

"Just another cup of tea, thank you. I am sure I am by far too fidgeted to eat."

Since Lady Langston had left no trace of the fish, the pudding, or the bread and butter with which she had been lavishly provided, her niece did not worry unduly at this alarming loss of appetite.

=8=

LADY LANGSTON RETIRED to the drawing room after luncheon, with the stated aim of applying herself to her embroidery. It was generally understood that on such occasions she did not require attendance; indeed, she positively resisted any offer to accompany her.

When this became clear to Octavia, she asked Sir Tristram to show her the bookroom.

"I am a little tired after our morning exercise," she claimed. "I shall be perfectly happy there while you stroll about the grounds, Julia."

"I can very well wait until you are recovered, cousin. There is no fashionable hour for the promenade here, after all. I will come with you to choose a book, for I have read nothing this age, I vow."

"It is not an extensive collection," warned Sir Tristram, leading them through the Great Hall and into the east wing. "Just a few volumes to while away the hours if it rains when the earl brings a house-party."

The room was too small to be described by so grand a term as library, but all four walls were lined with well-filled shelves. Octavia at once began to collect a pile of novels, biographies, histories, and poetry, all of which looked fascinating to her. Sir Tristram looked at the stack and laughed.

"Shall I call a footman to carry these to your room, Miss Gray?" he asked.

She flushed slightly, but smiled at him with a twinkle in

her eye. "I am not used to such bounty," she explained. "It is ridiculous, but I am half afraid that if I do not lay claim to these, they will disappear before I return."

"At the very least, a housemaid will return them to the shelves and you will have to hunt them out again. There is no reason you should not keep a private supply elsewhere. Do you care to choose one for now?"

"Yes, I shall take this life of Queen Elizabeth." She was about to sink into a chair with her prize when she realised that Julia was wandering discontentedly up and down the room, reading and rejecting title after title. Evidently literature held no charms in her present restless state. "Ju, the very sight of these books has revived me," she said. "Shall we go out now?"

Since her fatigue had been an unsuccessful ruse to allow Sir Tristram to be alone with her cousin, she was perfectly ready for the sort of leisurely stroll Julia preferred.

They walked about the upper gardens this time. Octavia was delighted with the wide green lawns, the shady shrubbery and the neat kitchen garden, tucked away behind yew hedges. There was another lily pond, a small meadow where cows were milked morning and evening and, at the top of the hill behind the house, a tall tower on the skyline.

"I should like to go up to that tower," Octavia said. "Did not the map show a hiding place there?"

Julia brightened. She had been walking without complaint, but equally without enthusiasm, indifferent to the beauties of the rural scene.

"The Prospect Tower is an interesting structure," said Sir Tristram. "I think you will be surprised when you reach it, even if we should not find the secret. Do you go on ahead, while I go back to the house for the map. I shall join you there presently."

He watched them start up the grassy path. Even in the sullens Julia was a diamond of the first water and when she smiled she was quite the most beautiful creature he had ever seen. And what a surprise the little cousin had turned out to be! At their first meeting he had thought her a plain, unpromising piece and she had looked infinitely worse the next time he saw her. Yet a haircut and a new gown had worked a miracle. She was really quite pretty, and her cheerful, obliging temper threw Julia's crotchets into strong relief.

Of course Julia had every excuse for her behaviour. Their situations were vastly different. Miss Gray had been granted a temporary reprieve from a life of toil in straitened circumstances. Julia had been exiled from her friends, torn from the entertainments of a successful season, parted from the man she fancied she loved.

He did not like to think of this last. Where the devil had he left that map?

When he rejoined them at the base of the Prospect Tower, both the girls were in whoops.

"I have never seen anything more worthy to be called a Folly," cried Julia. "Why ever did they build it in such a ridiculous fashion?"

Close to, the square-seeming structure was revealed to be three sided, and each side concave. The windows were false, bricked in, and when Sir Tristram unlocked the door with a key obtained from the housekeeper, they could see that the external division into three storeys was equally deceiving. The interior was hollow, with a wooden stair winding precariously up the stone walls, and no roof.

"A Folly with a purpose," Sir Tristram assured them, "as you may see if you dare climb up with me."

Somewhat to his surprise, both the young ladies were eager to go. The stairs looked solid, with a rail on the open side, but he went first in case there were any loose or rotten boards.

It was a long climb, the tower being some sixty feet high. Had there been windows, they might have contented themselves with the view from the halfway point. They were moving very slowly, with considerable panting, by the time they reached the landing at the top. It was worth the effort.

Octavia had thought the view from the gardens magnificent. This was overwhelming. The air was crystal clear. Every detail of the closer woods and fields stood out, and in the distance, to west and east, the high rolling hills of Bodmin Moor and Dartmoor stretched to the horizon. Southward the river twisted and turned, now hidden, now revealed, until it widened into Plymouth Sound.

She realised with a start that she had missed what Sir Tristram was saying.

"I'll try to point it out to you. You see where the headland seems to block the river? That is where Mount Edgcumbe lies. By river it is several hours distant, by land, a good day's journey, but as the crow flies ten or eleven miles. No, I believe you cannot see it without a spyglass."

"What am I looking for?" asked Octavia.

"The tower of Maker church, Miss Gray. That is the purpose I told you of. With the aid of a spyglass, or with lights at night, messages can be passed from one to the other."

"Smugglers?"

"I daresay. Officially, simply signals telling of arrivals and departures, or a warning in time of danger. The coming of the Spanish Armada, perhaps, or the Round-heads during the Civil War."

"But you think it might be used by smugglers?" she persisted. "That would explain the secret room."

"There is no room for a secret room," protested Julia.

"Underground," said Sir Tristram. "I inspected the map as I walked up from the house. Let us go down and see whether we can find the entrance." He sounded extremely skeptical.

Octavia's knees were shaking when she reached the bottom. They went outside and she and Julia supported each other, giggling, while the baronet unfolded the map. He , laid it on the grass and they all bent over it.

The ink was faded but perfectly legible. There was a loose brick in the wall directly opposite the door. Behind it was a lever, which would open a trapdoor.

They tried it. With a click and a scrape, a section of floor in the darkest corner moved downwards, leaving a black hole.

"But we have no lantern!" Julia lamented.

"I can fetch one in a moment. Wait here and do not go near the entrance." The hitherto imperturbable baronet set off at a run.

He returned shortly, breathless and dishevelled, bearing a lighted lantern. Lying full-length on the dusty floor, he held it down in the hole and peered over the edge.

"There are steps of a sort," he announced. "I can't see much else. I'm going down."

"I shall come with you," said Julia in a voice which brooked no denial.

Octavia looked wistfully at the hole, then down at her yellow gown, already besmirched from brushing against the wall. Julia, in keeping with her declared lack of interest in dress, was wearing a plain blue muslin, probably the plainest frock in her wardrobe. Besides, she had plenty more to choose from.

"I had best wait here, in case the two of you land in the briars," Octavia sighed.

Sir Tristram first, then Julia, they disappeared.

A squeal from Julia was followed by a thump and a muffled curse. She could hear their voices but not what they were saying, and there was no answer when she called a question. Frustrated, she turned to the map.

A dotted line led from the Prospect Tower diagonally past the corner of the house to a point opposite the centre of the east wing. Orienting herself on the river, Octavia decided it must be where the tunnel from lawn to valley garden passed under the lane. There was another secret room there, or rather a cave, she decided, peering at the writing. And the dotted line was marked "tunnel."

She went to stand beside the hole in the floor, bent down and shouted. "Can you see the entrance to a tunnel?"

"No. The walls are all solid stone." Sir Tristram's voice echoed.

"There ought to be one. Wait a minute, I cannot read it in this light. I shall go outside and see if there are more instructions."

The instructions were very simple. Close the trapdoor and the way to the tunnel would be clear.

"Not while I am down here!" cried Julia. Her head appeared, ringlets liberally decorated with cobwebs.

Sir Tristram came up too, brushing futilely at his filthy coat and filthier trousers. "I believe I have had enough excitement for one day," he admitted, slightly sheepish. "If you care to go down and try it, Miss Gray, we shall wait for you."

"Not I. What did you find?"

"A number of empty chests, labelled 'Darjeeling—Calcutta—London.' I would guess that the contents were divided into smaller packages before continuing their journey."

"They still smelled faintly of tea," Julia added as they walked down the hill, "so it cannot be very long since the place was used."

"Luggers meet the India clippers in mid-Channel," said Sir Tristram knowledgeably. "Most of the cargo is unloaded before they ever reach port."

"You know a great deal about it." Julia was curious. Octavia was about to tell her about Captain Red Jack Day when she caught a warning look from the baronet.

"There are reports in the newspapers from time to time," he said. "On the rare occasions when the Customs actually manage to catch them."

The afternoon had flown past. They had missed teatime, and Lady Langston had already retired to change for dinner. The girls hurried up to their rooms.

Ada was horrified at the sight of Julia's disarray.

"I hope her ladyship didn't see you like this," she clucked. "There's a gown laid out on your bed, Miss Gray. And if the gentleman was to see you, Miss Julia, it's off and away he'd be like a scalded cat. I'll fetch up some hot water."

"No such luck," said Julia gloomily. "He did see me."

Octavia had to agree with her. She thought her cousin's intrepid descent into the secret cellar had entirely restored the baronet's esteem, while the smudge on her nose only made her look more enchanting than ever.

The gown on her bed was another of Julia's, newly altered. Peach-coloured sarsenet, with a white lace petticoat, it was trimmed with tiny rosettes of white lace. Used to managing without a maid, Octavia slipped into it, ran a brush through her curls, and danced into Julia's chamber.

"That is quite perfect for you!" her cousin cried. "Ada, did I not have matching slippers? They were open-toed, as I recall, so they ought to fit. And I know the very thing to go with it." She darted to the dressing table and searched through her jewelry case. "Here it is. It is yours."

She clasped a gold chain around Octavia's neck. The oval gem depending from it glowed with a matching peachy hue, several shades deeper than the silk.

"Oh, no, Ju, I cannot take it!"

"It is only a carnelian. If your mama objects, I shall keep it for you and you may wear it when you visit. After seeing how pretty you are in elegant clothes and with your new coiffure, I refuse to let you sink back into drabness."

"You are a darling." Octavia hugged her. "Whatever happens in the future, I shall wear it now and enjoy it. Do you really think I look pretty?"

"Only look at yourself in the mirror. You cannot doubt your own eyes."

"I scarcely recognise myself."

"Those curls want some more brushing," said Ada severely. "Natural they may be, but they won't set right without you help 'em. Let me show you how, miss. There

now, if I don't have two young ladies fit to set the Thames
on fire!"

"The Tamar, you mean," said Julia, suddenly losing her
high spirits. "How I wish I were in London! At least among
so many people that odious Sir Tristram could not persecute me with his attentions."

"You are unjust. He does not persecute you, and I do not
think him in the least odious."

Julia sighed. "You are right. Isolated as we are his constant presence is inevitable, and I will even admit that he is
charming. But I do not love him and I wish he will go
away!"

Dinner was not a cheerful meal. They judged it wisest
not to disturb Lady Langston with the story of their
afternoon's explorations, so the conversation was an exchange of commonplaces in which Julia did not trouble to
join. When the ladies withdrew, Sir Tristram remained at
table long enough to fortify himself with a glass of brandy
against the evening ahead.

When he went up to the drawing room, Octavia was
reading, her ladyship had taken up her embroidery and
was actually setting a stitch, and Julia was at her favourite
post, gazing out of the east window. He joined her.

"Do you care to walk in the gardens, Miss Langston?"
he asked. "It will be light for an hour and more."

"These June evenings go on forever." She sounded as if
she thought the sun shone late deliberately to annoy her.

"Or a game of chess, perhaps?"

"Ask Octavia. I must help Mama sort her silks."

The baronet and Octavia set up the chess board by the
west window, while Julia pulled up a footstool by her
mother's sofa and took several skeins of thread from the
workbasket. For several minutes the quiet was broken only
by the murmur of the players.

"Julia! You are tying my silk in knots! Pray leave it alone
and go play upon the spinet. You have scarce touched the

instrument since we came and it has a prodigious pretty sound."

"What is the point of playing when there is no one to listen!" cried Julia.

My lady's shocked look was followed by a plea from Octavia.

"Do play, Ju. I love to hear it. Indeed I did not realise there was an instrument here or I should have asked you long ago. You will not blame us for being a smaller audience than you deserve."

"My playing is nothing beyond the ordinary," Julia disclaimed, but she looked ashamed of her outburst and went to the spinet.

The next few days passed in much the same occupations, except that without the excitement of the secret map Julia's fretful temper was still more marked. On the evening of the fourth day, she took her seat at the spinet without being asked, but she played with a mournful dreaminess clearly intended for her own ears only.

Sir Tristram and Octavia were playing backgammon. He threw a double five and knocked one of her most promising pieces off the board.

"Have you considered my request for advice?" he asked under cover of the music. "You have had ample opportunity to discover how your cousin regards my suit."

"I am certain that you do your cause no good by staying here. She sees only that you are not James Wynn."

"Does she truly love him? Here, it is your turn to toss the dice."

"Ha, a double six! Now I shall have my revenge. What is true love? She pines for him. If she saw him daily, who knows how she would feel by now? I believe my uncle was wrong to part them at this juncture, and still more wrong to separate her from all company and entertainment that might serve to direct her thoughts away from him."

"In his case, absence makes the heart grow fonder. I am afraid that in mine, it is more like to be out of sight, out of mind. Yet if I stay, it is only to give my head for washing. You advise me to go."

"She must regret your departure. She is a social creature, and if an audience of three is not enough, two will hardly suffice! Perhaps she will see your merits more clearly in your absence. But I do not mean to raise your hopes too high. Have you never thought of giving up the pursuit?"

"A feeble wretch I should be to give up so easily! I have some sense of my own merits, as it pleases you to call them, and Lord Langston is on my side. I must hope that time is, too. However, I will trust your judgement and make myself scarce for a fortnight or so. In fact, I have urgent business at home that cannot be well managed by correspondence. The sooner I go, the better."

Octavia rattled the dice thoughtfully. The game had scarcely moved during their discussion. "Do you mean to travel by way of Plymouth?" she asked.

"Yes. My horse is stabled there. Coming down I rode part of the way as a change from sitting in the Langstons' carriage, but I shall ride all the way home. It is cross-country, with poor roads from here. Is there something I can do for you in Plymouth?"

"If you do not care for company, I shall perfectly understand, but I have some few errands to perform in the town and I should be excessively glad of your escort down the river."

"I am entirely at your service, Miss Gray. Is tomorrow morning too soon for you?"

"That will answer very well. Let us finish this game, then I shall ask my aunt's permission."

"My play, I think." He threw a two and a three. "Alas, you have left me no room to move, ma'am, and I must forfeit my turn."

=9=

THE TRIP DOWNRIVER was very different from Octavia's journey upstream, though she once again found herself aboard the *River Queen*. Captain Pilway seemed like an old friend now, and accompanied by Sir Tristram and Ada she could have faced with equanimity another encounter with smugglers at midnight.

She was not called upon to do so. For one thing, they left at mid-morning. It was misty, with very little breeze, and the boat slipped quietly through the water carried by the combined efforts of the current and the ebb tide. The banks were scarcely visible, and Octavia was glad of the warmth of her grey and white striped pelisse.

Since it was no longer her best, she had ventured to wear the grey figured silk dress. Sir Tristram had thoughtfully provided a blanket to sit on, and the deck had been swept between unloading limestone and loading the present cargo of fruit. An irresistible odour of gooseberries, cherries, and strawberries rose from the well.

Shortly after they left Cotehele Quay, a rowboat appeared out of the mist. Octavia quite expected it to pull alongside and take aboard a bale or two of untaxed tobacco, but though Captain Pilway hailed the rower he did not slow down. A trail of bobbing floats followed the boat, circling out from the bank, and as they came closer she could see a net sliding into the water from its stern.

The rower headed for shore. A couple of men in thigh-high boots pulled the boat in, then all three started hauling on the net. As the circle grew smaller, the water within swirled and a silver-glinting fish jumped, twisting in the air and scattering droplets before it fell back with a splash.

"Salmon?" asked Octavia.

"Good guess." Sir Tristram had watched her intent face with slightly amused approbation. "If you are interested in the fishing, I believe you would enjoy a visit to Cotehele Mill. I shall take you there when I return."

"What is there to see at Cotehele Mill?"

"All the industries of a country estate, and all in one place. Much the same activities may be found at my place in Gloucestershire, but scattered about."

"I should like to see it. Tell me about Gloucestershire. Is it pretty country?"

He described Dean Park and its surroundings. She listened with interest, asking questions, until Halton Quay came into view. The mist had thinned somewhat and she scanned the washing line hopefully, but there was no sign of the scarlet petticoat.

"What are you looking for?" he asked.

"The smugglers' warning sign. It is not here today."

"You said something yesterday about trusting the evidence of your own eyes as to Jack Day's profession."

It was his turn to listen as she recounted her adventures. She made a comedy of the tale and several times he laughed aloud. However, when she finished with her escape from the Riding Officer, he said seriously, "You came to no harm, I know, but I wish you will not travel alone again. Promise me you will hire a private boat to return today. I am certain your aunt expects it."

"I have Ada to protect me this time." They both looked to where the abigail dozed in a corner of the deck, and she laughed. "I promise, if you will tell me how to arrange it."

"I shall arrange it myself, before I leave. Also before I leave, I hope you will honour me with your company at luncheon at some inn. Breakfast already seems long ago."

Octavia accepted both gracefully and gratefully. As if

reading their hungry minds, the sailor Tom made his way forward at that moment, bearing a tin bowl of cherries.

"Cap'n's compliments an' there be goosegogs an' strawb'ries too if 'e'd like 'em, miss."

A breeze rose, and with its aid the sun drove off the mist. By the time they reached the Sound, sparkling whitecaps danced about the *River Queen*. They had a superb view of Mount Edgcumbe, with its wide avenue leading up to the stately Tudor mansion. Sir Tristram pointed out a number of follies, ranging from a temple in honour of Milton to a Gothic ruin. Octavia longed to explore the grounds, though it seemed highly unlikely that she would ever have the chance. She was sorry when they turned away towards Plymouth.

As Sir Tristram helped her ashore, she saw the New Customs House on the quay.

"I must deliver a letter there," she said, pointing. "It will not take a moment."

She left him giving directions for his saddlebags, his only luggage, to be taken to the Golden Hind Inn, and with Ada following she went up to the gate of the Customs House. She handed her note to the porter, asking him to see it delivered to Lieutenant Cardin, and was turning away when he stopped her.

"Mr Cardin's within, miss, if ye'll bide for an answer."

"I did not expect an answer," Octavia said.

" 'Twon't take but a minute to find un. 'Tis right sorry the lieutenant'd be to miss his sweetheart." The man winked at Ada and hurried off, just as Sir Tristram came up.

Octavia crimsoned at the sight of his raised eyebrows.

"I am not his sweetheart, indeed I am not," she said indignantly. "He was kind to me when I arrived in Plymouth and I promised to let him know I had reached Cotehele safely. Then I did not like to send word to the Customs House by way of the Tamar smugglers."

"Perfectly understandable," said Sir Tristram, trying

unsuccessfully to hide his grin. "It must be awkward to have friends in both camps. Shall we see what the Golden Hind can do in the way of a neat luncheon?"

He offered his arm, but before she could take it Lieutenant Cardin dashed out of the Customs House. He saw them, looked around bewildered, then approached.

"Miss Gray? It *is* you! I can see you are perfectly recovered from that devilish stagecoach. I hardly recognised you, ma'am. I hope you'll let me show you about town this time?"

"Thank you, sir, I should be happy to accept but we are on our way to luncheon." Dimpling at the admiration in his eyes, Octavia presented him to Sir Tristram.

The young officer saluted. Sir Tristram shook hands with him and professed himself delighted to make the acquaintance.

"The name is familiar," he said. "If you care to join us, perhaps we can ferret out some connection."

"There is a connection, of sorts," Mr Cardin blurted out as they started up the street. "I have seen you at Mount Edgcumbe, sir. The earl is my patron."

"Ah, I have it. Your father was the midshipman who saved the first earl's life. At the Battle of Quiberon Bay, was it not?"

"That's right, sir. My father advanced to captain, but he died before I was old enough to go to sea. His lordship— the present earl, that is—helped me to enter the Navy, and then to obtain promotion. I transferred quite recently to the Customs service. The Navy is laying up ships, you know, since the end of the war with France."

Sir Tristram was pleased with the lieutenant's cheerful, sensible conversation. They enjoyed a luncheon of Cornish pasties and grilled mackerel with new peas, and then he commended Octavia to the young man's care without a qualm. If he understood her circumstances aright, it could prove a respectable alliance for both. While she might look higher on the social scale, and he for a bride with a more ample portion, with Lord Edgcumbe's patronage their prospects must satisfy their friends.

Sir Tristram counted himself their friend, and one not without influence to be used in their favour. Nonetheless, the idea left him vaguely dissatisfied.

Laughing at himself in the role of matchmaker when his efforts in his own behalf met with so little success, he went to find his horse.

Lieutenant Cardin had never shopped for a lady's parasol before, but he knew where the best shops were and was happy to lend his support and advice. After much dithering and laughter, Octavia emerged from the third haberdasher's with two pair of gloves and a beruffled parasol of white oiled silk, polka-dotted in black. The proprietor promised it would hold off a shower of rain as well as the rays of the sun, and Ada said it would go with any outfit.

A milliner provided a saucy chipstraw hat decorated with white artificial roses, ideal for the country, and they moved on to the shoemaker. Here Ada insisted that the lieutenant wait outside ("Ankles!" she whispered to Octavia), and they saw him through the shop window, striding impatiently up and down, while slippers, sandals, and half-boots bestrewed the floor. Feeling shockingly extravagant, Octavia chose a pair of boots and two each of slippers and sandals. She counted her money, found she had more left than she had supposed, and added a pair of stout walking shoes.

Ada nodded wisely. "Miss Julia can't resist a bit of lace," she said, "and I can see you're the same with shoes, miss. It's a good thing Plymouth prices are half what they are in town. We'd best be going now, afore you see anything else to take your fancy and afore the young gentleman comes in to fetch you out."

Mr Cardin happily relieved them of the packages and begged them to step into a nearby coffeehouse for a cup of tea. Refreshed, they left the parcels with the proprietor and walked about the Barbican, then strolled across the grassy Hoe with its spectacular view of the shipping in the harbour and Sound. All too soon it was time to fetch the shopping and repair to the quay to find the boat ordered by Sir Tristram.

"I have enjoyed myself prodigiously, sir," said Octavia, offering her hand to the lieutenant.

Instead of shaking it, he raised it to his lips. "You will let me know next time you come to Plymouth, won't you?" His pleading eyes made him look like a hopeful puppy. "There are still any number of sights to be seen."

"Your duties do not seem to occupy a great deal of your time."

"Unless I am at sea, I can always get away for a few hours. Much of our work is done at night. Please say you will come again?"

"I cannot be sure, because my cousin is not permitted to leave Cotehele and it is not fair to abandon her. But if I do come, I will call at the Customs House to see how you go on. There, does that satisfy you?"

"It will have to," he said sadly, and helped her into the boat.

The hired boat was much smaller than the cargo-carrying sailing barges, and much more comfortable. Octavia leaned back on the well-cushioned seat, her packages at her feet, and trailed her fingers in the water. Lieutenant Cardin stayed on the wharf, waving, for as long as she could see him.

"You've made a conquest there, right enough," commented Ada with a smile.

Octavia turned to her, startled.

"You mean . . . you mean he is *enamoured*?" she asked incredulously.

"Head over heels, if you ask me, miss. Nice young chap, but with his way to make in the world yet."

"If you are warning me that he is not like to offer marriage in the near future, you need not trouble, Ada. I have no thought of such a thing. Indeed, I can scarcely believe you are serious!"

"You're still used to thinking of yourself as an antidote, begging your pardon, miss. It's my belief that if you was to come out in society now, you'd have as many admirers as the most of them milk-and-water misses, and what's more, they wouldn't get bored, for you've a taking way with you and plenty of sense in your cockloft. You'll excuse me talking so plain, miss, but I can't abide to see you mistrust yourself so and I'd go bail the lieutenant is enamoured, as you put it."

Octavia put her arms round the maid's neck and kissed her cheek. "Be careful," she said, "or you will raise me so high in my own conceit you will be compelled to give me a sharp set down. If Mr Cardin has really conceived a *tendre* for me, I shall have to watch how I behave towards him if we meet again. I should not like to lose his friendship."

The return to Cotehele was tedious, though towards the end the setting sun painted the sky with crimson, gold, and green. Octavia missed Sir Tristram's conversation. She was sure that Julia must feel the same and that he had been wise to leave.

It was dusk when they arrived, and the gig from the house was waiting for them. Octavia took out her purse to pay the boatman, but he waved it away.

"T'gennulman paid," he said. "Not t'gennulman as seed you off, t'other gennulman." He laid his finger along his nose and nodded his head knowingly.

"Oh," she said, in some confusion, "well, thank you."

The Cotehele groom handed them into the carriage and they set off up the hill.

"All the same," said Octavia as they reached the top, "I wish you will not mention the lieutenant to Lady Langston. She might not understand that I regard him only as a friend, and I should not like to worry her."

"I misdoubt it's not my place to bear tales to her lady-ship," said Ada. "Will you be telling Miss Julia?"

"Oh, yes! And at once, for I cannot wait to see her face when I tell her I have a beau of my own!"

=10=

BEFORE THE WEEK was out, Julia was forced to admit that she felt the loss of Sir Tristram's company.

"There is something about the presence of a gentleman," she complained, seating herself listlessly on the bench in the arbour by the fish pond, "even if one does not care for him personally. Could you not invite your lieutenant to stay for a week or so, Tavy?"

"Heavens, no!" Octavia joined her, smoothing the skirts of the sea-green muslin which was the latest addition to her wardrobe. "If Ada is right about his feelings for me, it would be the outside of enough for me to encourage him so. Besides, though he is a true gentleman, he has none of those airs and graces you are accustomed to in town bucks."

"No more does my James. For that matter, I should not describe Sir Tristram as an out-and-outer. He has no idea of keeping up the style one expects of his position and wealth. Do you know he brought not a single servant to attend him here?"

"Shocking! I expect he knew there were enough servants attached to the house to take care of his needs."

"You may laugh at me, but what is the point of marrying a man with a vast income if he does not care to live up to it? I should be as well off wed to James."

"Have you seriously considered marrying Sir Tristram, then?"

"It would save such a deal of unpleasantness!" Julia burst out. "I hate being confined to this wilderness, and I hate being at outs with Papa. He has not written a single word to me since we came here. But if I changed my mind now, everyone would say it was creampot love, and besides I *do* love James."

Octavia caught a note of uncertainty in her cousin's last words. Was separation already weakening her attachment?

"I am sure that if you marry Sir Tristram, you will come to love him. He is all that is kind and considerate."

"A paragon of a husband! Sometimes I think James was only a dream, or that I dreamed he loves me. If only I might see him! Perhaps he has forgotten me. He is so brilliant, so dedicated, why should he spare a thought for a butterfly like me? He needs a wife who can help him in his work, and he has so many friends he is bound to find one sooner or later. You would be perfect for him, Tavy."

"I think not. A politician must be always entertaining, as I know all too well from experience, and I dislike excessively having an endless stream of guests in the house. You would be a superb hostess, and enjoy it too, and you would soon get in the way of joining political discussions, for I can do it, without having the least interest in the world. As for you being a butterfly, his character is sadly in need of lightening and a little gaiety about the house could only improve him."

Anxious to console Julia, and also to disclaim the possibility of being herself a fitting bride for Mr Wynn, Octavia found herself arguing on the wrong side.

"However, entertaining takes a deal of money," she added hurriedly. "If I am glad to accept your unneeded gowns, it is not because Papa's income is so very small, but because his expenses are large."

"Then you must marry a rich man when I marry James, and I will take your castoffs!"

"I hope you mean to introduce me to some rich, unattached gentlemen, for on those grounds, my poor lieutenant is quite ineligible!"

"I should be happy to, and I'm sure I can think of half a

dozen in London who are not seriously attached, but as long as we languish here nothing can be done. I am tired of sitting here, let us go in."

Nothing held Julia's attention for long. She read a little, played for a while upon the spinet, walked no more than a half mile with Octavia before she grew tired, and grew tired of sitting equally fast. Admonished by her mother, she would set a few stitches in a handkerchief she was embroidering for her father, and then lose the needle. She wrote long letters to James Wynn, then tore them into little pieces and burned them.

But for her cousin's unhappiness, Octavia would have thoroughly enjoyed the peaceful days.

With or without Julia, she loved to stroll in the gardens, and when her cousin would not accompany her she wandered for miles through fields and woods. One day she found herself near Cotehele Mill. She was tempted to visit it, but decided to wait in the hope that Sir Tristram might go with her to explain its business on his return. She talked to the country folk she met, at first understanding with difficulty the Cornish dialect; later, with familiarity, following it easily.

When the weather was bad, or she was tired of walking, she read avidly. Her education, under Julia's governess, had been excellent, and though she had had little opportunity to widen her book-learning since her emancipation from the schoolroom, she had a foundation of taste and discrimination to guide her reading.

The collection of books in the east wing, though not large, was wide-ranging, catering to the catholic tastes of the Edgcumbes and their guests. Learned histories and lively biographies abounded, and when she tired of heavier fare there were plenty of novels to turn to. She searched in particular for *Northanger Abbey*, having gathered from Julia's mention of it that it was suitable reading for a visitor in an ancient house full of secret hiding places. To her disappointment, it was not on the shelves. She wished she had thought to look for a copy in Plymouth.

Towards the end of June, they learned that the earl had arrived at Mount Edgcumbe with his family and a large house-party. A few days later, Octavia entered the drawing room to find her aunt fanning herself with a letter and looking thoroughly flustered.

"What is the matter, ma'am?" she cried, hurrying to her side. "Is it bad news, or are you unwell?"

"My dear, I hardly know," Lady Langston said querulously. "I am all of a flutter. Here is Lord Edgcumbe announcing he will bring his friends to stay at Cotehele for a fortnight and I do not know how I shall manage."

"You always manage at the Priory, Aunt, do you not?"

"But my housekeeper there knows very well how to go on without a great deal of direction. I must send for her at once. I will write to the Priory."

"Surely that is not necessary, when Mrs Pengarth is such an excellent manager. Besides, his lordship cannot expect you to act as his hostess. Does not his elder daughter perform that function?"

"Yes, I believe Lady Emma runs his household. He mentions that she will be coming, to be sure."

"Then you will warn Mrs Pengarth and leave all to her. There is no need to be in a pother about it."

"You are such a comfort, Octavia! I am very glad that you are here, I vow. Only what will your mama think? I promised her that I should not take you into company, for I knew she would dislike it excessively. Perhaps you ought to stay in your chamber while they are here? It will be only two weeks."

"I cannot suppose Mama would expect me to resort to such strong measures! Indeed, she said when I left that I had reached an age where I might be expected not to lose my head at a glimpse of high society. Nor can she blame you when it is none of your doing."

"You think not? I hope you are right. It will be pleasant

to enlarge our party. But Langston will be sadly displeased when he hears. He sent Julia here to be out of the way of meeting people."

"Of meeting one particular person, I believe, ma'am, and one who is not like to be found in my lord's train."

"No, of course not. His lordship is almost as strong a Tory as my dear Langston. Mr—what was his name?—is not like to come with him."

"I daresay Sir Tristram may, however. You will like to see Sir Tristram again, Aunt."

"Oh, yes. Such an amiable gentleman and so much in love with poor Julia. Langston will be pleased that he is come back."

"You see, you may be perfectly easy on all counts. Between us, Mrs Pengarth and I will make sure you need not be troubled with any of the arrangements, so you may look forward to enjoying the company. I shall go and see her at once."

"What a comfort you are, Octavia. I'm sure I am very glad you are here," Lady Langston said again.

Mrs Pengarth had already received her instructions, and said she needed no assistance.

"I take it kindly that you offered, miss, but Lady Emma and me have our own little ways of doing things. His lordship always sends up extra servants and plenty of supplies in good time, so there's no need for you to worry your head about anything."

"I never doubted that you could cope, Mrs Pengarth. Lady Langston was thrown into high fidgets and I promised her I would consult you."

"You can tell her ladyship it's all under control, miss. She's nothing to do but choose which gown to wear, and it's my belief it's her dresser as makes that decision, if you don't mind me saying so, miss."

Octavia laughed. "You may be right," she admitted.

Everything proved to be under control except Raeburn's feelings. The Langstons' butler was decidedly offended to learn that Lord Edgcumbe would bring his majordomo with him, and it took all Octavia's tact to smooth his ruffled feathers without referring him to her aunt. Julia helped by saying that her mother would be excessively put out if she had to share his services with a crowd of strangers.

Julia was in a high gig, her megrims vanished at the prospect of a lively gathering of members of the Haut Ton. Cotehele was transformed instantly from a wilderness to the perfect setting for a house-party. She planned picnics, outings to gather raspberries and cherries, musical evenings, and river cruises.

"I expect his lordship and Lady Emma will have their own plans," Octavia remonstrated.

"It can do no harm to have suggestions ready, in case I am asked," Julia answered gaily. "Do you think we ought to show them the map and the hidden room beneath the Prospect Tower? We might have a treasure hunt."

"By all means a treasure hunt, with cryptic clues such as you have told me you have at the Priory, but let us keep the secret of the tower to ourselves. It may be that Lord Edgcumbe already knows of it and would be displeased to have it generally discussed."

"The Edgcumbes came to stay at the Priory one summer, but it was before I was out, and though I have met them in town, I do not know them well. The earl has the reputation of a wit, and I believe he is partial to amateur theatricals. Only think, he once wrote an opera! Perhaps he will write a play for us to act in."

"I hope not! Surely your mama would not let you take part in a play? I am very certain mine would be excessively shocked at the thought."

"It would be perfectly unexceptionable, I assure you. It is not very different from charades, after all, which I have often acted in. Indeed, we were to perform a play at the Priory once, only the gentlemen quarrelled so about who was to be the hero that it all came to nothing."

"If you were to be the heroine, I am not in the least

surprised that they quarrelled, but it sounds vastly improper to me. I could not join in." Octavia was in a quake at the prospect.

"It is not as if you were being asked to make a living on the stage. What a puritan you are, Tavy! If you were needed I am sure there is no reason you should refuse, but I daresay Lord Edgcumbe will not suggest such a thing anyway. It is scarce a year since his son died. And besides, he is more likely to do so at Mount Edgcumbe, where he can assemble a larger party and there are nearer neighbours to be the audience."

Octavia was profoundly thankful. The idea of dressing up in peculiar clothes and parading in front of an audience filled her with alarm. She did not think it was delicacy of principle though. An examination of her feelings confirmed the melancholy suspicion that she was simply afraid of making a cake of herself in front of a selection of the *beau monde*.

She had been looking forward to the Edgcumbes' arrival as the nearest she would ever come to making a debut in Polite Circles. Suddenly her confidence was gone. New clothes and a different style of hair were feeble foundations on which to build a new image of herself.

Her governess's lessons on the niceties of correct behaviour in fashionable young ladies had passed over her head, as she had expected never to need them. She knew very well how to go on at one of her father's informal political gatherings, how to humour her mother's philanthropic friends. Now she was to be faced with terrifying creatures she had only heard of: Corinthians, Tulips, Wags and Dandies, perhaps even a Nonpareil. Did Lord Edgcumbe number a Court-Card among his acquaintance? What did one say to a Fop at the breakfast table? How was she to deal with a Coxcomb, or, God forbid, a Rake?

And the ladies! The ladies would see at a glance that she was an encroaching mushroom, a crow in peacock's feathers. They would laugh at her efforts to set herself up as one of them.

She could see only mortification ahead.

"Mama is right!" she blurted in a panic. "My aunt was right! I shall stay in my room while they are here."

"What fustian!" Julia exclaimed. "What has put you in such a tweak, Tavy? If it is only that you do not wish to act, of course you shall not."

Octavia tried to explain her apprehension.

"Fustian!" her cousin repeated. "It is not as if you have the patronesses of Almack's to turn up sweet. Even if they guess that you are not accustomed to go about in society, there is nothing in your manners to offend the highest stickler. Be yourself and you will be all the rage."

"I do not aim so high!" Octavia could not help laughing at the exaggeration. "If I can but rub through without putting you or myself to the blush, I shall be more than satisfied."

She hoped against hope that Sir Tristram would return with the other guests. It would be such a comfort to find a friendly face among the crowd.

Mrs Pengarth came in to ask if the two young ladies would mind sharing a bed, so that she could put another young lady in the little chamber. Julia declared that her bed was large enough for a family; sharing with her cousin was no hardship.

"But Octavia's room is scarce wide enough to turn round in," she added. "Who is to have it?"

"A Lady Cynthia Marlowe, miss."

"Cynnie! That's famous! You will like her, Tavy, I promise. She shall use our chamber for dressing."

"Thank you, miss. I was hoping you'd not mind."

"Is Lady Cynthia's brother coming?"

"So I understand, miss. Him and our Lord Ernest was at the university together."

This news sent Julia into a fit of the giggles. Mrs Pengarth smiled indulgently and departed, leaving Octavia to try to make sense of her cousin's gasped explanations.

"Never mind," she spluttered, "you will see. Cynnie is the dearest girl, but Lord Rupert . . . !" She wiped tears of merriment from her eyes.

For three days the house was filled with bustling maids bearing buckets and mops, dusters and beeswax, armfuls of linen, as the chambers in the rarely used east wing were prepared for habitation. Gardeners brought wheelbarrows full of vegetables and flowers; odours of baking and roasting filled the kitchen court and seeped into every room. On the third day, grooms arrived leading several riding hacks. The stables were soon as busy as the house.

The fourth day dawned windy but bright. It took Octavia two hours to decide which of her four new morning dresses was most suited to make a good first impression; she finally settled on an Indian mull with deep rose and white stripes. Julia, still lounging in bed with her morning chocolate, laughed at her as Ada brushed her curls.

"I shall wear blue," she said, "so as not to clash. Ada, there is a bit of pink ribbon somewhere which matches that gown. Thread my locket on it and it will be the perfect ornament. I believe I shall get up now. At last there is something to look forward to!"

The earl and his guests were expected to arrive with the tide early in the afternoon. Octavia was too apprehensive to eat any luncheon. Lady Langston, sighing, decided she must forgo her customary postprandial nap in order to be on hand to greet her host. Julia jumped up a hundred times, vowing she heard the wheels of the carriages carrying the company up from the quay.

The brief meal concluded, her ladyship decided they should sit in the Great Hall.

"Such an old-fashioned house," she lamented. "The drawing room is certainly more suitable, but tucked away as it is, and not half large enough, I daresay, for the whole party, and I do not care to be remiss when his lordship has been so kind. Yes, we shall wait in the Great Hall. I shall not regard the draughts."

Neither Octavia nor Julia could sit still. Octavia wandered about the hall, looking with unseeing eyes at the halberds and muskets on the walls. Her cousin stationed herself by the door into the courtyard, and gazed towards the gatehouse arch.

"They are come!" she cried at last, as a pair of horses crossed her view.

Octavia ran to her side. It seemed to her that at least a score of gaily chattering ladies and gentlemen passed under the arch and along the cobbled walk towards her. The introductions left her befuddled, aware only of Lord Edgcumbe himself, a fine figure of a man in his mid-fifties, of Julia's friend Lady Cynthia, and of Lady Cynthia's brother.

The sight of Lord Rupert Marlowe was enough to drive all the other guests from her mind. He was a young man of medium height but his hair was brushed up in such a way as to add at least five inches. His shirt collar reached nearly to his ears, and the stiff-starched points in front threatened his nose on either side. His neckcloth was a miracle of snowy intricacy reaching to his chin, his emerald green coat so tight that the slightest movement of his arms threatened to burst a seam. A waistcoat of cloth of gold embroidered in green silk with flourishing vines completed his upper half, while matching gold tassels adorned the green-dyed tops of his gleaming boots. Judging by his mincing walk, these latter were as much too tight for him as the coat.

He seemed to be unable to bend at the waist, for his bow consisted of a series of elaborate flourishes of the right hand.

Julia caught Octavia's eye as she gaped after this apparition. She bit her lip and tried to keep a straight face.

"Do not laugh, Miss Gray," said Lady Cynthia mournfully. "I assure you it is in the highest degree mortifying to be obliged to own that popinjay as my brother. Julia will tell you I have been trying these three years to disown him."

"I expect he will grow out of it," soothed Octavia, happy to see that his sister was a sprightly young lady dressed perfectly normally in sprig muslin.

"Certainly," agreed Julia. "Last year Lord Ernest rivalled him, but since his brother died and he became heir, his shirt points have shrunk quite three inches and he can breathe in his coats."

"Lord Ernest?" asked Octavia uncertainly.

They pointed out Lord Edgcumbe's heir, and his lordship's daughter, Lady Emma, a dignified woman in her late twenties who had run his household since her mother's death thirteen years earlier.

"That is her friend, Mrs Alverston, standing next to her," said Lady Cynthia. "She is a widow. An elegant creature, is she not? The elderly lady is her companion, Miss Matilda Crosby."

"Who is the gentleman talking to my aunt, Ju?"

"That is Sir Magnus Rayle. He is a friend of Papa's."

"Which leaves only the two most interesting characters to be described," continued Lady Cynthia. "The gentleman admiring the halberds and muskets is Mr Frederick Findlay, a noted Dandy, and his companion is Lord Wetherford, heir to the Marquis of Stoke and my betrothed!"

"Cynnie! Never say you have thrown your cap over the windmill. Lord Wetherford has been dangling after you this age!"

"That explains why he is regarding Julia and me with such a jaundiced eye," laughed Octavia. "We are keeping him from your side. You had best go to him before he takes us in dislike."

Lady Cynthia smiled invitingly at the young man, and he hurried over, dragging his friend with him. It was soon clear to Octavia that Mr Findlay was one of Julia's court of admirers. She thought him rather ordinary; certainly he was dressed with neat propriety, quite unlike Lord Rupert's excesses, but in spite of the recent boat journey, not a hair on his head was out of place, no smudge marred his glossy boots, and his brown coat showed nary a wrinkle. Feeling very much an outsider, she listened to the four exchanging reminiscences of the past season, and wished that Sir Tristram had come.

= 11 =

WHEN HE BROUGHT guests to Cotehele, Lord Edgcumbe liked to live in the style of his sixteenth-century forebears. He did not go so far as to ban forks from the table in the Great Hall, but dinner was definitely more on the lines of a Tudor banquet than an elegant modern meal. The highlight of the first course was a roasted swan, flanked by a pair of sucking pigs, and a huge bowl of syllabub appeared with the second course. Cider and mead flowed freely, loosening tongues, and when his lordship did his famous impression of a typical Cornish mayor the laughter was uproarious.

When Octavia woke the next morning, it was pouring with rain. The planned picnic was out of the question; even if it stopped raining, the ground must be sodden. She anticipated with dread a day spent trying to make conversation with a dozen people with whom she had nothing in common. Would it, she wondered, be shockingly discourteous to retreat to the bookroom?

Julia was disappointed by the weather, but she bounced out of bed nonetheless, already making alternative plans. James Wynn seemed to be entirely forgotten. Octavia was glad to see her happy, sorry to think her so fickle, and concerned at Sir Tristram's absence. If Mr Wynn's long silence had cured Julia of her *tendre*, it was a pity the baronet was not there to take advantage of it.

Despite the rain, Lord Edgcumbe and his son rode off to visit their tenants. Lady Emma suggested that her guests might like to tour the house and hear something of its history. Lady Langston and Miss Matilda Crosby declined, but all the rest followed her though Lord Wetherford and Sir Magnus had visited Cotehele before.

Octavia had seen all the public rooms already, except the chapel, which was entered through the dining room. She had never thought to wonder what was beyond the door in the corner. Lady Emma showed them the ancient clock, built of handwrought iron in 1485 and still sounding its hourly chime. She also pointed out a tiny balcony high on one wall. It was built so that elderly and sick family members could attend mass without leaving the solar, she explained.

"The solar?" queried Mr Findlay. "And what may that be?"

"A sort of withdrawing room, where the lord's family lived in medieval times. We shall go there next. It was divided more than a century ago into two bedchambers, the Red Room and the South Room."

"By Jove, ma'am," said Mr Findlay, startled, "if you mean to show off my chamber, I had best go check that it is fit to be seen!" He bolted like a frightened horse.

Lord Wetherford laughed. "I have the Red Room," he said, "but I hope I may trust my man to have left it decent. I have been through this before!"

As well as the closet-balcony overlooking the chapel, the South Room proved to possess a squint with a view into the Great Hall, to allow the lord of the manor to see what his retainers were up to. Octavia and Julia were particularly interested to learn that the walnut escritoire against one wall had secret drawers.

"I wonder if Sir Tristram knows about that one?" whispered Julia. "Did he not sleep in this chamber?"

"In the Red Room, I think. We cannot investigate it until they go back to Mount Edgcumbe."

"I'll think of a way," vowed Julia.

Lady Emma indicated the cabinet in the drawing room

as another place of concealment, but she did not demonstrate any of its secrets. Nor did she mention the possibility of hidden rooms or buried treasure. The tour of the house ended in the Punch Room, where the gentlemen were invited to examine the contents of the small wine cellar and sample what they would.

"Strictly a masculine room," said Lady Emma, smiling as she led the ladies out. "The host would retire here with his male guests to drink in peace."

They repaired to the drawing room, where they found Lady Langston and Miss Crosby enjoying a comfortable cose. Sir Magnus, Lord Wetherby, Lord Rupert, and Mr Findlay soon reappeared, having, they announced, split an excellent bottle of Madeira between them.

After a few words with Lady Langston, Sir Magnus approached Octavia.

"I understand your father is a colleague of mine, Miss Gray," he said, "though on the opposite side of the House."

"You are a Member of Parliament, sir?" She smiled up at him. Much as she disliked political discussions, which, she kenw from experience, all too easily deteriorated into argument and even squabbling, it was a subject on which she could hold her own.

Besides, it was gratifying to be sought out by a gentleman with such an air of distinction, a well-bred ease of manner. Though he must be over forty, his brown hair greying at the temples, his close-fitting coat of russet superfine revealed an athletic figure which might be envied by many half his age. According to Lady Cynthia's revelations in the privacy of their chamber the night before, Sir Magnus was fabulously wealthy and hanging out for a wife. Cynnie thought he was trying to decide between Lady Emma and her friend, Mrs Alverston. At his advanced age it was not to be supposed that he expected to fall in love.

"But he is only a knight," she had giggled, "so it is scarcely likely that Lady Emma would leave her papa's house for him, and besides Mrs Alverston is prettier."

The knight seated himself beside Octavia and showed no disposition to let his attention wander towards either of the supposed objects of his affections. She soon discovered that though a Tory he held moderate views on most subjects. More important, as far as she was concerned, he attended with respect to her own opinions, distilled from many hours of listening to her father's friends. He even enquired as to her reasons, especially where she differed from her father's known position.

Accustomed to automatic male disparagement of a female's intellectual capability, she thought him delightful.

Julia had taken a seat close by. She listened in silence for some time. When she decided to join the conversation, Octavia was half amused, half horrified to hear her expounding James Wynn's extreme views as her own. Once recovered from his initial astonishment, Sir Magnus was merely amused. Octavia recognised the odiously familiar signs of condescending superiority.

Failing to hush her cousin, she left her explaining the necessity for revolution and went to the window to see if there was any sign of the rain letting up.

Here she was joined by Lord Rupert. The young man's sartorial splendour was somewhat dimmed today, his coat being maroon, waistcoat striped maroon and grey, and boots of normal hue. His shirtpoints, however, were as dangerous as ever, and he was forced to turn his whole body to transfer his gaze from the weather to Octavia.

"Dashed miserable day!" he announced.

"Not for ducks," she said, watching a family waddling across the lawn towards the upper pond.

"Oh, I say, very good!" He laughed heartily. "Ducks like the rain, you mean to say. Daresay they do, at that. Can't say I ever cared for it myself. Nothing to do."

"I will show you the bookroom, if you like, sir. There is an excellent selection of literature."

His plump face took on a hunted look.

"I say, books?" He laughed again, but nervously. "No

time. Don't you think it must be nearly time for luncheon, ma'am?"

Octavia took pity on him and agreed that luncheon must certainly be served shortly.

He brightened. "Jolly good feast last night, warn't it? Must say, Edgcumbe's pater knows how to put on a feast."

"It was interesting. I had never considered how so simple a thing as the etiquette of dining has changed since Elizabethan days."

"Changed no end," he agreed vaguely.

Octavia struggled through another ten minutes of attempted conversation before luncheon was announced. Lord Rupert seemed pleased to have held her attention so long, and insisted on escorting her down to the dining room and helping her to turtle soup from the buffet. She could not make out whether he was really a knock-in-the-cradle, or had simply no idea in his head beyond his clothes. On the whole she was sorry for him.

She compared him with Lieutenant Cardin, who was much the same age. Lord Rupert was second son of an earl and the lieutenant's father had been a simple sea captain; in many eyes those facts would determine their relative worth. Perhaps England really did need a revolution!

In the middle of the afternoon most of the party were gathered about a roaring blaze in the fireplace of the Great Hall when Lord Edgcumbe and his son returned, soaked to the skin. With them came Sir Tristram, also wet through. He had arrived at the quay aboard the *River Queen* just as they crossed the Tamar after visiting the Edgcumbe holdings at Bere Ferrers.

Octavia's breath caught in her throat when she saw him. As the others fussed about the sodden trio, she hung back, concentrating on convincing herself that it was for Julia's sake she was so glad of his return.

Mrs Pengarth appeared.

"My lord!" she exclaimed. "Lord Ernest, you'll catch your death! What can you be thinking of to stand about in such a state! Sir Tristram, I did not expect you, sir. You'll not mind sharing the South Room with Mr Findlay? Off with you all at once!"

The gentlemen took her scolding in good part and allowed her to shepherd them out.

When Sir Tristram returned, he made his way straight to Octavia's side and presented her with a book.

"A small contribution towards the Encouragement of Literacy," he quoted himself.

"*Northanger Abbey!* How I have been wishing to read it! It is excessively kind in you to have brought it."

"I wanted you to read it while staying in this historic house. We have bettered the heroine already, of course, having found gold and a secret map instead of a laundry list."

Julia came up in time to hear his softly spoken comment.

"Do you know about the other desk with secret drawers?" she asked eagerly. "Lady Emma showed it to us this morning when we toured the house. It is in the South Room. How fortunate that you are to sleep there!"

"Why, Ju, have you been unable to come up with a plan for you and me to investigate it?"

"It is not so easy. The only access is through the Red Room, and while we might be able to sneak into one gentleman's chamber, two is rather more of a challenge."

"Never fear, Miss Langston, you may leave it to me. I shall drug Freddy's port tonight, and as soon as he is sleeping soundly I shall rise and tiptoe stealthily to the desk . . ."

"Oh, no," interrupted Octavia. "You must wait until the stroke of midnight to carry out such nefarious activities. Have you no sense of the Gothic proprieties?"

"You are roasting me," Julia complained. "I am sure you need not drug Mr Findlay's port."

"Indeed you need not!" exclaimed Mr Findlay indignantly, overhearing her incautiously raised voice. "Thank you, Miss Langston, for those kind words. What is this wicked plot against me that you have so neatly foiled? Is Deanbridge planning to assassinate me in order to have you to himself?"

"Perhaps he has found a love philtre and means to try its effects on you." Julia laughed merrily, her blue eys sparkling with enjoyment.

"Then you are right. No potion is needed to make me fall in love with you."

"If I had a love philtre, I should put it in Miss Langston's tea, not waste it on your port, Freddy," Sir Tristram said with a smile. "Besides, I daresay Lord Edgcumbe would regard it as an insult to his excellent port."

"And Lady Emma would object to the adulteration of her precious tea," pointed out Mr Findlay. "With the duty so high, it costs near as much as port, I believe."

Remembering the empty tea chests below the Prospect Tower, the other three would have been surprised to learn that duty had been paid on any tea at Cotehele. Julia giggled and Sir Tristram exchanged a glance with Octavia.

"Since I have no philtre, both tea and port are safe," he said quickly. "And Miss Langston's heart likewise, I fear.

The joking chatter continued, with Lord Wetherford and Cynnie joining them. Sir Tristram made an effort to include Octavia in the conversation, but she wished she had run off with her book to her chamber.

Julia was in her element, surrounded by congenial companions. Her face bright, golden ringlets shining in the flickering firelight, she could not have been more different from the mopish creature of the past few weeks. Nor did she make any attempt to hold aloof from Sir Tristram. She gave him a large share of her smiling attention and he responded with evidently increasing admiration.

Octavia was glad when the time came to change for dinner, though she was not looking forward to the turmoil of another Tudor banquet. Once had been interesting and amusing; the prospect of a whole week made her long for a return to nineteenth-century decorum.

"Are you going to marry Sir Tristram, Ju?" demanded Lady Cynthia as soon as they reached their shared room.

"Perhaps."

"He is quite a catch! Prodigious handsome and Wetherford says he is well able to buy an abbey, though not so plump in the pocket as Sir Magnus. Why have I never met him before?"

"He does not care for London. This is the first year he has been there in an age, except on business."

"Of course that will change when you marry him. He will not expect you to miss the season. Wetherford and I mean to spend every spring in town." Cynnie prattled on about her plans for married life.

Julia was silent. Octavia read unhappiness in her eyes and wished she could talk to her privately. Lady Cynthia did not retire even momentarily to her own little chamber, and they went down to dinner without exchanging a word.

Mr Findlay attached himself to Octavia. Although he had scarcely noticed her existence previously, he insisted on escorting her into the Great Hall, sat beside her, and helped her to all the choicest morsels.

She thought him rather dull, but she could not fault his persistence. He made straight for her side when the gentlemen joined the ladies in the drawing room, and cast not a glance at the corner where Julia and Sir Tristram were laughing together. She was almost tempted to believe that he had indeed taken a love potion, and that it had miscarried and fixed his interest on her. The only alternative was that he had been dazzled by her evening dress of garnet silk, newly trimmed with smuggled French lace.

In the course of the evening she gradually lost her shyness of him and stopped trying consciously to behave like a demure young lady of fashion. By the time the tea tray was brought in she was perfectly comfortable talking to him, though her opinion of him had not changed.

"Dare I taste it?" he said as he passed her a cup of tea. "Perhaps you too should beware, Miss Gray."

"I can think of no reason why anyone might choose to put a love philtre in my tea," she answered, sipping.

"Can you not? You are an exceptionally modest young lady."

Octavia could not make out whether he was laughing at her or merely flattering her because flattery was a habit. She drank her tea in silence, thinking that her mama had been quite right to shun society.

She would have liked to consult her world-wise cousin about Mr Findlay's strange behaviour when at last Lady Cynthia retired and left them alone together. Julia was engrossed in her own wretchedness.

"James has forgotten me!" Her ringlets tightly confined in curlpapers under her lacy nightcap, tears running down her face, she looked like a small, lost child.

Octavia hugged her. "Surely not! He has not written lest the letter be intercepted, and you know yourself the difficulty of his coming here."

"He has forgotten me. When next Sir Tristram offers, I shall accept him."

Her own heart sinking inexplicably, Octavia protested. "Is it fair to accept him when your heart is given to another?"

"If Mr Wynn spurns it, it shall not remain long in his keeping," said Julia proudly. "I like and respect Sir Tristram, and Papa says that is sufficient foundation for a happy marriage. Perhaps I may learn to love him once we are wed." She blew out the candle.

"Oh, Ju!" Kissing her cheek for lack of words of comfort, Octavia lay down. She was aware of her cousin lying rigidly wakeful beside her, but exhausted by a difficult day she soon drifted into sleep.

She found the next day no easier. The rain continued, confining everyone to the house. Mr Findlay once again devoted himself to her amusement, though they had no interests in common that she could discover. Still worse, Lord Rupert had overnight conceived a puppylike admiration and followed her everywhere, to Lord Ernest's obvious annoyance.

She managed to escape for long enough to enjoy a rational conversation with Sir Magnus; to retire with her book, as she longed to do, was out of the question.

If Sir Tristram had not already declared his intentions, Julia might have been accused of setting her cap at him. She exerted all her arts to charm him. Octavia thought her more charming when she was being natural, but Julia had spent two seasons successfully attracting gentlemen so she must be supposed to know what she was about.

Lady Emma was heard to ask Lady Langston when an announcement was to be expected.

By the time everyone dispersed to change for dinner, Octavia was desperate for a few moments of solitude. She dressed quickly and hurried down to the chapel. She was not of a religious turn of mind, but she would be out of the way of the servants and no one else was likely to find her.

She sat down in a pew at the back, behind the rood screen, and tried to bring order to her confused thoughts. Suddenly she heard Sir Tristram's voice.

Looking round in surprise, she realised it was coming from the alcove above, where the old solar opened onto the chapel.

"I must thank you, Freddy," he said, "for taking care of Miss Gray. I should think you might safely leave her to Marlowe now."

"Shouldn't dream of it," came Mr Findlay's reply. "That mooncalf would bore her to death within the day."

"I didn't mean you to devote every minute to her for the rest of your stay. Just to entertain her now and then so that I might have a clear field with Miss Langston."

"But it's a pleasure, my dear chap. The Incomparable's cousin is a taking little thing, 'pon rep, and something of an Original when you come to know her. It's for me to thank you for forcing me into her company."

Octavia was paralysed. She longed to flee, feared her footsteps might be heard, and could not help wishing to hear the rest of the conversation.

"An engaging young lady, is she not?" Sir Tristram's voice.

"Can't imagine why I've not seen her about town."

"I understand she has never made a formal debut in society," said the baronet. Octavia knew he was thinking back to their first meeting, or the second, when she had presented a still more deplorable appearance. "I am glad you like her, but all the same it is good of you to forgo Julia's company in my favour."

"Your intentions are serious, Deanbridge; mine are not," said Mr Findlay simply. "I've neither the funds nor the temperament to step into parson's mousetrap. Matter of fact, I've a notion I've heard you say you'd no thought of getting leg-shackled."

"Nor did I. Know my brother-in-law? No? Glad to hear it: he's a curst rum touch. Well, the thing is, my sister's produced a son. My heir. I've nothing against the child, you understand, it's not a year old yet. But I'll be damned if I'll have my nodcock of a brother-in-law taking over Dean Park if I slip my wind before the boy reaches his majority, and I'll tell you, Valletort's death last year made me think."

"Nothing for it, you need a son of your own. And having made up your mind to it, you head for town, fall for the Incomparable, and Bob's your uncle. I'll be first with my congratulations. When do you pop the question?"

A note of caution entered Sir Tristram's voice. "I've been refused once and I don't care to trust my luck again till I'm sure of the outcome."

"Dash it, man, the chit's casting out every lure in the book! It's plain as the nose on your face she means to have you."

"There's no hurry," said Sir Tristram obstinately. "Are

you ready? Let's go down. Oh, and Freddy, don't you go trifling with Miss Gray's affections, raising any hopes in her breast that you don't mean to satisfy, or it'll be pistols at dawn!"

= 12 =

OCTAVIA FOUND IT impossible to meet either Sir Tristram's or Mr Findlay's eyes when she saw them in the Great Hall. With a skill she did not know she possessed, she manoeuvred to sit between Lord Rupert and Sir Magnus, both of whom were happy to oblige.

When Lady Emma led the ladies up to the drawing room, leaving the gentlemen to their port and brandy, she at last had leisure for consideration of what she had overheard. Claiming a letter to be written, she retired to a corner to think.

On reexamination, it was not so bad after all. To be sure, Mr Findlay's attentions had started as a favour to a friend, but he had expressed gratitude for the push and described her as "taking." Sir Tristram had been his wonted kind self in wishing to see to her comfort, and he had said she was "engaging." To a young lady unaccustomed to compliments, these moderate words of praise meant a good deal.

Besides, she was glad to find elucidation of Mr Findlay's puzzling behaviour, and Sir Tristram's reason for wishing to marry brought a smile to her lips. Having taken that decision, it was scarce surprising that he should have formed a serious passion for Julia. It did surprise her that he meant to delay offering for her hand when she so obviously had decided to accept him.

If Mr Wynn should suddenly turn up, Sir Tristram might find he had missed his chance. On the other hand, what if he turned up when they were already betrothed, and Julia found she still loved him?

She was puzzling over this question when the gentlemen came in. Mr Findlay headed directly for her side. When she explained that she was writing to her parents, he insisted on dictating to her a paragraph describing a certain "exquisite and charming fribble," namely himself. She laughed but did not write it down.

"Mama would be excessively shocked," she said, "to learn that I am consorting with a gentleman who is both 'complete to a shade' and 'bang up to the knocker.' If she knew that it takes you two hours to tie your cravat, and that you discard five or six in the process, she would request the spoiled ones to convert into clothing for the natives of the South Sea Islands."

He raised both hands to protect his superbly arranged neckcloth. "Never!" he declaimed. "I am ready to defend my cravat against any number of South Sea Islanders, with my life if necessary. This, Miss Gray, is the style known as the *Trône d'Amour*. Does it please you?"

"To tell the truth," she said, regarding it critically, "I believe only another Dandy could tell the difference between that and any other style."

He sighed and shook his head mournfully.

In the days that followed, the weather improved. The gentlemen and several of the ladies went riding, leaving Octavia, who had never had the opportunity of learning, with Lady Langston and Miss Crosby. She was perfectly happy to stay behind. Though she had nearly overcome her fear of committing an inexcusable *faux pas*, she regretted the quiet days she had passed before the arrival of the house-party, and looked forward to their departure.

She wandered alone about the gardens, now bereft of the glory of rhododendron and azalea but blooming with flowers she could not name. There was time for books, and she read *Northanger Abbey* with great enjoyment, the more particularly because Sir Tristram had reported in disgust that the second mysterious cabinet held a varied but not in the least mysterious collection of buttons.

"How clever of Miss Austen to sympathise with Catherine even as she laughs at her!" she exclaimed to Julia and Sir Tristram. "It is quite the most amusing book I have read."

"Amusing!" cried Julia. "I thought it monstrous disappointing. Every time Catherine thought she had discovered a mystery, it turned out to be nothing!"

"Therein lies the humour," said Sir Tristram.

"It was not a proper Gothic novel at all." Julia sounded cross. "Nor yet a romance, for I do not remember that Catherine fainted even once and Henry Tilney was far too dull to be a proper hero." She turned away to talk to Mr Findlay, who had vocally expressed his dissatisfaction at not having read the book.

"I have read one or two Gothic novels," said Octavia. "*The Castle of Otranto* of course, and *The Monk*. I confess I thought them excessively silly, but I beg you will not tell Julia so!"

They discussed the essential ingredients of a good novel, until Octavia guiltily realised she was keeping him from Julia and claimed the necessity of attending on her aunt.

Lady Langston greeted her with an exclamation of relief.

"Octavia, dear child, you will know what I ought to do. Such a comfort to me as you are! Here is Lady Emma, just this moment, inviting us to go with them to Mount Edgcumbe, for you know they go tomorrow, and what I am to say I'm sure I don't know. I daresay Langston will dislike it vastly. 'Take her to Cotehele,' he said to me, meaning Julia, of course, 'and there she shall stay until she comes to her senses.' "

"I believe my cousin has come to her senses, ma'am. Have you not noticed how obligingly she behaves to Sir Tristram?"

"Do you think she will have him? I wish he will ask her

113

again quickly! But until they are betrothed, I cannot like to go against Langston's wishes."

"Does Sir Tristram go or stay?"

"He will hardly care to stay here if we go. Should you like to go, Octavia? Mount Edgcumbe is a prodigious pretty place. I daresay they can make up quite thirty beds! And Edgcumbe is such a hospitable gentleman, he does not like to see them empty."

Octavia shuddered mentally at the idea of being one of thirty guests, but she had longed to visit Mount Edgcumbe since seeing it from the Sound. Among so many, perhaps she would be able to escape and explore on her own.

"We might go for a few days, Aunt," she said. "If you see anything in Julia's manner to alarm you, it will be easy enough to return here."

"You are right! I should not know at all how to go on without you, I declare. Now if only you will beg Lady Emma to step over, I shall tell her we are happy to accept. You are a dear, good girl, Octavia, and so I shall inform my sister." In an access of energetic enthusiasm, Lady Langston leaned close and kissed her niece.

Lord Edgcumbe's sailing barge was provided with every comfort, and the voyage down the river was more like a pleasure outing than a necessary journey. Octavia told Mr Findlay about her dawn arrival on the limestone boat, though she omitted the story of the smugglers' rendezvous. When they passed Halton Quay she saw the notorious scarlet petticoat hanging out to dry. Wondering where the Riding Officer was meddling today, she exchanged a glance of complicity with Sir Tristram.

There were open carriages waiting at the Cremyll ferry landing. They drove up the long, straight avenue towards the mansion. The square Tudor facade of pinkish stone had been embellished by succeeding generations, as Lady Emma explained to Octavia, with a classical entrance and octagonal towers at each end. Octavia thought it magnificent.

They reached the house just in time to change for dinner. For that first evening there were no additions to their company, but the atmosphere in the elegant dining room was very different from that of the Great Hall at Cotehele. To Octavia it seemed to have swung to the opposite extreme, making her father's political dinners seem positively casual. Conversation was carried on in politely lowered voices, and entirely with one's immediate neighbours, while servants passed the dishes so efficiently that one need never ask for anything.

Julia told her later that compared to the strict etiquette of a London dinner party, it had been quite informal. Once again she was seized with a dread of falling into some mortifying error which would expose her lack of aquaintance with the ways of society.

The next day's arrivals added considerably to Julia's court. She flirted determinedly with every male who seemed disposed to pay her the least attention, and Octavia found it hard to blame her, since Sir Tristram had not yet renewed his offer for her hand. The baronet soon abandoned his first efforts to compete for her favour, and disappeared frequently on long solitary walks or rides.

Octavia found the house less interesting than Cotehele, but the grounds superb. She too often wandered alone, escaping from her own minor court. There were miles of carriage drives with views over the busy Sound to Plymouth, or out into the English Channel, as far as the Eddystone Lighthouse; follies and monuments galore, including the fake Gothic ruin and the temple to Milton which she had seen from aboard ship; formal gardens in the Italian, French, and English styles; and fortifications which bore witness to the many threats of invasion from Spanish or French fleets over the centuries.

In a gloomy dell hung with ferns and creeping ivy, set about with Roman urns, she found, surrounding a dripping fountain, a number of gravestones erected in memory of family pets. Most of these, unsurprisingly, were dogs, but one was a pyramidal monument to a favourite pig by the name of Cupid. The Edgcumbes were undoubtedly animal lovers: in the Garden House in the English garden stood the skeleton of a dog, the bones whitened with age.

Octavia asked Lord Ernest about it.

"That was the first baron's animal," he told her. "Somewhat macabre, ain't it? They say he was a favourite of George II because he was the only courtier shorter than the king, but he was made a baron to save him from some enquiry about the management of Cornish boroughs. If you think he was a dirty dish, though, let me tell you about the second baron."

"Do you think you ought, my lord?" Octavia objected anxiously. She remembered that Sir Tristram had mentioned the "bad baron," who had been a gambler.

"No harm," insisted the young man. "It's ancient history, and everybody knows, and besides, everyone has the odd skeleton in the closet, if not in the summer house. The second baron was the black sheep of the family. He was sent abroad to try and stop his gambling. He brought back the orange trees in the Italian garden, though he continued to gamble as badly as ever. He never married, but he had four b . . . children by his mistress . . ."

"I am quite certain you should not be telling me this, my lord!" Octavia turned away, blushing. "Thank you for telling me about the dog skeleton, but I believe I have heard enough of the family history for the present."

"Just come to me if you have any more questions," he said genially, grinning at her. "M'sister's the expert though."

"I shall ask Lady Emma in future," she said hastily.

So that was the bad baron's secret! The son mentioned in the scrap of paper they had found with the gold coins was a love child. And Sir Tristram had claimed to know to whom the money belonged, so there must be descendants still acknowledged by the family.

She would have liked to ask him about it, but it was too delicate a subject to be approached in company. Though she often saw him in the distance while out walking, he never came close, seeming to avoid her deliberately.

She wished he would ask her advice again about Julia. She would tell him to propose at once, for she saw in her cousin's flirting the gaiety of desperation.

One morning she walked down to the tiny hamlet of Cremyll to make enquiries about the ferry. She still had a few guineas left, and thought to make a shopping expedition as an excuse to see Lieutenant Cardin. Smothered by the rarified atmosphere of Polite Society, she longed to talk to an ordinary person for once.

Doubtless she had only to hint of her desire to Lady Emma and a private vessel would be put at her disposal. She preferred to take the common ferry.

Under a grey sky, grey swells rolled shoreward, tacking a lacy fringe of white froth around the grey rocks. Herring gulls swooped about the shipping in the Sound.

Looking out across the Tamar to Devil's Point, she saw a dark shape arc out of the water, reentering with scarcely a splash. Another followed, then two in unison.

"Dolphins," said a voice close by.

She turned to find Sir Tristram at her side, holding the reins of his horse.

"They are beautiful! How carefree they look!"

"Should you like to go closer? There is a rowboat moored by the quay that we might borrow."

"I should like it of all things, but would it not be dangerous?"

"You do not care to trust yourself to my rowing?" he asked with a smile. "I assure you I was used to row right across when I was a boy."

"I did not suppose you would offer if you had no faith in

your own seamanship. I meant, are the dolphins not dangerous?"

"Since the ancient times they have been reputed friendly creatures. There are even stories of them helping shipwrecked mariners. Certainly I have known them to play about a moving boat with every evidence of enjoyment and no threat of harm to the passengers."

"Oh, let us go, then!"

He gave a small boy sixpence to take his mount back to the lodge, and in no time they were several hundred feet out in the channel. Sleek grey shapes twisted and turned in the water, so close to the dinghy that Octavia could have leaned over the side and touched them. She was fascinated by the intelligence in their eyes, and the smiles on their long-nosed faces brought an answering smile to her lips.

Sir Tristram rested his oars and watched her.

"Why cannot humans be so natural and joyous?" she asked rhetorically.

He chose to take her literally. "Because they cannot swim so well, and besides, a diet of fish would soon grow monotonous."

"You are in a teasing humour today, sir. Oh, look!"

Not twenty feet from the boat a dolphin shot vertically into the air, descending with a splash which would have drenched them had they been any closer. As if excited by the display, nine or ten of the animals rose to the surface in a humpbacked chain that mimicked a monstrous sea serpent.

With a cry of delight, Octavia rose to her feet for a closer view. The little vessel tilted, her cry turned to alarm, and with a splash only slightly less than that of the acrobatic dolphin, she landed in the river.

Before Sir Tristram could react, a hitherto unnoticed current had moved the dinghy several feet away from her. Her ballooning skirts buoyed her momentarily, but within seconds they must soak through, leaving her to sink.

If he dived in and swam to the rescue, the boat would

float away, stranding them in mid-channel. With two powerful strokes of the oars he moved closer, then unshipped one of them and held it out towards her, trying to steady the boat at the same time.

She reached for the blade, caught it with both hands, hung on desperately as he drew her in. She grasped at the gunwale, and he abandoned the oar to pull her over the side into the bilge.

For a moment, neither of them could speak, then Octavia gasped, "They held me up. The dolphins, they held me up. I felt them beneath me."

He looked at her blankly, still stunned by her narrow escape.

"It's true!" she insisted. "Their skins are leathery, not slimy at all. I felt them." She began to shiver convulsively.

He took off his coat and wrapped it around her, though it was scarcely less wet than her gown.

"We must get back to the house quickly," he said. "The dolphins? Are you sure?"

She nodded. He reached out and clasped both her hands, gazing into her eyes as if trying to read something in their depths, then turned to the oars.

Or rather, to the one oar.

The other, the one he had held out to her, was nowhere to be seen.

"So much for my seamanship!" he said in disgust. "The first emergency and I lose my oar! Well, I have seen boats propelled by one so I know it is possible."

She grinned, wrinkled her nose at him, and shook her head.

"Alas, sir, you persuaded me to trust you. How am I deceived!"

"That is no way to speak to your rescuer! I was not to know you had no more common sense than to fall overboard."

Sir Tristram placed the remaining oar over the stern and stood up, balancing carefully. With no rowlock to hold it, it slid about haphazardly, and no matter how hard he waggled it, he merely rocked the dinghy without making the slightest forward progress.

"Sit down!" ordered Octavia in alarm. "If *you* fall overboard I shall never have the strength to pull you in."

"There is more skill involved than I expected," he sighed, obeying. "There is nothing for it, we shall have to shout for help. How excessively humiliating!"

"Yes, but how fortunate that we are in the middle of one of the busiest shipping lanes in the world. I wish we had the scarlet petticoat from Halton Quay. We might tie it to the oar and wave it." She tried to stop her teeth chattering.

"You are not wearing scarlet petticoats? Pity. I trust that after this you will never leave home without one. My neckcloth will be better than nothing, I daresay." He pulled it off, tied one end to the oar, and raised it amidships like a mast. "Halloo!" he shouted, then stood up and shouted again, "Halloo!"

"Help!" cried Octavia. Shivering, she pulled his coat closer about her. If she had to be marooned at sea in an open boat, she had rather be marooned with him than with anyone else she knew. Coatless, his shirt open at the neck and his dark locks ruffled by the breeze, he only wanted sword in hand to present the very picture of a pirate chief. "Help!" she called.

They drifted slowly seaward on the ebbing tide.

It seemed like an endless time before a sloop sailed across their bow within hailing distance and a faint "Ho there!" answered their hoarse shouts. Octavia was white-lipped with cold, though Sir Tristram's damp clothes had dried on him and he tried to persuade her it was a warm day.

"Not long now," he said in anxious reassurance as the sloop lowered its sails, lost way, and came round. "Good God, I believe it is the *Seamew!* Yes, they are lowering a boat and even from here I recognise Jack Day's dimensions. Your favourite free-trader is coming to the rescue, my dear!"

"D-don't tell anyone about the d-dolphins," begged Octavia. "I m-mean about them saving m-me. P-please don't."

He smiled understandingly. "I shall take all the credit to myself, never fear. It will in some degree atone for my subsequent stupidity. Ho, Captain Day! I have never been more glad to see anyone in my life!"

Octavia was passed across into the *Seamew*'s gig like a bale of smuggled silk, Sir Tristram followed, and their dinghy was tied on behind. Red Jack insisted on substituting his own warm dry coat for the baronet's wet one. It covered her to her knees. Already several degrees warmer, the colour returning to her face, she sat on a bench among the rowers while the two men discussed whether to take her aboard the *Seamew* to dry off, or to head straight for Cremyll.

The rowers were a mixed crew. Two looked no different from any honest seaman, but one was a villainous fellow with long mustaches and a black-patched eye, while the fourth had a hook in place of his left hand and a hugely muscular right arm. They all nodded and smiled at Octavia.

"Tha'lt soon warrum up, I'll warrant, miss," said the one-eyed man encouragingly in the slow, soft accents of a Yorkshireman. "T'air's warrum enow for all t'water's coldish."

Sir Tristram turned to her. "I believe we will go directly to Mount Edgcumbe, Miss Gray," he said. "The captain vouches for his men's silence . . ."

"Aye," "Aye," and "Right enough," were heard from the crew.

". . . But I think it best you do not board the *Seamew* without a female companion."

"Oh yes, let us go back at once. I am hardly cold at all now, and perhaps my aunt is worrying."

The gig turned and headed towards the ferry landing, the one-handed rower pulling as hard with his right arm as the others with two.

Red Jack noticed Octavia's interest.

"Dan Small was in the navy till he lost his hand," he said. "Now he's my right-hand man."

Dan Small grinned at her, and the rest laughed as at a time-honoured joke.

"Ahoy, Cap'n Day!" came a booming hail. "Avast there, *Seamew's* gig!"

They all looked round. A cutter bearing the flag of the Customs service was bearing down on them, a figure on the bow raising a speaking trumpet to call again.

"Avast there, boys," Red Jack ordered. "For once, we've nothing aboard to upset the revenuer."

"Lay to for searching!"

The voice was distorted by the loudspeaker, but Octavia thought she recognised it. She had meant to visit Lieutenant Cardin; it seemed that he had come to her.

The cutter pulled alongside and threw down a rope ladder.

"Come aboard, if you please, Captain," requested Lieutenant Cardin, leaning on the rail. "All of you, one by one."

"If you insist, Lieutenant," said Red Jack genially. "We've nothing to hide. But I've a young lady here has taken an unwanted swim and I'd prefer to put her ashore without delay."

Mr Cardin scanned the group in the boat, his gaze passing over Sir Tristram in his shirtsleeves and wet-haired Octavia swathed in Red Jack's coat. He raised his eyebrows in disbelief. "Young lady? Come now, Captain!" Octavia waved to him and he took a second look. "What the devil . . . . Miss Gray!"

"Correct, Lieutenant," said Sir Tristram dryly. "And I am prepared to vouch that there is no contraband aboard, at present."

"Sir Tristram! Sir, I beg your pardon, I did not recognise you. Of course I accept your word. But Miss Gray . . . is she all right?"

"I shall do very well," Octavia said with a smile, "but I should like to get home and dry quickly. I shall come and see you tomorrow, if you will be ashore?"

"All day!" he said fervently. "Nothing shall make me stir from the Customs House until you come." He flushed at the interested looks of both the smugglers and his own men. "Carry on, Captain Day."

"Until next time, Lieutenant." Red Jack saluted, grinning, and the rowers took up their oars. "A good lad," he commented as they pulled away, "and though I've not yet tried to insult him, the word is he'll not take a bribe."

"Of course he will not," said Octavia indignantly.

When they reached the Cremyll quay, Red Jack lifted Octavia in his arms and carried her ashore, despite her protests that she was perfectly able to walk. He carried her all the way to the gates of Mount Edgcumbe, waited while Sir Tristram retrieved his horse from the lodge, and then passed her up to him.

"This," said Sir Tristram in mock severity, smiling down at her, "is becoming a habit!"

His strong arm holding her safe, he cantered up the avenue.

= 13 =

LADY LANGSTON WAS thoroughly alarmed by her niece's
adventure. In fact, Lady Langston was altogether unhappy
with the results of her decision to come to Mount
Edgcumbe. Sir Tristram had not proposed, Julia flirted
wildly with every gentleman she saw, and now Lord
Edgcumbe was planning to mount a production of a play
he had recently completed.

"Yes, I know we were to have a play at the Priory," she
said to her disappointed daughter, "but it is quite different
in one's own home with one's friends about one. Not to
mention your father. No, my mind is quite made up. We
shall return to Cotehele tomorrow."

"If Tavy has not caught her death of cold," said Julia, not
without hope.

"Sorry, Ju, I am never ill. If you do not object, Aunt, I
should like to do some shopping in Plymouth on the way.
My slippers are nearly worn through."

"I suppose that would be unexceptionable, my dear, if
Ada goes with you. You came to no harm last time."

"May I go too, Mama? I am sure if no harm comes to
Octavia, it cannot possibly come to me."

"Certainly not!" Her irritation at her daughter's recent
behaviour roused her ladyship to unusual sharpness.

Julia went off with a sulky face.

When Sir Tristram heard of Lady Langston's decision,
he asked her permission to return to Cotehele with them.
It was granted with relief, the anxious mother being half

convinced he had given up hope. She was also pleased at his offer to escort Octavia to Plymouth.

"I know she goes about alone in London," she confided, "but what I should say to her mama if something happened, I cannot think."

"I believe Plymouth to be safer than London," he said, "but the tides are such at present that she will arrive at Cotehele after dark. I promise you I shall not strand her in mid-channel again."

"Oh, no, for Edgcumbe has offered us the use of two of his barges. One will take Julia and me directly to Cotehele, and the other will take Octavia to Plymouth and bring her after us when she is ready. What a very hospitable gentleman Edgcumbe is!"

Sir Tristram was pleased to agree with this praise of his godfather, and went off to tell Octavia that he would accompany her on the morrow.

"To lend you countenance," he teased, "which you will certainly need for I expect half Plymouth knows by now that the lieutenant is smitten."

"Mr Findlay has offered to escort me too," she answered, her colour heightened. "I refused him, because I was afraid he might laugh at Mr Cardin. I know you will not, and I shall be glad of your company."

Sir Magnus next sought her out. He had continued kind to her, and besides finding him an interesting person to talk to, she had come to regard him as a friend among the crowd.

"I am sorry you are going, Miss Gray. May I call on you at Cotehele?" he requested.

"Of course, if you wish to, sir. Only I expect you ought to ask my aunt, and I believe she will not care to receive visitors. Though of course as a friend of my uncle, you must always be welcome."

"Thank you, ma'am, but perhaps it will be best if I do not disturb her ladyship." He sighed. "You will convey my greetings to your father when you return to town." He kissed her hand, and as he turned away she thought she heard him say as if to himself, "I am too old for her. Mrs. Alverston will suit me very well."

She looked after him, startled. Had she heard aright? Did his words mean what they seemed to mean?

No, she scolded herself. She was growing conceited with too much attention. Mama would be shocked to learn what ideas two weeks in exalted company had put into her head. But at least she had two friends whose kindness she had no excuse to misinterpret. With Sir Tristram in pursuit of Julia and Red Jack Day so firmly attached to his Martha, only good-natured generosity could explain their willingness to assist her.

She was sitting in the magnificent drawing room that evening, listening to the more talented members of the party performing a variety of musical offerings, when a footman made his way to her side.

"Beggin' your pardon, miss, there's two persons to see you. That is, not wishful of disturbing you, only to know are you quite recovered. I put 'em in his lordship's library. What will I tell 'em, miss?"

"Who are they? Did they not give their names?"

"It's Captain Day and Mr Cardin, miss. I know 'em both."

"I will come down at once."

She slipped out of the room and was halfway down the grand staircase when Julia called to her from the top.

"Tavy! What is it? Are you all right? I saw you leave and thought maybe you do not feel quite the thing. But why are you going downstairs?"

"I am perfectly well, Ju. I have visitors."

"Visitors? How extraordinary! Who is it? May I come with you to meet them?"

Octavia considered. The footman had referred to them as "persons." Clearly in his view they were not gentlemen. However, she could see no harm coming from Julia meeting them.

"If you wish," she agreed. "It is Captain Day, who rescued Sir Tristram and me this morning, and Lieutenant Cardin, the Customs officer I have told you about."

"The one who is in love with you? I cannot wait to meet him! Come!"

To Octavia's relief, her callers were not at daggers drawn. Indeed they seemed on remarkably good terms, considering their positions on opposite sides of the law. She put it down to their mutual, if vague, connection with the Edgcumbes. The lieutenant, younger and less sure of himself, was somewhat confused at being introduced to so elegant a young lady as Miss Langston, but there was nothing to blush for in his manners.

They both made enquiries about her health and were pleased to hear she had suffered no ill effects from her ducking. The lieutenant confirmed their appointment on the morrow, looked disappointed on learning that Sir Tristram would go with her, and took his leave with the lowest of low bows to Julia. Red Jack lingered a moment longer, to press into her hand a folded paper which he asked her to deliver to Mrs Pengarth.

"I shan't be coming up to Cotehele for a while," he explained.

"How did you know we are to return there?" asked Octavia.

"Oh, his lordship mentioned it," said Red Jack evasively. "I must be on my way, miss. Good-bye, Miss Langston, a pleasure to have made your acquaintance."

He left Octavia wondering just how close was his relationship to the Edgcumbes.

The next morning it was Julia's turn to press a folded paper into Octavia's hand.

"Take it to the post in Plymouth," she entreated. "I must find out for certain whether James has forgotten me."

"I ought not." She looked at the letter uncertainly.

"You have not given your word to thwart our love?"

"No, but I am sure my aunt does not expect that I should

encourage it. Oh, don't cry, Ju! That was horrid of me. Of course I shall post it for you. It is miserable for you not to know how he feels."

Julia blinked back tears. "It is much worse than knowing he does not love me. At least, I think so now. Perhaps I will change my mind if that comes to pass." She tried to smile. "I shall see you this evening then, at Cotehele. Thank you, Tavy."

A stylish barouche carried Lady Langston, her daughter, and her abigail down the avenue to Cremyll quay. With them went Miss Matilda Crosby, Lady Emma Edgcumbe's companion. For some years now Lady Emma had not felt the need of a chaperone, and the small, wispy grey woman, a poor relation, was in no wise suited to become her friend. She suited Lady Langston perfectly, being always willing to fetch and carry, sort tangled silks, or carry on a conversation without requiring more response than an occasional "tut tut," or "really?"

Five young gentlemen went down to the quay to wave farewell to Julia. They had all angled unsuccessfully for invitations to Cotehele, and looked with envy on Sir Tristram. Not only had he received the coveted invitation, but he had also sufficient confidence in his expectations to spend the day with Miss Langston's little cousin!

Octavia overheard one or two remarks hopeful of his suffering a severe set-down when he rejoined the Incomparable.

Her own departure, some hours later, was far from mortifying in comparison. Sir Magnus, Mr Findlay, and Lord Rupert, spectacular in blue and orange, all rode down to Cremyll to take their leave. Nonetheless, she stepped aboard the small sailing barge with the light-heartedness of a child waking to the first day of the holidays.

The crossing was swift, a stiff breeze chopping the water into wavelets which sparkled in the sun. They landed at Phoenix Wharf again. Octavia took Sir Tristram's arm and they were walking towards the Customs House when Ada pulled at her sleeve.

"Look, miss!" She pointed along the quay. "Isn't that Mr Wynn?"

"Surely not!" Octavia turned to look. Some hundred feet off, a tall, thin man was talking to a seaman. His hat was in his hand, and that reddish bush of hair was unmistakable. "Heavens above, you are right, Ada! Whatever shall I do?"

She was given no time to decide. Mr Wynn jammed his hat on his head, swung round, and started towards them at a rapid pace.

Dithering, she put her hand on Ada's arm as he approached. The gesture caught his eye and he glanced at the maid. A puzzled frown crossed his high forehead: he thought he knew her but could not identify her. His gaze moved on to Octavia.

Always oblivious of clothes, he had not the slightest difficulty in recognising her face.

"Miss Gray! What a happy chance!"

"Good afternoon, Mr Wynn." Her mind spinning with conjecture, Octavia could think of nothing to say but, "Sir Tristram, you remember Mr James Wynn?"

The gentlemen bowed to each other, the baronet looking as stunned as Octavia felt.

"Your servant, sir," said Mr Wynn. "I am looking for passage to Cotehele. Perhaps you can advise me?"

Sir Tristram glanced at Octavia, his eyebrows raised. If he expected her to send Mr Wynn to the rightabout, he looked in vain. She had promised Julia not to interfere. As for Mr Wynn, he showed not the least sign of awkwardness. It did not seem to dawn on him that there could be any objection to his arrival at Cotehele, nor that Julia might not welcome him after his long silence.

"Perhaps you would like to join us," Sir Tristram offered politely. "We sail for Cotehele this evening."

Octavia turned to him in exasperation. Why was he

deliberately sabotaging his own chances? Was he so over-whelmingly certain of eventual success?'

At that moment, Lieutenant Cardin hurried up. He had expected to see Sir Tristram but was clearly displeased to find that yet another rival for Miss Gray's attention had appeared. Mr Wynn flung a look of scorn at his uniform, symbol of the oppressing class, and ignored him.

"Thank you, sir," he said to the baronet. "I shall gladly take advantage of your kind offer. Miss Gray, allow me to escort you about the town in the meantime. I have never visited Plymouth before and should like to see any monu-ments to the days when the Parliamentarians so bravely held it against the power of Charles I."

"I have shopping to do, Mr Wynn," said Octavia crossly. "Perhaps you can persuade Sir Tristram and the lieutenant to show you the sights."

Mr Cardin looked at her with hurt in his dark blue spaniel eyes. Sir Tristram grinned.

"We are a troublesome bunch," he said cheerfully, "but I must regretfully inform you that you will not find it so easy to dispose of us. Lead on, Miss Gray, and let milliner and mantua maker beware!"

Octavia wished she had never expressed a desire to shop. If the state of the tide had allowed, she would have insisted on returning to Cotehele at once. With the few guineas left to her, she made her trifling purchases last as long as possible. The Customs officer and the politician were plainly ripe for a quarrel, but the public bustle of the busy shopping streets kept them from each others' throats.

At last she could pretend no longer that she intended to buy one of the sprigged muslins displayed by an obliging draper.

"I fear it is not quite what I was looking for," she said apologetically, and led her procession out of the shop.

"Allow me to buy you an ice!" suggested Mr Cardin eagerly. "There is a new confectioner just opened around the corner."

"Miss Gray will prefer tea and cakes," said James Wynn in a cold voice. "That coffee shop appears respectable enough."

Sir Tristram merely steered her gently towards a nearby inn. "Since we shall be on the water at the usual hour of dining," he said, "I took the liberty yesterday of ordering a neat dinner at this excellent hostelry. Doubtless it will stretch to include Mr Wynn. Allow me, Miss Gray." He held a chair for her as the landlord hurried up, beaming.

"One extra, Sir Tristram? Of course, sir, not the slightest difficulty. I'll bring the soup this instant."

Mr Wynn and the lieutenant were seated perforce, and to judge by their appetites must have been well satisfied not to have to subsist on ices or tea and cakes.

On the walk back to the wharf, their mutual antagonism at last found voice. Deep in argument, they soon outpaced Sir Tristram, Octavia, and Ada. Phrases floated back:

". . . lackey of the Hanoverian repression . . ."

". . . dangerous revolutionary ideas . . ."

". . . starving widows and children . . ."

"By the time Mr Cardin is an admiral," observed Sir Tristram, "James Wynn will be a minister of the Crown."

"How can you laugh!" cried Octavia. "Why ever did you invite him to go with us? What will my aunt say when he appears? You will have no one but yourself to blame if Julia runs off with him."

"I find them amusing. He would have found some other way to reach Cotehele. He shall hide in the chapel by the river and your aunt need not know. And you cannot suppose that I wish to be married to someone who would prefer to run off with another man. Does that answer all your questions? Come, do not look so distressed! I do not mean to tamely hand over Miss Langston to my rival, I assure you. If I am lucky, she will find that he does not live up to the picture her imagination has painted during his absence. In any case, I fancy the world would not counsel me to despair. Are you so certain she will prefer him?"

"I cannot imagine why she should, except that they say love is blind. Surely she will not be so foolish as to choose him!"

"You are a fervent supporter of my cause, Miss Gray."

"I am very fond of Julia; how could James Wynn possibly make her as happy as you could?" Octavia's throat felt strangely tight. She walked faster, trying to catch up with the others.

They found them on the quay. They had apparently discovered common ground somewhere for they were chatting with every appearance of amicability. Octavia heard Julia's name mentioned, and guessed that once the lieutenant had discovered that the object of Mr Wynn's affections was not herself, he had dropped the quarrel. Even James Wynn must find it impossible to carry on a dispute with so friendly and open a young man.

Mr Cardin begged for permission to visit Octavia at Cotehele. She felt it unwise to encourage him, but Julia was going to have two lovers in hot pursuit and she felt entitled to have an admirer of her own. The glow in his eyes made her glad to have given him pleasure, though sorry to have given cause for hope when, much as she liked him, she had no intention of marrying him, if it were to come to that.

The barge was ready to leave. As she stepped aboard, Octavia wondered why she was so sure she did not want to be Mr Cardin's wife. She had no doubt that he would be a kind and loving husband, and though the disadvantages attached to his profession were daunting, the alternative of returning to her parents' house in London was anything but inviting.

She shook herself mentally. What a fool she was to build such speculations on so few meetings! He had not even offered for her. And if she wished to marry only to escape returning to her parents, why had she so firmly discouraged Sir Magnus? She had liked him equally, and he had a vast fortune to make up for the disadvantages of his age and Toryism!

"You are very silent, Miss Gray. Are you sorry to leave Mount Edgcumbe?" asked Sir Tristram.

She looked up, startled, to see that they had already tacked away from the harbour and were approaching St. Nicholas's Island.

"Mount Edgcumbe? The place, yes. It is very beautiful, the setting, the way the park is laid out, the gardens. It must take longer than a single week to tire of it. But I find I enjoy a fashionable crowd no better than the constant coming and going at home. I look forward to the peace of Cotehele."

"I do not expect much peace there!" lamented the baronet, glancing at their fellow passenger, who sat with his nose buried in a political treatise. "Mr Wynn, you do not care for scenery?"

There was no response.

"He has not heard you," Octavia said, laughing. "He told me once that when he is concentrating nothing can distract him. I have seen him at my father's table, with his dinner before him, so lost in thought that everyone else had eaten and left before he came to himself."

"Surely you exaggerate! A man who . . . Wait a moment. What is going on?"

The barge had slowed nearly to a stop, and their captain was leaning over the side, talking to someone who must be standing in a smaller vessel, since only his head was visible.

Sir Tristram jumped up and hurried aft. She heard his exclamation, "What the devil?" and then he called to her, "Miss Gray, come here, if you please, and quickly!"

James Wynn did not stir as she hastened to join them.

"It's Jack Day," Sir Tristram said as she approached. "It seems the *Seamew* has been taken filled to the scuppers with contraband, and he has been shot. His men have got him away, but he is badly hurt."

She looked down and saw the giant lying inert and bleeding in the bottom of his gig. The one-eyed man leaned over him, wrapping one of his wounds in a dirty rag, while the hook-handed ex-navy seaman, Dan Small, held the rail of their barge.

" 'Tis the young lady as fell in the water," he said in surprise. "We c'n trust the cap'n to her."

"Of course you can," Octavia assured him. "We shall take him to Cotehele to Mrs Pengarth. It will be easy to hide him there."

"If 'e don't slip 'is anchor afore we gets 'im there," said their boatman gloomily. " 'Urry up, now. Think what 'is lordship ud say was we taken red-'anded."

"His lordship will most certainly approve your aid to his relative," Sir Tristram assured him.

"Relative?" Octavia was momentarily distracted, until the injured man moaned as he was lifted. "Oh, be careful! He is bleeding dreadfully!"

The commotion had at last attracted Mr Wynn's attention. He wandered up, book in hand, and watched with interest as Red Jack's red-stained bulk was laid gently on the deck.

"Tha'lt take care on 'im!" the one-eyed Yorkshireman begged Octavia. "We mun go back, see if there's aught to do to help t'others."

"I shall take care of him," intervened James Wynn firmly. "I studied medicine for two years before I found my vocation. I shall need water, and clean linen, plenty of clean linen."

Sir Tristram offered his spotless neckcloth, and the captain his grubby one. Mr Wynn was examining Red Jack, ruthlessly ripping off his clothing. He took the cloths and demanded more.

"Turn your backs, gentlemen," ordered Octavia. "Ada, come and help me." She pulled off her petticoat. Several feet of the French lace Captain Day had given her went to staunch his wounds.

"Good girl," said Sir Tristram approvingly, then looked at her closely. "Are you going to faint? You are shockingly pale."

"I ought to help," whispered Octavia, "but I cannot bear to see it. The men are needed to sail the boat."

Sir Tristram's arm was about her waist, supporting her, leading her to a seat well away from the carnage on the aft deck. "I ought not to have let you see!" he said in self-accusation as Ada clucked in alarm and searched for her smelling salts. "Stay here. Ada, look after her. I shall assist Mr Wynn. I must admit, he has surprised me!"

"And me. Oh, how could I be so foolish! Hurry back to him, sir, I shall do very well."

The crew was crowding on all possible sail. They were swinging northward towards the narrow strait between Cremyll and Devil's Point when a Customs' cutter hailed them.

"Lord Edgcumbe's private ship, with guests for Cotehele!" shouted the captain. "If I lose the tide you'll answer to his lordship!"

The cutter turned away.

=14=

As they approached Halton Quay, Octavia peered apprehensively through the dusk towards the washing line. No red petticoat. She sighed in relief.

A hazy half moon rose. By its glimmering light, they saw a gig waiting for them on the quay at Cotehele.

"We will have to trust the groom to drive us up to the house," said Sir Tristram, consulting Octavia in a low voice, "but I think it best not to let him see where we take Jack from there."

"The room under the Prospect Tower?"

"Yes. Do you think Wynn can be relied upon to keep his mouth closed?"

"Judging by his hauling poor Mr Cardin over the coals for his profession, his sympathies lie with the free-traders, not the law. We will need a lantern. I had best fetch one as soon as we arrive, and warn Mrs Pengarth. I'll meet you at the tower."

The captain ordered his men to carry Red Jack ashore, swathed in bandages, but showed no further disposition to help. The three of them disappeared into the Edgcumbe Arms as the gig started up the hill.

Their driver, a dour, elderly Cornishman, showed no interest after his first glance at Red Jack's recumbent form. Without demur he followed instructions to go straight to the end of the lane instead of turning to the front of the house.

They stopped at the gate to the tower field. Octavia and Ada slipped into the house through the kitchens.

"Ada, you had best go to your room and do not come out until we are known to have returned. I know I can trust you not to tell anyone what has happened."

"Can't I tell Miss Julia, miss?"

Octavia thought for a moment. "No, best not. At least until I have asked Sir Tristram. And do not tell her about Mr Wynn, either, not yet."

"Very well, miss. Here's Mrs Pengarth's parlour. Take care, miss. If there's anything I can do to help . . ."

"Thank you, Ada. Hurry now, and try not to be seen." She knocked on the door.

Lady Langston's dresser was with the housekeeper, both enjoying a small glass of port as a nightcap. Mrs Pengarth jumped to her feet as Octavia went in.

"Miss Gray! Goodness, I had no idea you were back. What can I do for you, miss?"

"I must speak with you privately." She looked at the lady's maid, who curtseyed and left the room. "Pray sit down, Mrs Pengarth. I fear I have bad news for you."

"Jack!" The woman did not sit down, but she leaned against a table and held her hand to her heart. "Is he dead?"

"Oh, no! But badly hurt. We have brought him here, to the Prospect Tower. There's a secret cellar where he can be hidden. Will you come with me? We need a lantern."

"Bless you, miss! I'll fetch a lantern and come with you, but that cellar is known to everyone, even the Customs. It's been searched a hundred times. Whatever shall we do?"

"The secret passage: we will have to risk it! Come quickly."

As they hurried up the hill, Octavia explained how they had found out about the passage. Mrs Pengarth had heard no more than rumours that such things existed. She thought it should be safe, if the untried entrance worked, the passage had not collapsed, the cave and the other end had not been filled.

"Hush now!" said Octavia sharply. "If that is not possible we will think of something else. Sir Tristram will not let Captain Day be taken easily."

"I knew this was going to happen one day. You don't know what it's like, miss, always looking over your shoulder, wondering if this'll be the day he gets caught. Are the revenuers close on his trail, miss?"

"I don't believe so, but they saw us pass and may well be suspicious." A figure detached itself from the shadow of the tower and moved towards them. "Sir Tristram? How is he?"

"Extraordinarily weighty. Martha? Jack is still unconscious, but Mr Wynn says that at present he is suffering only from loss of blood. Nothing vital was hit."

"Mr Wynn, sir?"

"I'll explain later," said Octavia impatiently. "Come in and light the lantern. Sir Tristram, Mrs Pengarth says the cellar is common knowledge. We must try the passage."

"It was four years ago, sir, the Customs found it."

"The passage it is, then." He closed the tower door behind them and held up the flickering lantern. "Wynn, I fear we have some way to carry your patient yet."

James Wynn, sitting tiredly on the floor beside Red Jack, raised his arms in warning as Mrs Pengarth flung herself on her knees beside him.

"Don't touch him, ma'am. You will disarrange my makeshift bandages. It is bad enough that he must be moved. Where to now, Deanbridge?"

Sir Tristram was examining the wall for the loose brick, not easy to find in semidarkness and without the map.

"Where the devil is it?" he muttered as he broke a fingernail on the wrong bit of masonry. "Aha, here we are." The trapdoor opened. "Now how are we going to manage this? I wish I had thought to ask for two lanterns, Miss Gray!"

"I will go down first and hold the light so that you can see the steps," offered Octavia.

"Are you not afraid?"

"Just because I am a trifle squeamish at the sight of blood, you must not think me altogether hen-hearted! Where you and Julia have been I do not fear to follow." She took the lantern and held it up while the gentlemen struggled to lift Captain Day.

He groaned and opened his eyes.

"The devil has got me fast by the legs!" he cried. "Pray for me, Martha!"

Mr Wynn, his thin face and wiry red hair lit by the wavering lantern, did look somewhat devilish. Mrs Pengarth, overjoyed to hear his voice, hastened to reassure him as the master of Hades lowered his legs and Sir Tristram laid him gently on the floor again.

The situation being explained to him, Red Jack vowed his own two legs, if the doctor/devil would leave them to him, were fitter to carry him than anybody else's. He staggered to his feet, and with Sir Tristram and Mr Wynn supporting him on either side he managed to descend into the cellar.

"Don't put me down, gentlemen," he warned, "or it'll be more than we all can do to get me up again. Where to next?"

Octavia set the lantern on an empty tea chest and tried to close the trapdoor. Mrs Pengarth had to help her. As it swung up, it revealed a door-latch, much larger than most but otherwise perfectly ordinary. She lifted it and pulled hard. A section of the wall swung out, revealing a black opening from which dank, musty air blew in her face.

"Ugh!" she said stepping back, then quickly, before she could imagine the terrors ahead, she seized the lantern and marched in.

"Slowly, Miss Gray!" There was laughter in Sir Tristram's voice. "Much as I admire your boldness, we cannot go so fast."

Mrs Pengarth followed last, closing the door behind

them. Octavia heard it slam and wondered whether they would ever be able to open it again.

The tunnel's rock and earthen walls were reinforced here and there with timber. It was far too narrow for three men abreast, especially when one of them was Jack Day. They had to walk in a sort of crabwise shuffle. At least the roof was high enough, the footing was firm and smooth, and the downward slope helped them to keep moving. It also took much of Red Jack's weight off Mr Wynn's shoulders, laying it instead on Sir Tristram's, which were much fitter to bear it.

A cobweb brushed Octavia's face and she lost all desire to hurry. Spiders, she thought, and bats and rats. She held the lantern higher and peered ahead into the darkness. Suddenly a drip splashed her forehead and she could not repress a squeal.

"What is the matter?" asked Sir Tristram sharply. "Are you all right?"

"Yes. I'm sorry. There is water coming through the ceiling here but judging from the stains on the wood it has been dripping forever. I do not see why it should choose to collapse just as we pass." Cautiously she went on.

There was a long flight of stone steps. By the time they reached the bottom, Captain Day was barely conscious, eyes glazed, his legs moving automatically. James Wynn was not in much better case.

"Now I see . . . the benefits . . . of exercise!" he gasped, his face pale and sweating. "How much . . . farther?"

"It is levelling off," reported Octavia. "We must be nearly there."

A few paces farther on the passage widened, then opened into a small chamber, no more than ten feet on a side. It was half room, half cave, three walls being unevenly carved from the hillside, shored here and there with wood, and the fourth built with neatly laid blocks of stone. The ceiling was strongly constructed of rough-hewn timber. Octavia remembered that the map showed the lane passing directly overhead. She hoped it was not much used by heavy farm carts.

Sir Tristram and Mr Wynn carried the captain in and laid him on the damp ground as gently as their aching muscles allowed. Mr Wynn sank down, exhausted, and sat leaning against the wall, breathing heavily. Sir Tristram stretched as widely as he could in the limited space.

"You've a large suitor, Martha," he said wryly.

"Aye, and it's a pity he hasn't the sense to match his size. But ye may call him my betrothed, sir, for if he comes out of this alive I'll drag him to the altar afore I let him go back to free trading. Now I'd best fetch bedding, for it won't do to let him lie in the damp." She turned towards the passage.

"Wait!" said Octavia. "There is supposed to be a way directly to the outside. Let me look."

Sir Tristam took the lantern and they both scrutinised the stone wall, which seemed the logical place for an exit. It was featureless.

"I hoped not to have to return through that horrid tunnel," sighed Octavia in disappointment, turning away. "Oh dear, and who is to have the lantern?"

"Look!" James Wynn was pointing at one of the corners on the other side of the room from the stone wall. "Surely that is a door, though it looks like part of the reinforcement. Hold the lantern closer, Deanbridge."

Sir Tristram stepped over Red Jack's recumbent form.

"You are right. Martha, hold this, if you please." The housekeeper took the lantern and he pulled on a rusty iron bar set in the wood. With a creaking groan the door opened, revealing a curtain of ivy. He held it aside and stepped forward carefully. "Ouch! It opens into a tree. Bring the light closer. Yes, it must have grown since this place was used—it has probably had two centuries of peace!—but I think we can squeeze past it. The entrance is well hidden, at all events."

He turned back, and Octavia saw that a twig had scratched his cheek.

"Keep still," she ordered, going to him and holding his chin with one hand while she cleaned it with her handkerchief. "Now how do you propose to explain that away?"

"It will not be half so difficult as explaining why we are so late, if we do not go up to the house very soon." He took the blood-smeared handkerchief. "I doubt I shall die of it, but thank you, nurse. I will buy you a new one. Now, you and I must go with Martha. Wynn, you will stay with Jack for the present. All in all, it is quite the best place for you. Martha and I will return as soon as we can. We shall bring blankets and food. Is there anything else you require?"

"Linen for bandages. He is bleeding again, unsurprisingly. What I crave most is rest and sleep!"

"You have done a good day's work. I confess it is more than I would have expected of a political essayist! We will leave you the lantern and bring more fuel for it. Come, Miss Gray, let me hold back the branches for you."

Octavia slipped out into the night, followed by Mrs Pengarth. The moon had set, and the sky was bright with more stars than she had dreamed existed. Their faint light showed black silhouettes of trees and bushes but left the ground in obscurity.

As she hesitated, she felt Sir Tristram's arm about her shoulders. He guided her after the housekeeper, who went round by the gate not, Octavia was glad to see, through the stone passage under the lane.

They walked in companionable silence until they came to the corner of the house, where Mrs Pengarth awaited them.

"Sir, I had best go first to be there to meet you. The staff will wonder if we go in together."

"Go ahead. We shall sit here for a few minutes. You are not cold, Miss Gray?"

"No, not at all." She could feel the warmth of his arm all the way down to her toes.

They sat on the bench and he pointed out constellations to her: the Plough, Orion, Cassiopeia. She would have been happy to stay there forever; all too soon he stood up, took her hands, and pulled her to her feet.

Suddenly she was tired.

The lights from the house illuminated their way. In no time they were going up the stairs and through the inside porch into the drawing room.

Julia turned from the window and came eagerly to greet them. Lady Langston looked up from her embroidery frame.

"It is very late. I was growing quite worried," she said placidly.

"Oh, Sir Tristram, you have hurt your cheek!" cried Miss Matilda Crosby, jumping up. "Let me fetch you a court plaster at once!"

"A mere scratch, ma'am. Pray do not disturb yourself. I—ah—now how did I come by this scratch, Miss Gray? I cannot remember, I vow."

He raised his eyebrows at Octavia, who repressed a giggle.

"How could you forget, Sir Tristram? You were taken by surprise when a big wave made the barge roll, lost your balance, and fell against a—a spar!"

"Of course, a spar it was."

What exactly was a spar? Octavia wondered. She was sure it was part of a boat but whether it might inflict such an injury, she had no idea. However, her aunt and Miss Crosby raised no demur, though Julia was looking at them with suspicion.

"What did you buy in Plymouth?" she asked.

Octavia looked blank. "Good heavens!" she said, "I must have left all my packages in the carriage. I am by far too tired to do anything about it now. If you will excuse me, Aunt, I believe I shall go up to bed."

"We were all about to retire," said Lady Langston.

"Thank you, Sir Tristram, for taking care of my niece. How fortunate that you did not fall overboard."

"Very fortunate, ma'am. It might have proven difficult for Miss Gray to explain my absence had she left me to drown."

As soon as they reached the bedchamber, where Ada awaited them, Julia turned to Octavia.

"Did you post my letter?"

She had forgotten all about it. It had lost its purpose when Mr Wynn appeared. However, she had not consulted Sir Tristram about how much she ought to tell her cousin. If she said that Mr Wynn was here, Julia would want to see him at once.

Catching Ada's eye, she nodded. "I am sure James will very soon give you his answer."

"Tavy, what have you been up to today? I would wager that you and Sir Tristram are sharing some secret. That business of the scratch on his face!"

"Wait till the morning, Ju. I am quite worn out."

"We'll have you fast asleep in your own chamber in no time, miss," said Ada, hurrying to help her undress. "There's no need to share with Miss Julia now."

Good, thought Octavia sleepily. All the same, by the morning she must come up with a story to satisfy her cousin.

= 15 =

JULIA WAS STILL asleep when Octavia went down the next morning. As she had hoped, Sir Tristram was at the breakfast table, and he was obviously waiting for her.

Unfortunately, Matilda Crosby had also risen early. She was methodically consuming a plateful of kidneys, kippers, and kedgeree which made Octavia feel bilious.

"Tea and toast, please, Raeburn," she requested, averting her eyes.

Sir Tristram looked up in disapproval. He himself was provided with two hefty slices of cold beef, several marmaladed muffins and a tankard of cider.

"Must eat more than that," he said. "You are growing quite thin."

"Am I?" asked Octavia, pink with pleasure.

"Yes. Have some buttered eggs, they are excellent."

"You have tried them already, have you? Bring me just a little of the buttered eggs, then, Raeburn, if Sir Tristram has left any. Thank you."

"In my day," said Miss Crosby with a titter, "young ladies would not dream of being seen to break their fast in public."

Sir Tristram stared at her plate with raised eyebrows.

"How quaint old-fashioned customs sound," Octavia hurriedly intervened. "I wonder what they ate for breakfast in Tudor times?"

"Larks' tongue pies and lampreys," suggested Sir Tristram with a grin. "I wonder if Lord Edgcumbe has ever served larks' tongue pie at one of his banquets."

"It sounds horrid. Sir, I must ask your advice on one or two matters."

"I am at your service, ma'am, as soon as you are finished breaking your fast . . ."

She glared at him and he left off the words "in public" which she had seen on the tip of his tongue.

"That is like to be long before you," she pointed out, sipping her tea. "Raeburn, pray do not refill Sir Tristram's plate."

Miss Crosby was heard to sniff and mutter something indistinct about modern manners. She ate slower and slower, as if determined not to leave them alone together. The baronet finished his sirloin, washed it down with cider, and stuck two half muffins together."

"Shall we walk outside?" he proposed. "It is a beautiful morning."

"Is it? I did not take the time to look. Yes, let us go out. You will excuse us, Miss Crosby."

Muffins in hand, he ushered her out.

"What is the connection between Captain Day and Lord Edgcumbe?" she demanded as they crossed the courtyard.

"Unf!" he said through a mouthful of muffin.

"Do not try to evade the question! You told the sailor his lordship would approve any aid given to his relative."

"Did I! He is some sort of distant cousin, I believe."

"I do not believe you, sir. Or at least, there is more to it than that. And if he is a descendant of the Bad Baron, I know all about him so you need not fear to tell me."

"Oh, do you! And who told you that story?"

"Lord Ernest. I promise you I was very cross with him for revealing to a stranger his own family's scandalous behaviour."

"And shocked, I hope, at a tale unfit for a female's ears. Yes, Jack Day is the second baron's grandson. The present earl sent him to school and bought him the *Seamew*, though

I daresay he did not foresee the use that would be made of her!"

"Did you give him the gold that we found in the cabinet?"

"No. I gave it to Martha Pengarth."

"Very sensible," applauded Octavia. "Shall you . . ."

"It is my turn to ask a few questions. What have you told Miss Langston?"

"Nothing. Not even about Mr Wynn."

"Good. She is to know nothing of Jack. The fewer people who can connect him with this place, the better."

"My cousin is no chatterbox, sir."

"I place less reliance on her discretion than I do on yours, ma'am. Shall we sit down? I fancy there will be enough walking to be done once you have revealed Mr Wynn's presence. I took him to the chapel in the woods early this morning."

They sat on the bench at the corner of the house. Considering how best to tell Julia the news, Octavia neither noticed the view nor recalled last night's starry sky.

"She guessed last night that we were hiding something. I shall tell her I have a surprise for her," she decided, "and we shall take a picnic lunch. Then we can leave the food for him."

"Must I come with you?"

"Of course! Oh, I see what you mean. Will it be very painful to you if she rushes into his arms?"

He pulled a face. "It is not a spectacle I look forward to with pleasure."

"No. I am heartily sorry for it, but I think you must come, if only to carry the picnic basket! We cannot trust a servant to go with us. Besides, it will look very odd if you stay behind."

He sighed but acquiesced. "We had best take twice as much food as we need. We can leave some with Jack. By the way, Martha has received an urgent message calling her to the bedside of a sick relative."

"That is all very well, but who is to run the house in her absence? I am sure my aunt will not know what is to be done."

"She has left an upper housemaid in charge. Doris, by name, I believe. Satisfied? Martha will stay in the cave until Jack is able to care for himself, so it is up to us to supply them."

"You will have to make a habit of walking out of the breakfast room with a handful of muffins! I fear Miss Crosby disapproves of me, though I cannot think how I have offended."

"Like her, you are a poor relative. However, unlike her, you are young and beautiful. Enough cause for envy."

"I must strive to be kinder to her," Octavia said, her cheeks flushed. "Oh! What is that noise?"

Round the corner of the house rode four scarlet-coated dragoons. Harnesses jingling, their massive horses' ironclad hooves chopped the lawn into a muddy morass.

"What the devil do you think you're doing!" demanded Sir Tristram in an icy voice that cut straight through the noise.

The cavalrymen had passed without seeing them. They reined in and looked back, then one of them rode back and saluted.

"Orders to surround the 'ouse, sir," he said reasonably. "Beg pardon, ma'am if we frighted ye."

"Whose orders, sergeant? What damn fool told you to ruin his lordship's lawn?"

The troopers looked around in dismay. Clearly the difference between a rough meadow and a greensward with several centuries of care behind it had never dawned on them.

"The Riding Officer, sir," said the sergeant, his voice sullen. "We're seconded to the Customs. 'E never warned us 'bout no lawn. I'll 'ave to ask 'oo you are, sir. Orders to hindentafy hevery male hin'abitant."

"I am Sir Tristram Deanbridge, a guest of the Earl of

Mount Edgcumbe. Where is this impertinent Riding Officer?"

Two of the horsemen sniggered.

"In the 'ouse, sir, directing the search. Please to go in, sir. No one's to leave. I *got* to surround the 'ouse, sir!" He sounded almost desperate.

"At least go round by the path, man! Come, Miss Gray, let us see what is toward. This could prove most amusing!"

"Amusing! You have an odd sense of humour, I vow! What if they find Jack? They will know we must have helped him."

"Do you regret it?"

"No, but that does not mean that I am not terrified!"

They walked back through the gatehouse, passing a dragoon stationed there, and into the courtyard. Octavia recognised the Riding Officer at once: it was the tall, thin, elderly man who had ordered her trunk opened on her arrival at Cotehele Quay.

She pulled on Sir Tristram's coat.

"That's him!" she whispered. "The one I told you of. I made everyone laugh at him. He is certain to hold a grudge."

The baronet laughed aloud and patted her hand. "My dear, I cannot think of anything less likely than that he should recognise you. Remember, I saw you then! Act the haughty wellborn miss and he will never think to have seen you before. Chin up, now!"

Everyone in the courtyard, the officer, seven troopers, Raeburn, two footmen, and a maid, turned to gape at that laugh.

The stout butler, his voice filled with dignified outrage, appealed to the baronet.

"Sir, this person insists on searching the house in the King's name. Her ladyship has not come down yet."

"I've a warrant!" declared the Riding Officer, his high voice belligerent, waving a large sheet of paper. "I have reason to suppose a dangerous criminal may be concealed in this house!"

"A dangerous criminal?" said Sir Tristram with assumed interest. "A highwayman, perhaps, or even a murderer?"

"A smuggler, sir, and badly wounded when his ship was taken in Plymouth Sound yesterday."

"A dangerous, badly wounded smuggler? I suppose he swam up the Tamar, climbed the hill, and broke into the house while we slept. Truly a formidable man!"

"You may laugh, sir, but I've a warrant. I'll thank you not to obstruct me in carrying out my duties."

"Am I obstructing you? I do beg your pardon. Raeburn, you will allow this—ah—person and his men to go where they please. You will instruct the staff to observe their every move and notify you of any damage incurred. You may head the list with a badly cut up lawn, the destruction of which I myself witnessed. That will be all." He turned to Octavia. "Shall we go in, ma'am?"

"Yes. I had best go at once to Lady Langston. I hope this outrage will not give her a Spasm." She almost giggled at the thought of her aunt finding enough energy to indulge in a Spasm. "I daresay Lord Langston will raise questions in the House of Lords, if Lord Edgcumbe does not."

The Riding Officer glared at her as she passed him, but showed no sign of recognising her.

"It is indeed shocking when the house of a peer can be ransacked with impunity," agreed Sir Tristram smoothly. "However, if there is indeed a dangerous criminal on the premises, we must hope that he will be found."

Lady Langston was mildly ruffled to hear that the house was full of troops searching for a fugitive. She sent her dresser to fetch Julia, Ada, and Miss Crosby.

Soon a heavy tread was heard trudging up the granite steps to the White Bedroom. The beefy corporal who entered, his face as scarlet as his uniform, found her holding court, reclining in her walnut four-poster bed, swathed in a dressing gown of a startling shade of mulberry.

If there had been a fugitive under the bed he would have been perfectly safe. Confronted by six pairs of accusing female eyes, the corporal squawked a strangled apology and fled.

Despite protests from a scandalised Matilda Crosby, Julia and Octavia soon followed him. They went to the Great Hall, where Sir Tristram sat at the long table writing while the Riding Officer stalked up and down impatiently. He scowled at them, oblivious of the charming picture they made, arm in arm, Julia in blue Indian muslin and Octavia in green.

The baronet, more appreciative, set aside his letter and welcomed them with an admiring smile.

"Shall we plan our picnic, ladies?" he suggested.

"What . . . ?" Julia started to ask, then caught Octavia's eye and finished, ". . . a good idea."

"I am excessively hungry after all this excitement," said Octavia. "I shall tell cook to pack enough food for six."

"Where shall we go?" enquired Julia, realising that something was afoot.

"The day promises to be hot," Sir Tristram said. "Shall we go down to the chapel in the woods? There is plenty of shade thereabouts."

"Oh, yes, I have never been there. Is there not some romantic story about the chapel? Lady Emma mentioned it but I did not hear the whole."

Wondering why the baronet apparently wanted the Customs officer to know where they were going, Octavia told her the story of Sir Richard Edgcumbe's escape from his enemies.

"It is just like my dream!" exclaimed Julia, much struck. "You remember I told you, Tavy, about Hero and Leander."

"Not in the least! There are no lovers in the tale and no one was drowned." Octavia saw that her cousin was not listening. "Now attend, Ju. If Sir Tristram carries the picnic basket and I carry a rug to sit on, will you take some cushions?"

"There are plenty of servants to carry everything," Julia protested, then caught herself. "But of course they will be all at sixes and sevens after this morning's disturbance, and it will be more fun on our own."

She was obviously bursting with questions, nobly suppressed.

"Let us go and tell cook what we want," suggested Octavia, taking pity on her.

There was a dragoon stationed in the kitchen court. Octavia pulled Julia aside into an empty scullery.

"It's Mr Wynn," she hissed. "He's hiding in the chapel."

Julia turned white. "James is the fugitive they are hunting?" she said faintly. "Is it something he wrote?"

"No! They are looking for a smuggler! James came to see you, and Sir Tristram has hidden him. Surely you do not want everyone to know he is here?"

"They are not after him? Thank heaven! Oh, Tavy, is he really come? I must go at once."

Octavia managed to persuade her to wait until they had a picnic, pointing out that Mr Wynn could not be expected to survive on love alone. They went on into the kitchens to consult the cook, then back to the Great Hall.

Julia was walking on air.

As they entered the hall, the corporal came in through another door. The Riding Officer approached him eagerly.

"Nary a sign, sir," reported the trooper.

Furious at his disappointment, the officer turned away.

"Search the grounds," he ordered curtly.

"No luck?" asked Sir Tristram with great affability. "Perhaps your felon was too badly wounded to swim so far and went to ground in Plymouth."

"If he's in Plymouth, he can watch the *Seamew* being sawn in three pieces this afternoon," said the officer with a sneer. "You'll excuse me, sir." Smugly satisfied at the shock on Octavia's face and Sir Tristram's tight-lipped disapprobation, he stalked out.

"Cut up the *Seamew?*" cried Octavia. "They cannot!"

"They can, and undoubtedly will. Such is the law."

"What a dreadful waste! She is a beautiful ship. Remember how she looked when she came to rescue us that day."

Sir Tristram shook his head sadly. "We must not tell Jack while he is ill," he said, forgetting Julia's presence. "The *Seamew* has been his life."

Julia had not heard a word. She had sat down in a chair, hands folded in her lap in the correct posture for a young lady in company, and was gazing into the middle distance with a dreamy smile on her face.

Octavia sighed. "Ju, come and change your shoes. We shall be able to go soon."

=== 16 ===

IT WAS NOT a merry party that made its way down the paths of the valley garden. Sir Tristram was glumly silent and Julia was still lost in a happy dream. She kept dropping cushions, until Octavia, exasperated, gave her the rug and took the cushions herself. Not that they were truly necessary for the picnic, but she had thought Mr Wynn might appreciate them in his uncomfortable hiding place.

The undergrowth seemed to be full of troopers. One scarlet coat guarded the little arbour by the fish pond, and another the dovecote. A wizened gardener, grumbling at having his work interrupted, was being interrogated by the red-faced corporal. He denied everything, from having seen a wounded stranger to deliberately speaking in Cornish dialect to confuse the city-bred soldier.

When they came in sight of the tiny chapel, Julia dropped the rug and ran forward.

"James!" she cried, pushing open the heavy wooden door. She looked around, then came out disconsolate. "He is not there. Tavy, you were not teasing me?"

"Of course not! He must be somewhere close by. Are you sure he is not inside?"

"There is hardly room to hide in there. James! Where are you?"

There was a rustling in the shrubbery and Mr Wynn's thin face and bush of dark red hair appeared around a tree trunk.

"Hush!" he hissed. "The dragoons are searching for me."

"No, they are not," said Octavia. "They are after someone completely different."

"Are you sure?"

"Quite sure," Sir Tristram confirmed. "They are hunting a smuggler."

"Oh, yes, of course." Mr Wynn emerged from the undergrowth, decidedly tousled, and opened his arms just in time to catch Julia, who flung herself at him. "My love!" he exclaimed, no whit disconcerted.

Julia burst into tears. "James," she wept, "I thought you had forgotten me."

He tenderly kissed her wet eyelids. Sir Tristram turned away, his face set.

"Why should you think the dragoons are chasing you?" asked Octavia loudly, shocked by the impropriety of their behaviour. To think that Miss Crosby was scandalised by her breakfasting with a gentleman! "Mr Wynn, why should they chase you?"

He emerged from Julia's fervent embrace.

"An article I wrote in the *Review*," he explained, "attacking the Hertfords' pernicious influence on Prinny."

"I never liked Lady Hertford," agreed Julia. "She has such a way of looking down her nose at one. Lord Hertford is a friend of Papa's, though."

"I regret having descended to personalities," said Mr Wynn. "It is beneath me, and quite unnecessary. Principles are the thing. As a matter of principle, I ought to have stayed in London to become a martyr to the cause if necessary, but having just discovered my Julia's direction, I was forced to come away."

He spoke with such straightforward simplicity that it was impossible to suspect him of ulterior motives. With the same simplicity he added, "Is that a picnic basket I see? I am very hungry."

To Octavia and Sir Tristram it was a thoroughly uncomfortable meal. Their companions had eyes only for each other and conversation languished. Octavia realised she was eating faster and faster. She forced herself to stop, and sat sipping a mug of cider, scarcely aware that it was not lemonade, half listening to Julia telling her beloved a muddled version of the story of Sir Richard, in which Leander figured largely.

"Shall we walk down to the quay, Miss Gray?" asked Sir Tristram at last.

"To the quay?" she asked stupidly, startled out of her daze. "Oh, yes, that is a good idea. At least—perhaps I ought to stay with Julia?"

"There is not the least need," said her cousin. "James will protect me if those soldiers come near."

Octavia wanted to ask who would protect her against James, but it seemed like too much effort. She accepted Sir Tristram's aid in rising, and they set off down the woodland path.

It was shady, but not at all gloomy, and she could not understand why she kept falling over tree roots. Sir Tristram offered his arm to steady her; she took it gratefully. They walked for some time in silence.

"Why did you do it?" she asked accusingly, when they were well out of earshot. "Why did you help Mr Wynn to come here and hide him and leave Julia alone with him? You are sato . . . shabo . . . saboging . . . dash it, *what* is that word?"

"Sabotaging? Miss Gray, I regret having to tell you that you are definitely bosky. I should have noticed sooner that you were drinking scrumpy." Sir Tristram's face was serious but his voice was full of hidden laughter.

"Crumpy? Whash crumpy? Whash bosky mean?" Octavia clung to his arm. "The worl's going roun' an' roun'. Hol' me up."

"Scrumpy is the strongest kind of cider there is. In half a moment you are going to fall asleep, so be a good girl and hold on to this tree while I take off my jacket. There. Now sit down on it, here on the bank. Whoa, careful!"

"I fee' te'ble. Don' go 'way."

"I won't, I promise."

"Ho' my han'." The last thing Octavia knew was his hand grasping hers comfortingly as she sank into black depths.

Her hand was still in his when she woke.

"Have I slept long?" she asked, perfectly clearheaded.

"Not more than an hour. How do you feel?"

"Perfectly well." She sat up, turned greenish white, leaned over sideways, and was violently sick.

He held her forehead until she stopped retching, and then offered her his handerchief. She wiped her face and put it in her pocket.

"Thank you. Now I owe you a handkerchief. I think I shall be all right now; shall we go?"

"If you are sure you can manage?" He helped her up, picked up his coat, and shook the dry, crumbly leaf mould off it. "No headache?" he asked, putting it on.

"No, I do not think so. Was I . . . was I *foxed?*"

"I'm afraid so." He grinned at her. "Don't worry, yours is not the first head to be taken by surprise by Cornish scrumpy."

"It was perfectly horrid. I cannot believe that men sometimes drink too much on purpose! You will not tell anyone?"

"No more than I did about your dolphins. What a lot of secrets we have between us, Miss Gray!"

They walked back towards the chapel. As they neared it, they heard men's voices raised in anger, and then Julia screamed.

Sir Tristram broke into a run. Octavia followed as quick as she was able, cursing her long skirts.

James Wynn was struggling in the grip of a couple of redcoats, while Julia hit one of them with both fists, screaming, "He is not a smuggler, indeed he is not!"

The baronet slowed to a saunter and Octavia caught up.

"What is going on here?" he asked, in a quieter version of the voice he had used on the lawn-desecrating sergeant.

The troopers jumped to attention, letting their prisoner go.

"We've caught that smuggler, sir," reported one of them, saluting.

"No you have not. Mr Wynn is a writer, not a smuggler."

" 'E's jist like wot we was told ter look fer," said the other sullenly, grabbing James's arm as he stepped back. "Tall, like, wi' red 'air an' talks eddicated."

"Nonetheless, he is not the man you are looking for. Let him go. Does he look as if he is badly wounded?"

"Naw." The dragoon doubtfully let go.

"Was not the description of a *big* man, rather than merely tall?"

"Aye, sir, it were," said the first. He studied James's lanky figure dubiously.

"Might I suggest that one of you remains here to keep an eye on Mr Wynn, while the other fetches the Riding Officer. I assume he will know whom he is looking for?"

"Aye, sir. Go on, man, do what the gennelman says. I'll stay and watch this 'un."

The sullen soldier left unwillingly as Julia threw her arms about James's neck.

"There, there, beloved, all is well," soothed the young man with his habitual calm. "Thank you, Deanbridge!"

"Not at all," said Sir Tristram politely, and offered the remaining dragoon a mug of cider.

It was some time before his comrade returned. Before they saw anyone, they heard the Riding Officer's high voice rising in an indignant squeak, to be answered by another, calming, voice.

"Lieutenant Cardin!" cried Octavia. "What on earth is he doing here?"

The lieutenant and the Riding Officer appeared, followed by five cavalrymen, all looking unhappy without their mounts.

"Ha, I knew it!" snorted Mr Cardin, regarding the waiting group. "I told you it was the political fellow. Miss

Gray, Miss Langston, I most humbly apologise for my colleague upsetting you!"

"Blockheads!" snarled the Riding Officer at his troops, without a word to the victim of mistaken identity. "I might have known you'd pick the wrong man. Have you searched the tower yet?"

The corporal came forward. "Sir, we couldn't find no way into the secret cellar as you said were there."

"Fools! Must I do everything myself? Come with me!" He turned and marched back towards the garden.

"How does he know about our secret cellar?" asked Julia indignantly.

"Is there really a secret cellar?" asked Mr Cardin with boyish enthusiasm. "I should like to see it."

There was no reason he should not have gone by himself, but Octavia saw that he did not want to leave them and suggested that they should all go. Besides, if by some terrible chance the tunnel should be discovered, perhaps they might somehow be able to save Red Jack. They stowed the cushions, the rug and some food in the chapel, hastily packed up the rest of the picnic, and followed the dragoons.

When they reached the top of the garden, Sir Tristram left the picnic basket under a tree that grew against an ivy-covered wall.

"It is by no means as heavy as it was," he declared, "but there's no sense carrying it up the hill and back down again. I'll send someone for it later."

Only Octavia read a hidden meaning in his words. Mr Wynn was occupied in exclaiming over his Julia's bravery in going down into the mysterious cellar, while Julia and Mr Cardin passed the tree without dreaming that it hid the entrance to a still more secret hiding place.

They caught up with the dragoons halfway up the tower hill. The cavalrymen were still on foot, in deference to Lord Edgcumbe's lawns and paths, and being used to regard walking as exercise fit only for the infantry, they moved slowly. The Riding Officer was still berating them, and their initial sheepishness was turning to resentment.

Everyone crowded into the tower, and the Riding Officer went straight to the loose brick as if he had done it many times before. The trapdoor opened and the corporal peered doubtfully into the dark hole.

"We'll need lanterns," he announced.

"Of course we need lanterns, clothhead!" screeched the unhappy officer. "Why the devil are there none here? Fetch some!"

The corporal saluted, turned smartly about, and marched out, followed by all his men. Octavia stepped out into the sunshine and watched them troop down the green hillside. The others joined her, leaving the Riding Officer fuming inside.

Sir Tristram spread his now somewhat grubby coat on the grass and invited Julia to sit on it.

"I have a feeling they will not return for some time," he said with a grin.

She accepted gracefully. Mr Wynn and Mr Cardin hurried to offer their coats to Octavia, who refused. She desperately wanted to talk alone with Sir Tristram, to propose a plan of action in case the tunnel should be found, but she could not think how to separate him from the group.

"What a magnificent day it is!" he said at that moment. "I believe I shall climb the tower while we await the return of the troops. Do you care to go with me, Miss Gray?"

He did not ask Julia. Octavia was sure he had the same possibility in mind and eagerly agreed, starting towards the door.

"There must be quite a view from up there," said Mr Cardin, shading his eyes as he peered upwards. "I'll come too."

"It is well worth it," Sir Tristram said cordially, but Octavia thought she heard him groan.

As they entered the tower, the Riding Officer pounced on the lieutenant.

"Cardin, I've a bone to pick with you. This is my territory and I was sent to take Red Jack Day. You're supposed to be at sea. What the devil are you doing here?"

Mr Cardin cast a harrassed glance at Octavia. "Come outside," he said in embarrassment, "and I'll tell you."

The Riding Officer unwillingly followed him out again, and Sir Tristram urged Octavia to the stairs.

"For the first time today I am in charity with that man," she said, starting to climb, "but poor Mr Cardin, having to explain that he came to see me!" She giggled.

Soon she had no breath for anything but climbing, going as fast as she could in case the lieutenant came after them. She reached the top and turned as Sir Tristram joined her. He put his finger on his lips.

"Speak quietly, they may be able to hear us."

"I have made a plan," she whispered, "in case they close the trapdoor and find the tunnel. You must create a diversion, and I will run down the tunnel and help Mrs Pengarth to get Red Jack out at the other end before they come."

"I doubt I could divert their attention enough that they would not notice you opening the door, and still more I doubt that the two of you can move Jack. No, if you are willing, and I see that you are, let us try this. You must stay close to the trapdoor, pretending to be fearful. They do not know how courageous you are and will not be surprised. I shall stay above, having seen the place before. Then if they decide to close the trap, you refuse to stay and call to Cardin to help you out. When I hear you, I shall run down the hill to help Jack escape. I can go much quicker than they will be able to in that tunnel."

"That is a better plan," said Octavia regretfully. "Only what if Mr Cardin sees you go? He will be suspicious. I know! I shall pretend to hurt my ankle and keep him by me in the tower! You must be careful not to twist yours as you go down."

"If it comes to that, I shall take care," promised Sir Tristram, "but I doubt either of our plans will be needed. The cellar has been searched a hundred times without . . . Quick, admire the view! Hallo, Cardin! Has our friend forgiven your presence?"

"Look!" cried Octavia, leaning over the parapet and pointing down the hill. "Here come the dragoons, and each of them has several lanterns. I wonder where they found so many? I am afraid they are mocking the poor Riding Officer."

Mr Cardin laughed, but said rather angrily, "The man's a pompous fool. The appointment of such as him does not make our task any easier." He accorded the panorama his perfunctory admiration, then offered to escort Octavia down the stairs. "I would not miss seeing the secret room for anything," he explained.

"I have seen it already," said Sir Tristram lazily. "I shall follow shortly." He leaned on the parapet and studied the valley garden, where a red uniform was still visible beside the dovecote.

When Octavia reached the bottom, the dragoons were methodically stacking lanterns against the wall. The corporal winked at her and shook his head. He lit two of the lanterns, handed one to the Riding Officer, and descended the steps into the cellar. His men followed, brought up at the rear by the officer. Mr Cardin helped Octavia down the steps after them.

"What a horrid place!" she exclaimed, staying close to the exit. She had not had time on her last visit to look about her, nor to hesitate before attempting the tunnel. Now she was glad Sir Tristram had rejected her plan to run down it alone.

The Riding Officer was standing in the middle of the room, holding up his lantern and peering around with a look on his face of mortal disappointment. There was no wounded smuggler, and no place to hide one.

Mr Cardin and the soldiers opened the empty tea chests. They found nothing of interest.

"Perhaps there is another room opening off this," suggested the young man to Octavia's alarm. "Corporal, try tapping on the walls to see if they sound hollow anywhere."

"These men are under my command!" cried the Riding Officer. "I was about to try that."

The corporal shrugged, and motioned to the dragoons to spread out along the walls. Mr Cardin shrugged and joined Octavia. He watched restlessly as the soldiers thumped without result. As the corporal approached the Riding Officer, saluted, and reported no hollow sounds, she realised that her companion was eyeing thoughtfully the trapdoor and its folding steps.

"Sir Tristram!" she called instantly in a weak voice, praying that he was near enough to hear. "I feel faint. Please help me out of here!"

The baronet appeared above as the lieutenant anxiously begged her to lean on him. Feeling thoroughly foolish, she allowed them to lift her out of the cellar, carry her outside, and fuss over her. Julia hurried up in alarm, and Sir Tristram stood back to leave her room to reach her cousin.

He winked at Octavia and went back into the tower. Moments later he came out again, followed by the gloomy Riding Officer and the six dragoons.

Octavia, who had begun to feel really unwell with suspense, breathed easily again.

"It is past time we returned to the house," said Sir Tristram, watching the searchers plod wearily down the hill. "Miss Gray, are you well enough to walk?"

"Yes, indeed, if Mr Cardin will be so kind as to support me." She rose to her feet with an artistic wobble and leaned heavily on the lieutenant's arm. "Ju, do not look so long-faced. You will see James tomorrow."

At the bottom of the hill, Julia bade her lover a tearful good night. As he walked away down the lane he drew a book from his pocket and started to read it, but to Octavia's astonishment he turned and waved before disappearing into the valley. He must indeed love her cousin if the thought of her could distract him from his reading!

═17═

LADY LANGSTON WAS pleased to welcome Lord Edgcumbe's young protégé and invited him to dinner, assuring him that it made not the least difference to her that he was unable to change his clothes. Miss Crosby sniffed, but she had seen Mr Cardin at the earl's table and could not protest.

"A well-meaning young man," she said condescendingly. "His lordship tells me he has great hopes for his future."

Sir Tristram looked skeptical, not of the lieutenant's future but of the lady's claim to have discussed it with Lord Edgcumbe. Octavia guessed his thoughts and frowned at him across the drawing room. He was far too ready to take Miss Crosby up when she made her more questionable statements, and Octavia was doing her best to be charitable towards the poor woman.

Though she was hungry after the exercise and emotions of the day, when they went down to dinner she found she was even more tired than hungry. Mr Cardin anxiously plied her with food, but it was Sir Tristram's watchful eye that persuaded her to eat. He must not think that the dreadful business of the scrumpy had spoiled her appetite.

The lieutenant made a hearty meal. He had had no luncheon, he explained bashfully. The tide had brought him to Cotehele at mid-morning; having heard that fashionable ladies never rose before noon, he had waited until that hour, and then decided that it would be encroaching to make his appearance just before a mealtime. Octavia admired his restraint in not falling upon the remains of their picnic when he finally joined them.

Julia, seated beside the baronet, was aglow with happiness and behaved charmingly towards him. Even her mother noticed it.

"I am glad you have taken my advice as to fresh air and exercise, Julia," she said. "Your looks are improved already, I vow, and your spirits also. Pray continue to take advantage of this delightful weather."

"I mean to, Mama," said Julia with a sparkling, mischievous smile. "I intend to be out of doors from breakfast until dinner every day."

"But do not on any account get brown, my love. You must remember to take your parasol. Matilda, what lotion was it you recommended for freckles?"

"Denmark Lotion and crushed strawberries are both excellent, Lady Langston, though I do not consider Distilled Water of Green Pineapples to be efficacious. However, Miss Gray is more in need of such remedies than Miss Langston, for her complexion is much browner."

Julia, Sir Tristam, and Mr Cardin all leaped indignantly to the defense of Octavia's complexion, leaving Miss Crosby cowed and her victim biting her lip in an effort to avoid dissolving in helpless giggles.

She was hoping for a private word with the baronet, but when he and the lieutenant rejoined the ladies after their port, Julia again bestowed her attention upon him. She did not care to interrupt their tête-à-tête, though Sir Tristram did not appear to be enjoying it particularly. In fact, he looked somewhat bored.

Of course, he must know that he owed Julia's complaisance to her happiness at James's appearance, not to her pleasure in his company. Behind the mask of boredom, he was undoubtedly suffering the pangs of unrequited love. Octavia hoped he was also making practical plans to win her from the politician.

Mr Cardin left to catch the ebb tide back to Plymouth.

Julia decided to retire early, "in order to rise early and not waste the sunshine." Lady Langston regarded her daughter's departure as a good excuse to follow suit. Miss Crosby sat on, chattering aimlessly in the face of Octavia's sleepy yawns and Sir Tristram's all too obvious irritation.

Octavia was ready to surrender and go to bed when Lady Langston's dresser providentially appeared. Her ladyship wished to consult Miss Crosby on some little matter. Would Miss Crosby be kind enough to attend her ladyship in the White Bedroom?

Miss Crosby would, reluctantly. Bestowing a parting admonitory frown, she flounced off.

Sir Tristram heaved a sigh of relief. "That woman," he said awfully, "is enough to drive a saint to murder. I have been waiting all evening for an opportunity to congratulate you on your quick thinking in the tower."

"Why, thank you, kind sir! Mr Cardin was looking with the greatest suspicion at the trapdoor, and I had to divert him without making you think all was discovered. I must confess I myself was impressed with my acting ability, though I felt like the veriest widgeon, swooning away like that. Are you going down to take the food to Mrs Pengarth?"

"In a while, when the household is asleep."

"Were you not afraid, when you left the hamper under the tree, that it might attract attention? I did not think of it at the time."

"I left it under the wrong tree," he said smugly. "It was at least thirty feet from the secret door. I only hope I can find it tonight in the dark."

"Well, if that was the wrong tree, I should certainly never find the right one! Ada! What is it?"

The abigail had peeked round the drawing room door. She came into the room.

"Excuse me, miss, I was just thinking, with last night and Mrs. Pengarth going off and all and the troopers all over, if she was to be somewhere where she couldn't get about, like, is there anything I can do to help? Like if you was to bring me her linen to wash, or I could make some soup for the captain while nobody's in the kitchen. I don't mean to presume, sir. I'd like to help."

"Both excellent ideas, Ada," approved Sir Tristram. "If you can have soup ready in about an hour, I will come to the kitchen for it. Thank you!"

Octavia hugged the maid, who looked at her with concern.

"You're worn to a shadow, miss, and half-asleep! Off to bed with you!"

"In a minute. You go on and I shall come in just a minute, I promise." Ada went out and she continued to Sir Tristram, "There is just one more thing I must ask you. What are you going to do to persuade Julia to love you instead of James?"

"I believe my best course is to leave them alone together as much as possible. Do not frown! Did you not hear them talking? He lectures her on politics! Today there were enough interruptions to make it bearable, but a steady diet will pall very soon. Tomorrow there will be no interruptions—you and I are going to visit Cotehele Mill, without them."

"Are we indeed?"

"Your pardon, ma'am! Miss Gray, may I beg the pleasure of your company on an expedition to the Mill?"

"That sounds delightful, sir. If I ever wake up." She yawned hugely, smiled sleepily, and wished him good night.

She was fast asleep as soon as her head touched the pillow, even before Ada had blown out her candle.

It seemed scarce a few minutes later that she gradually became aware that Ada was shaking her.

"Miss Gray, wake up! Wake up, miss!"

Octavia blinked and rubbed her eyes. "Is it morning already? What is the matter? What time is it?"

"It's just past eleven, miss. I'm that sorry to wake you

when you're so tired, but Sir Tristram needs you. It seems the Riding Officer left dragoons posted in the gardens."

"Oh dear, how excessively awkward of him!" She sat up, wide awake. "But how can I help?"

"He said he had a plan, miss, but he wouldn't tell me. He said to wear a dark gown and a dark cloak with a hood, so I got these from Miss Julia's room. I don't know what he's up to, miss, but you will be careful, won't you?"

Octavia dressed quickly and hurried down to the Great Hall. By the light of a single candle, Sir Tristram was pacing impatiently up and down. He came to meet her and took her hands in his.

"I was sure you would come. Did Ada explain? I *must* go to Jack and those damned dragoons are everywhere. I hope that if you are with me they will think we have a lovers' rendezvous. It is a great deal to ask of you, I know, though if you keep the cloak close about you they cannot be sure who you are. But they will guess, after seeing the four of us today, and there may be talk." He searched her face.

"I hardly think soldiers' gossip is likely to reach my aunt," she said calmly, "still less my parents in London!"

"I knew you were game! It is bright moonlight, which lends colour to our story. Leave all the talking to me."

"You take care of her, sir!" ordered Ada, who had followed Octavia in and was listening, arms akimbo, a disapproving look on her face. "Why Miss Gray should risk herself for a smuggler she don't know from Adam beats me, related to the earl or no, but if go you must, miss, take these here flasks of hot soup for the poor man. They'll fit nicely in the pockets of your cloak."

Laughing, Octavia took the flasks and stowed them away.

"Why, Ada," she said, "until I came here I never had an adventure in my life, so I am making up for lost time."

"That's my girl!" approved Sir Tristram. "Let's be off."

The moon was shining brightly, though hidden now and then behind racing clouds driven by a brisk wind from the west. Octavia was glad of her muffling cloak even before they came upon the first sentry, at the corner of the house.

"Halt, who goes there?"

"Hush, man, it is I, Sir Tristram Deanbridge. Do you want to rouse the whole house?"

Octavia clung to his hand, pulling back as if afraid. Having heard the sentry's challenge, the corporal strode up with a lantern and she turned away.

" 'Tis Sir Tristram, right enough," he said. "Beggin' your pardon, sir, but what are you a-doin' up and about at this . . . Ah, I didn't see the young . . . Very good, Private Jones, all's well. Good night, sir."

"And a fine moonlit night it is," agreed Sir Tristram breezily. "Come, my love, shall we go down to the garden?"

Octavia's hand tightened involuntarily at his words. Suddenly she wished they were not acting, that their only purpose was in truth a lover's tryst. He put his arm about her waist and she shivered.

"Are you cold, sweetheart?" he asked, deliberately loud enough for the dragoons to hear.

She shook her head, not trusting her voice. Tears rose in her eyes and she blinked them back. If only he meant it when he called her sweetheart! If only he loved her, not Julia! If only . . .

"I think there is another dragoon by the dovecote," he whispered. "We shall go through the passage under the lane, then down the path past his post, so that he knows we are about and does not challenge us at the wrong moment. Then back up to the cave. The lower sentry will think we are going back through the passage, and Private Jones, that we are still in the garden."

Forcing herself to concentrate on their mission, Octavia followed him down the stone steps into the passage to the valley garden.

The second sentry ventured a remark about all women being hussies at heart. Octavia felt her face burning as Sir Tristram delivered a blistering reproof. When they passed the man again a few minutes later, on their way back, he saluted smartly, his eyes fixed on a point above their heads.

"He won't trouble us," Sir Tristram murmured as soon as the solid stone of the dovecote was between them. "I'll wager he'd not investigate any noise now unless you called him by name. Look, here is the hamper. I hope it is not full of ants. This way."

Octavia looked around carefully as she followed his broad back. She wanted to be able to find the cave herself in case it was ever necessary. Leaves fluttered and branches swayed in the wind, creating a confusion of moving shadows; rustling foliage and the gurgling rill masked the sounds of their footsteps on the gravel path. An owl hooted close by, making her jump, and a cloud covered the moon. She bumped into Sir Tristram.

"This is it."

"I shall never be able to find it," she whispered back.

"I'll show you tomorrow in daylight. Come on, I'll go first to open the door. Under the branches here. Careful."

She heard him knocking very softly, then a darker patch appeared in the blackness. A thud and a clink as he put down the picnic basket, a muffled oath, and he reached back to take her arm and guide her in.

The door closed behind them and Mrs Pengarth uncovered a lighted oil lamp.

"Oh, sir, thank heaven you've come! Jack's in a bad way. He's come over feverish and don't hardly know me. What am I to do?"

Captain Day's eyes were glazed, his face red and sweating. He kept shifting restlessly, muttered under his breath. Octavia stepped to his side, lifted his huge hand and felt for a pulse in the thick wrist. When she found it, it was rapid and fluttering.

"Have you ever done any nursing?" she asked Mrs Pengarth.

"No, miss. It's nursery maids and abigails do such, and

I went from chambermaid to housekeeper. What shall I do?"

"I have never done any either, being the youngest in the family. Sir Tristram, his pulse feels bad to me. We ought to bring Mr Wynn to see him."

"Through a garden full of dragoons!" groaned the baronet. "How do you propose we manage that?"

Octavia looked about the cave in search of an answer. It looked more like a room now, with cushions and rugs on the ground, a pitcher of water in one corner, Martha Pengarth's grey cloak hanging from a nail, partly concealing her carpetbag.

"Mrs Pengarth, have you a light-coloured scarf here? Something white, even a petticoat would do!"

"There's an old woollen shawl, miss. It's warm yet but a bit tattered."

"That does not matter, it is dark outside. Sir Tristram, I shall need your neckcloth for a sash, too." She scrambled out of her cloak. "No, I have not run mad. Take it off."

"Here, miss." A puzzled look on her face, the housekeeper offered her well-worn shawl and helped Octavia drape it over her head and shoulders.

Sir Tristram handed her his cravat, shaking his head. "If I could think of any other way!" he said in frustration.

"How quick you are!" marvelled Octavia, tying the long white cloth about her waist like a sash. "There! He did not see my face, only the dark cloak. He will think I am Julia, or at least a different female, going to meet a different lover. What a shocking opinion of our morals he will have! Well, it cannot be helped. Pray open the door for me."

He shook his head again, racking his brains for an alternative, then glanced at Red Jack and moved to obey. "Bring him to the bower by the pond," he said. "I will come to show you the way. Be careful, Octavia."

Mrs Pengarth doused the light. She heard the door open and slipped out, pushing through the ivy, ducking barely visible branches, emerging into moonlight that seemed to make her white garments glow.

She tiptoed quickly away from the cave entrance.

The sentry gaped as she hurried past him, but said not a word.

How dark it was in the woods! On every side, tree trunks menaced her with the threat of concealed dragoons. A dog howled in the distance. Down by the river something whistled, paused as if to listen for an answer, and whistled again. Man or beast?

A fox bounded onto the path. Her breath caught in her throat as it eyed her warily before trotting off about its business.

She picked up her skirts and ran.

At last the chapel loomed black before her. She beat on the door with all her strength, her bare hands making little noise on the solid oak.

"Who?" came a voice behind her.

She whirled, pressing her back against the door. An owl floated by on silent wings.

"Who?" it asked again.

"Wha'?"

This time the question came from the chapel.

"Mr Wynn!" Octavia's voice emerged as a compromise between a shout and a whisper.

"Who's 'at? Wossamarrer?"

"Mr Wynn, it is Octavia Gray. Captain Day is ill and the garden is full of soldiers. Oh, please, open the door!"

"Miss Gray! Come in, it is not locked. Just a minute, it is confounded dark in here. Where is my candle?"

She found the door handle and opened the door. James Wynn was standing by the altar, lighting a candle. He was in his shirtsleeves, excessively rumpled, his hair more than ever like an untrimmed bush.

Her terror forgotten, she looked at him with a new curiosity. Julia loved this man, had been thrown into despair when parted from him. What had drawn her to him? His brilliant intellect, his dedication to a cause, his fiery nature, these seemed such unlikely qualities to have attracted a spoiled beauty who had refused the most eligible bachelors without a second thought.

He turned to her. "The smuggler is ill? Feverish?"

"Yes, he is hot and restless and his pulse is fast and weak."

"Let me put my coat on and I shall come at once."

And he loved Julia. That was more understandable: everyone loved Julia. Yet it had taken him weeks to discover where she was, when all he had to do was ask Mr Gray, who would surely not have withheld the information. He had been writing his article; love was not all-important in his life. And Sir Tristram, who also loved Julia, had left her to attend to business on his estate.

"Where did I put that flask of brandy Deanbridge left me? Ah, here it is. Let us go, Miss Gray."

Octavia stumbled after him, trying to keep up with his long strides. It had not dawned on him to offer her his arm, any more than it had dawned on him to refuse to go out on this cold, windy night to help a man he knew nothing of except that he was a hunted outlaw and injured. What a strange creature he was!

The whistling came from the river again. Pushing her tired legs to the limit, she caught up with him and tugged at his sleeve.

"Did you hear the whistles?"

"Otters. I expect the river is full of them."

"How do you know it is otters?" she asked. "There are surely none in London!"

"I was brought up in the country, Miss Gray," he said patiently.

"Oh!" She was surprised, having thought him as much a Londoner as herself. She really knew very little of him, except that he had long legs. "Pray do not go so fast, I cannot keep up."

He slowed his pace, and she held on to his sleeve. Even

his unsatisfactory company held at bay the terrors of the night, and she resumed her thoughts.

She was sure it was not from kindness that James Wynn was doctoring Red Jack. It was simply something that needed doing and that he could do. His championship of the poor and oppressed rose from an abstract sense of injustice, not because he cared about his fellow man in any more personal way.

In that he was the opposite of Sir Tristram, who was the kindest man, no, the kindest person she knew. How could she help but love him?

She ought to have been more sympathetic to her cousin. Now she understood the aching misery of unrequited love. Though at least Julia had had hope, whereas she had none. Sir Tristram had already given his heart.

With a shiver she pushed the knowledge away. They were going uphill now and it was time to think of practical matters.

"Mr Wynn, stop a moment," she whispered. He obediently came to a halt and she arranged Mrs Pengarth's shawl more securely over her head. "There is a sentry by the dovecote. We must make him think we are sweethearts." To her annoyance she felt herself blushing, and wished he would realise what he had to do without her spelling it out. "Put your arm around me and do try to walk more slowly. He is certain to be suspicious if we race by him like hounds after a fox."

He settled his arm uncomfortably about her waist. As they stepped out of the woods and into the moonlight, Octavia was suddenly acutely aware of the impropriety of what she was doing. To wander about the garden at midnight with a gentleman's arm embracing her was bad enough. To permit two gentlemen the same familiarity—and on the same night!—was nothing short of disgraceful.

She was no noble heiress to be forgiven an occasional lapse from the highest standards, so the least hint of such behaviour could ruin her reputation forever. She shrugged.

There was only one person whose opinon she cared for, and he knew exactly what she was doing and why.

James Wynn's arm tightened in warning as the sentry, lounging against the dovecote, caught sight of them and straightened to attention. His eyes fixed stonily on a point some six inches above their heads, he let them pass without challenge. Octavia wanted to giggle, wishing she could recall the exact words of Sir Tristram's reproof. With luck, it might also stop the man gossiping about the havey-cavey goings-on in the gardens of Cotehele.

The baronet was waiting for them by the arbour.

"You can let go of her now!" he growled at Mr Wynn in an undertone.

The awkward arm was hurriedly removed, and they followed him to the cave.

Octavia saw at once that Red Jack was worse. Martha Pengarth was cradling his head, wiping his face with a wet cloth and trying to soothe his restless tossing. She looked up at James Wynn with a frightened face.

"Probably an infected wound," he grunted, pulling back the blanket that covered the big man. "Let me see if I can find any swelling without taking off all the bandages. Deanbridge, the lamp."

Octavia sank tiredly down onto a cushion and leaned back against the wall.

"You are burning the candle at both ends," said Sir Tristram, looking at her in concern. "Perhaps I should take you back to the house now."

"No!" said James Wynn sharply. "I may need all the help I can get. Yes, here it is, just above the elbow." He unwrapped the bandage. "Scarcely a scratch, but see how red and swollen it is. It is too far gone for brandy to disinfect it. I shall have to cauterise. I need a sharp knife, and a fire." He took off his coat and rolled up his sleeves.

"Jack's knife is with his clothes," said Mrs Pengarth. "I'll get it." Very gently she moved his head from her lap and went to a corner, returning with a sailor's all-purpose knife in a leather scabbard.

Mr Wynn drew it. The blade glinted wickedly in the light of the lamp, which Sir Tristram held towards him.

"This is the only fire. We could build one, but the smoke would suffocate us."

"It will have to do." He held the blade in the flame, plunging the room into a nightmarish, flickering red light. "Deanbridge, you will have to hold his arms, and you sit on his legs, ma'am. Miss Gray, if you will be so good as to come and help wherever help is needed?"

"I hope you can do without her help, Martha," said Sir Tristram grimly. "Jack is going to cry out when the red-hot steel touches, and he'll bring a pack of dragoons down on us. Octavia, find a cloth and hold it across his mouth with all your strength. If there's more than a peep out of him, all is up with us."

Numb with horror, Octavia untied the neckcloth which had served her as sash and folded it into a pad. She knelt by Red Jack's head and laid it loosely over his mouth.

The writer-politician lifted the knife. Its blade glowed dull red. He adjusted the lamp to give the best light and bent towards his patient. Octavia looked away.

"Octavia!" Sir Tristram's voice was commanding. "You must watch or you will not know when to exert your full strength."

Biting her lip, she turned her head and watched the knife descend. Just before it touched the angry flesh, she pressed hard with both hands on the captain's mouth.

The great body convulsed. Martha Pengarth and Sir Tristram barely managed to hold him down, but only a muffled moan emerged through the cloth.

"Once more."

Again she forced herself to watch, fighting down nausea. The smell of burned hair reached her as she braced for the struggle. There was none. Red Jack went limp.

Sir Tristram lifted her to her feet. She leaned against him, shaking.

"Brave girl," he murmured, "oh, my brave girl! It's over, that's all. I'll take you home now. Wynn and Martha can manage. Come now, here is your cloak."

He left her in Ada's care and went back to the cave. She staggered up the stairs, stood like a statue while Ada took off her filthy gown, tut-tutting, and fell into bed.

She expected the memory of Red Jack's agony to keep her awake in spite of her tiredness, but her last thought before falling into a deep, dreamless sleep was of Sir Tristram.

Whatever happened in the future, they had worked together this night and nothing could take away her memory of it. He had counted on her aid; she had given it freely and seen the admiration and gratitude in his eyes.

That must suffice.

=18=

Octavia woke to the sound of the ancient clock striking noon. Her first sensation was of hunger, and she rang the bell quickly. If she hurried she would be in time for luncheon.

Ada appeared at once.

"Morning, miss," she said cheerfully, drawing back the curtains to reveal a sunlit hillside. "I was right next door, in Miss Julia's room, working on that dress you wore last night. It won't be fit for much, I misdoubt."

"Perhaps I shall need it again tonight! It was one of my old ones, and I mean never to go back to such dowdy stuff, whatever Mama may say, so it does not matter."

"That's the spirit, miss. Can I get you a tray? You must be right sharp set after all that running about."

"I am starving, but I shall go down." She threw back the covers. "Where is Julia?"

"She went down to breakfast, miss!" said the abigail in a marvelling tone, as they went through to the other chamber. "If that's not a sign of true love, I'm sure I don't know what is. Then out right away, leaving word to my lady she was gone a-walking in the gardens. Them dragoons are gone, I'm glad to say. What will you wear today, miss?"

Octavia chose one of her new walking dresses, an amber muslin trimmed with straw-coloured lace. She hurried down to the dining room, where she found Raeburn putting the last touches to the cold buffet.

"Morning, miss," he answered her greeting. "My lady and Miss Crosby will be here any moment."

"And Sir . . . the others?"

"Miss Julia went out early, miss!" Unaware of James Wynn's arrival, the butler was still more astonished than the maid. "Sir Tristram got up uncommon late, not more than an hour ago, I'd say, and he took a hamper and went after her. They'll be picnicking in the garden again, I daresay."

"I am too hungry to go looking for them now," said Octavia in disappointment. "Pour me some tea, if you please, and I shall wait for my aunt."

Miss Crosby and Lady Langston came in almost immediately. Miss Crosby made a spiteful remark about gentlemen being obliged by good manners to stay up till all hours listening to the chatter of thoughtless young women.

"Octavia is less given to idle chatter than any young lady I know," said Lady Langston fondly, putting an end to that line of attack.

"Then she and Sir Tristram must have had matters of import to discuss," said Miss Crosby brightly. "What business, I wonder, had *dear* Miss Langston's suitor with Miss Gray?"

Her ladyship came to the rescue once more, her placidity unshaken. "Books, I expect, for they are both amazingly fond of books. Raeburn, I will take one of those currant tarts. I am particularly partial to blackcurrant tarts."

"A bluestocking! Of course, a gentleman may discuss literature with a lady, but nothing is less likely to lead to an offer of marriage than an excessive acquaintance with books." Satisfied with this thrust, Miss Crosby allowed Octavia to complete her meal in peace.

This she did with a hearty appetite, but scarcely noticing what she ate. Sir Tristram had changed his tactics and followed Julia, after saying he intended to leave her alone with James Wynn. She read a message in his actions.

He was warning her not to refine too much upon their

closeness last night, reminding her that she was not really his sweetheart. "My brave girl," he had called her. She was to ignore the first word though the last two could not be retracted. Had she done or said something that revealed to him her discovery that she loved him?

Her only clear recollections were of the glowing knife descending and of his reassuring arms about her afterwards. "My brave girl," he had said. "It is over."

"Are you quite well, Octavia?" asked her aunt. "You look a little pale. You had best go out in the fresh air with Julia."

"Yes, ma'am," she said obediently, but she chose to wander alone about the upper gardens, brooding on the unreasonableness of life.

Julia was in high spirits when she came in to change for dinner.

"I wish you had been with us, Tavy," she cried. "We quite expected you to join us. James and Sir Tristram were talking politics and I learned such a lot! Did you know Sir Tristram is a Whig? I'll wager Papa does not know or he would not be so eager to have him for a son-in-law."

"I expect he does know. It is James's radicalism and poverty to which he so strongly objects. He cannot insist that you marry a confirmed Tory!"

"Well, Sir Tristram said as we came up, that he has a most respectable friend whose ideas differ little from James's. He thinks it is James's eloquence which makes him seem so extreme. Actually, he said James's words run away with him." Julia giggled. "Can you not picture them, on little spindly legs, scampering off as fast as they can go?"

"You did not feel Sir Tristram's presence as an intrusion?"

"Heavens, no. James likes someone to argue with and I am still too ignorant. Besides, I agree with everything he says; his views seem perfectly reasonable to me. And Sir Tristram did not act like a rejected lover, which would have made me uncomfortable."

"Though James would not have noticed. No, Sir Tristram's manners are far too good, and I daresay he has not quite given up hope yet."

Octavia determined that her manners should prove as good as the baronet's. No one should guess her unhappiness; she would join the others and endeavour to be cheerful. She might never see Sir Tristram again once she left Cotehele, but until that dread moment, he must have no reason to think her anything other than a sympathetic friend.

When they went down to the drawing room, Lady Langston called her niece to her. Once again her ladyship had reason to congratulate herself on the effectiveness of her remedy; fresh air and exercise had restored the bloom to Octavia's cheeks, the smile to her lips.

Sir Tristram came in, slightly out of breath, his cravat arranged with less than its usual neatness. Octavia thought he must have gone to the cave after escorting Julia up to the house. The dinner gong rang at once, so she was not able to ask for news of Jack Day. He smiled at her as he led Lady Langston down to the dining room, but to her relief made no comment about her absence. She did not want her aunt to know she had been alone all afternoon.

Private conversation at the dinner table was impossible. Sir Tristram did not linger over his brandy, but by the time he came up, Miss Crosby had entangled Octavia in a discussion of the works of Hannah More. She upheld her bookish reputation admirably, since the philanthropist was her mother's favourite writer. *The Religion of the Fashionable World* and *Practical Piety* she was thoroughly acquainted with, and she had even read *Moral Sketches*, published as recently as 1818.

Since Miss Crosby had been unable to obtain a copy in the year since its appearance, this was momentary defeat. However, she was not about to admit it. Though Octavia offered to have her mother send a copy, she persisted in questioning her on every detail of the work.

Sir Tristram threw Octavia a glance of commiseration and spent the evening at Julia's side.

It was still quite early when Julia stretched and yawned and declared that there was nothing like a day in the open to make one sleepy.

"Come on, Tavy," she added. "We cannot have you sleeping the day away again. What a waste of the countryside you longed for!"

Miss Crosby's face was full of triumph as Octavia unwillingly said her good nights and retired.

Having risen so late, she was not in the least sleepy. She sat up in her bed, leaning against a pile of pillows, and tried to concentrate on the first part of Byron's *Don Juan*, a poem Julia said every lady of fashion must be acquainted with. She did not like it, but it seemed an appropriate rebellion against Hannah More.

There was a knock on the door and Ada came in.

"Here's a note from Sir Tristram, miss," she announced in a conspiratorial whisper. "He said as you'd be wanting to hear how the captain goes on." She handed over a much-folded sheet and slipped out.

Octavia held it for a moment without opening it. She wanted to press it to her heart, but could not bring herself to do anything so suggestive of a Cheltenham tragedy. With carefully steady fingers she unfolded it.

No salutation. He had not wanted to write "Dear Miss Gray." And it ended simply, "In haste, Deanbridge."

"You will be glad to hear," it said, "that Jack's condition is much improved. The fever is diminished, though naturally his arm pains him greatly. I am deeply grateful to James Wynn; I had rather be grateful to anybody else in the world, as you may imagine.

"My humble apologies, ma'am," she imagined the laugh in his eyes at such formality, "for the postponement of our outing. Even had you not been too fatigued for it, I must have remained close to Jack until his improvement was certain. Tomorrow I must go down to Mount Edgcumbe to inform the earl of what is toward. I beg your indulgence for the day after, which shall not pass without a visit to Cotehele Mill.

"Wynn is not the only person who has my heartfelt gratitude, together with my undying admiration for her courage.

In haste, Deanbridge."

Perhaps there was good reason to press it to her heart after all. She folded it and put it under her pillow, and fell asleep with her hand upon it.

Julia was once more up betimes. They went down to breakfast together and were arguing the relative merits of tea and chocolate as a morning drink when Sir Tristram came in.

"Good morning, ladies," he said. "You may think yourselves early risers, but I have been before you. Since I shall not be here today, I have got you a picnic packed up already, and taken it down to the arbour by the fish pond."

Julia clapped her hands in delight, while Octavia smiled at his ingenuity. Undoubtedly a goodly portion of the hamper's contents had already found its way to the cave.

"Where are you going?" asked Julia. "I hope you will not be gone for long?"

"I have business with Lord Edgcumbe. I shall return late tonight."

"Good. We shall miss you, shall we not, Tavy?"

Sir Tristram looked surprised at her words. Octavia saw that he still did not realise that Julia simply enjoyed company, even when her James was with her, and not merely to avoid political lectures.

Miss Crosby came in and took a seat beside Julia, whose attention she engaged with compliments about her fine suitor, accompanied by significant glances at the baronet.

Julia answered her politely, while her suitor seized the opportunity for a quick word with Octavia.

"Are you looking forward to tomorrow?" he asked.

"Yes, indeed. After all, I have been waiting for several weeks now! You have seen our friend this morning? How does he go on?"

"Still improving. I hope to arrange his future today. I beg your pardon, ma'am?" He turned to Miss Crosby. "But certainly Miss Langston's gown becomes her admirably. However, Miss Langston would be beautiful in rags. Her beauty is of the type that needs no adornment."

Julia sparkled at him. "Pray do not tell Papa such a thing!" she exclaimed. "How shocking if he were to take your words seriously. Now if you will excuse us, ma'am, Octavia and I are eager to take the air while it is fine. Do not miss the tide tonight, Sir Tristram. I look to see you at breakfast tomorrow."

They walked down through the passage into the lower garden, and went to the bower to check on their picnic.

"Shall we take it with us?" asked Octavia doubtfully. "There are two handles, I expect we might manage."

"No, James shall come up here with us. I'm sure all the servants know he is here, and neither Mama nor Miss Crosby ever stirs from the house. What an odious woman she is! Always disparaging you and toadeating me."

"Her position is difficult, enough to sour any temper."

"You are too charitable! We shall not think about her. How I love this garden with its twisting paths and bridges over the streamlet, and all the flowers! Shall we run? Do let us pick up our skirts and run."

"Be careful, Ju!" Octavia followed her light-footed cousin more slowly.

As she had feared, Julia came to grief on a bend, sliding on the gravel and landing on her knees. She sat back and pulled up her petticoats to inspect the damage, biting her lip.

"Drat!" she swore and blinked back tears. "I had forgot

how a skinned knee hurts. It is ten years since I did such a thing." She smiled ruefully at Octavia.

"We must go back to the house and have Ada bandage it. And look at your hand! You have scraped that too and there is dirt in the cuts. Can you get up? Let me help you."

"Thank you. Ouch! How it stings! We need not go back, though. James will know what to do."

"You know that he has medical training? I only found out by accident, and also that he grew up in the country. I had thought him as much a Londoner as I am."

"His father has an estate in Surrey but he has lived in town for near ten years." Julia limped along holding her skirts away from the sore knee with her undamaged hand. "To think he was there all that time and I only met him less than four months ago!"

"His father has an estate? You have found out more in those few months than I did in four years! Is your papa aware of the estate?"

"I do not know. No, I expect he is not. I only found out myself two days ago, when James mentioned that he had been in Surrey since I left London. It is not something he talks about, because he disapproves of great landowners, but he is the only son and will inherit it. Not that he will be a *great* landowner. It is quite small, I believe."

"All the same, I expect it will change Lord Langston's feelings towards him. You must write at once."

"I cannot. I would have to reveal that James is here! And if Papa did not relent, that would be the end of everything."

"What are you going to do then? Will your papa make you stay here until you accept Sir Tristram? I do not see what you are to do."

"If only Sir Tristram would withdraw his suit! Surely Papa would look more kindly on James if it were not for his rival. Sometimes I think the only thing to do is elope."

"No! Oh, Julia, do not say so. Promise me you will not."

"I cannot promise, though it would do James's career no good, so we shall not act precipitately. But if nothing has changed by the end of the summer . . . I cannot promise, Tavy."

Shocked, Octavia walked on in silence. If Julia caused a scandal by eloping, the tattlemongers would say she did it to escape from Sir Tristram's unwelcome attentions. He would be doubly hurt, by losing her and by the world's censure.

She saw James sitting under an oak tree near the chapel, reading as usual. Looking round, she realised she had outdistanced her cousin, who was toiling along uncomplainingly some way back down the path.

"Mr Wynn!" she called. No response. Louder, "Mr Wynn!"

Buried in his book, he did not stir.

"James!" came Julia's plaintive voice faintly from behind her.

He jumped up, dropping the book on the carpet of last autumn's leaves.

"Miss Gray?" he asked, looking bewildered, then saw Julia. "My love, what is the matter?"

He hurried to his beloved, passing Octavia with scarce a nod. She followed. She found it hard to restrain her amusement as the man who had unflinchingly cut open Jack Day's arm with red-hot steel carefully examined her cousin's childish injuries. With soothing words he led her to the rivulet. He washed hand and knee in its clear, cold water and bound them up with strips of cloth torn from her already ruined petticoat.

He could not have lavished more symapthy on the most dangerous illness, yet Octavia had received a still more convincing proof of his passion: though lost in his reading, he had heard Julia's voice.

In spite of the indecorous intimacy occasioned by the necessity of examing his beloved's shapely leg, James did not permit himself any untoward familiarities. Octavia was relieved to note the propriety of his behaviour, since she had been feeling somewhat guilty about conniving at her cousin's clandestine meetings.

Still, she could hardly protest at Julia's spending the days alone in the gardens with a gentleman. Not after her own midnight adventures in these same gardens!

After a while, Julia announced herself sufficiently recovered to stroll along the level path towards the quay. They had not gone far when they saw Lieutenant Cardin coming towards them. Octavia, already weary of playing gooseberry, greeted him with pleasure.

Julia and James were equally delighted with his company. The four of them spent an enjoyable day together, which came to an end only when they heard the medieval clock up at the house striking six.

"We must go and change for dinner, Ju," said Octavia. "Mr Cardin, you will dine with us, will you not?"

"Thank you, but will not Lady Langston think me presumptuous?"

"Mama is happy to entertain guests as long as they do not require her to put herself out," Julia assured him, "and she does dislike to dine in exclusively female company. Since Sir Tristram is gone, you will be doubly welcome."

Octavia and the lieutenant walked on, leaving Julia to take reluctant leave of James.

"I shall be very glad to get a good dinner," Mr Cardin confided. "The tide does not turn until near midnight."

"Yes, Sir Tristram said he would be late returning from Mount Edgcumbe."

"I met him at the quay when I arrived. He seemed displeased to see me, so I hope he will not take it amiss that I stay to dine."

"I am sure you mistook his meaning," Octavia reassured him. "Besides, if Lady Langston chooses to invite you, I am sure it is none of his affair."

And far better that the young Customs officer should be safe within the house instead of wandering alone about the garden finding clues to Red Jack's whereabouts!

=== 19 ===

IT RAINED DURING the night. By morning, a cool, blustery wind was chasing clouds about the sky like a flock of grey sheep chivvied by a sheepdog.

"A perfect day for a long walk in the country," said Octavia as she and Julia dressed.

"The lanes and fields will be all muddy!" objected Julia.

"Confess!" laughed Octavia, who had expected this reaction, "you do not care for long walks whatever the weather. I mean to go, though. If I do not take more exercise I shall grow fat again. Ada, I shall wear one of my old brown dresses, so it will not matter if I dirty the hem, and my stoutest shoes, if you please."

"I wonder if James will like to go?"

"Excessively unlikely. Did he not abandon country life years since? You must resign yourself to doing without me today, Ju."

"I wish you will take Sir Tristram with you. You ought not to walk alone. Suppose you fall!"

"And scrape my knee? I shall be glad of his company if he wishes to join me."

"You need not ask him; I shall tell him to go with you. He is too obliging a gentleman to refuse."

Octavia was well satisfied. Without telling her cousin about the projected outing to the mill, she had arranged to leave her alone with James all day, as Sir Tristram had planned. And she had made her think it was her own idea, so she could not feel ill-used at being abandoned.

They went down to breakfast. Raeburn, at his most stolid, was listening to a stream of complaint from Miss Crosby. The kippers were cold, the tea too weak, the sideboard undusted, and the housemaids pert. It was perfectly shocking how things went to rack and ruin while Mrs Pengarth was away, and still more shocking how she took advantage of his lordship's kindness to prolong her absence.

"Yes, madam," said Raeburn woodenly. "Good morning, Miss Julia, Miss Gray. Tea and chocolate as usual?"

"If you please, Raeburn." Julia turned to Miss Crosby. "How right you are, ma'am," she said with the greatest affability. "My mother has simply no notion how to hold household without a competent housekeeper in attendance."

"Oh no . . . I did not mean . . . Lady Langston is certainly . . . Indeed, Miss Langston, you mistake . . ."

Octavia choked on a bubble of laughter and took a hurried sip of tea. It was too hot, and she choked in reality. While Julia and the butler fussed over her, patting her back and offering napkins, Miss Crosby slipped red-faced from the room.

"Ju, that was brilliant and perfectly horrid of you," gasped Octavia, at last regaining her breath. "I have never heard such a masterly set-down. And true too! If Raeburn were not here, the house would be at sixes and sevens for all my aunt could do."

"She's right, though, Miss Julia," confessed the butler. "Leastways, there's not a speck of dust on the sideboard, for Doris does keep the maids to their work, but I made the tea weak because Miss Gray likes it weak, and the housemaids are pert because they don't like her, and the kippers are cold because she's the only one as eats them and Cook doesn't like her neither!"

The girls crowed with laughter.

Nibbling on a muffin, Julia remembered that Sir Tristram would not be taking care of today's food supply.

"Raeburn, do you think Cook has a small picnic basket? Miss Gray and Sir Tristram will not be with me, so I need enough just for me and . . . just for me. But I shall be very hungry!"

"Just for you and, Miss Julia," assented Raeburn gravely. "I understand perfectly and I'll inform Cook."

Julia smiled at him sunnily, perfectly aware that he knew of her suitor's presence.

Sir Tristram had still not come down when they finished eating.

"I cannot wait for such a slug-a-bed," Julia declared. "James expects me. Do you still intend to go walking today? If you change your mind, come and join us." She went off with a spring in her step.

Octavia dawdled over a third cup of tea. It was provoking of the baronet to sleep in on the day of their expedition, when he was usually such an early riser. She supposed he had gone to see Red Jack after arriving on the late tide. In fact, she thought, he had missed a vast deal of sleep recently. Perhaps he was too tired for the visit to the mill.

He came in, his stride as firm and purposeful as ever, and sat down to his usual hearty breakfast.

"I was thinking," said Octavia tentatively, "that you have not had a full night's sleep in an age. We need not go today if you prefer to rest."

He looked up with a grin from his bacon and eggs. "What a poor creature you must think me! It is not much more than a mile to the mill; I believe I shall manage it if you promise to slow down when I grow weary."

"Wretch! I promise."

"The paths will be muddy after the rain."

"That is why Julia does not come," said Octavia with satisfaction. "I am wearing an old gown so that mud will not show. All my old gowns are mud-coloured."

He looked at her in surprise. "So you are. I had not noticed, though I shall never forget the picture you presented when you first arrived at Cotehele!"

"That was limestone, not mud. Now do stop talking and finish your breakfast, or we shall never leave."

The baronet refused to be hurried, so it was half an hour later that they set off. As they passed the stables, the horse Lord Edgcumbe had provided for Sir Tristram's use whickered a greeting. A groom looked out reproachfully.

"Ah's not been rid sin' ye cam back fro' Mount Edgcumbe," he pointed out.

"I know. I shall try to take him out later today. Have you a nice, quiet hack suitable for Miss Gray?"

"I do not ride, sir."

"I know, but it is time you learned. We shall be able to escape further afield."

"Julia rides, and I expect James does too, since he grew up in the country, so that will not serve. I should like to learn, though, if there is quite a small horse for me. They always seem so very large."

"We'll talk of it later. Thank you, Sutton." Sir Tristram hurried her away. "Now what is this? Wynn country-bred? I thought him a thoroughgoing townsman."

"As did I. It turns out his father has a small estate in Surrey which he will inherit! Julia thinks her papa does not know. It will surely change his opinion of James's merits as a son-in-law."

He frowned. "Has she written to inform him? How is it she had not told him before?"

Octavia explained why she could not enlighten Lord Langston. "Who knows what he would do if he knew James was here! I daresay he would find some kinsman in the Scottish Highlands with a castle suitable for incarcerating poor Ju, like Mary Queen of Scots at Lochleven."

"I cannot like it that Langston is misinformed as to Wynn's prospects," he said, still frowning. "It would be dishonourable to rely on such an advantage over my rival."

"Fustian! His future inheritance of a small estate cannot change my uncle's opinion of your advantage as present possessor of a large one. Nor does it make the least difference to James's only advantage, which is Julia's opinion, or rather, feelings."

Instead of walking down the drive, they took the upper lane. To their left mixed woods of oak and ash and sycamore fell steeply towards the river, trimmed with an edging of flowers among which Octavia now recognised red campion, golden St. John's wort and purple vetches. On the right a steep bank and drystone wall were overgrown with sweet-scented honeysuckle and dog rose. Sir Tristram seemed oblivious of the delightful surroundings, his forehead still wrinkled.

"I must tell you that I have little faith in the success of your present plan of isolating them together." Octavia hated to add to his uneasiness, but felt she must warn him. "Julia showed every sign of enjoying his company and conversation when I spent the day with them yesterday."

"And with your lieutenant! Was he snooping after Jack?"

"I do not believe so. He was with us all day and came up to the house to dine in the evening, so he had no opportunity."

"So he came merely to visit you."

" 'Merely' to visit me," she agreed. "Do you wish to return to the garden and interrupt Julia's tête-à-tête? I have not the least desire to keep you here against your will."

"Are you tactfully telling me that I am out of reason cross? I beg your pardon. I find myself in something of a quandary over the best course to pursue, but I will set aside my deliberations until a more suitable time."

"Good! Tell me about Jack. You saw him last night?"

"Yes, and he is improved beyond recognition. I would say he is very well, but his left arm is near useless after that infection. Wynn cannot be sure that he will ever regain full strength in it. You know, Wynn's medical ability is unlikely to weigh with Langston, but my respect for him is much increased. Does Julia know of it?"

"Yes. What are Lord Edgcumbe's plans for Captain Day?"

"There is a small house at Mount Edgcumbe, near Fort Picklecombe. You probably saw it while you were there; it is not far from a sort of Gothic pavilion with a magnificent view of the Channel. He means to offer it to Jack on condition that he gives up smuggling and marries Martha."

"He will need some occupation."

"The fort needs an overseer. It is little used in peacetime and is falling into disrepair since the end of the war with France. Do you think the situation will suit him?"

"A man who spends his life breaking the law is in no position to quibble when offered an honourable situation by his friends! But how will he be able to settle down without the Customs arresting him?"

"The Customs Service is grossly overworked and already the hunt has died down. It is too late to take him red-handed, or to say they followed him directly from the scene of the crime. The earl means to come here in a few days and take him under his protection back to Mount Edgcumbe."

"Oh dear!" exclaimed Octavia. "Will he bring a party this time? Mrs Pengarth is not here to prepare for them and my aunt will be panicked again!"

Sir Tristram laughed. "Martha will return to the house this evening. Jack can manage now with an occasional visit."

"Thank heaven! Miss Crosby will be relieved."

He looked enquiringly and she told him of Matilda Crosby's complaints, Julia's set-down and Raeburn's confession. He whooped with laughter, blue devils forgotten.

They crossed another lane and entered the woods. The air was still, damp, rich with odours of leaf mould and sap. From the bottom of the steep slope to their left came the sound of rushing water. A squirrel dashed past them, raced up a tall, straight larch and sat scolding them.

The centre of the path was black mud, but the edges, less worn by foot and hoof, were drier. Octavia balanced her way along the narrow strip with an occasional helping hand from Sir Tristram, who strode on regardless of the mire splashing his top boots. They descended the gentle slope until the path doubled back in a hairpin bend, where a rough bench invited them to pause awhile.

"Am I going too fast for you, sir?" asked Octavia in mock concern. "Here is a place where you may rest."

"Set here for those going uphill!"

"Come and sit down. Listen!"

The stream in the valley splashed and gurgled. Invisible among the tree trunks, a woodpecker hammered, paused and hammered again. The sounds only accentuated the hushed peacefulness.

"How quiet it is. I dread going back to London." She made a moue of distaste. "But that is a bridge I will not cross until I come to it. Shall we go on?"

The path sloped more steeply now. Below them they could see where it doubled back again. As they neared the next bend, Sir Tristram showed her a precipitous shortcut that he and Lord William had always taken as boys.

"We had to hang on to those bushes, there and there, on the way down," he pointed out. "It is more of a scramble than a walk."

"It must cut off at least a hundred yards."

"An important difference when you are twelve or four-teen years old and always in a hurry. In actual fact it cuts off nothing, for the bridge over the stream is very close to the bend."

"But it is more fun. Let us go that way!"

"If you like, but I must warn you that we invariably returned home with muddy seats to our breeches."

"I told you, I am wearing my mud-coloured dress."

"Then allow me to go first, to catch you if you fall."

He started down, sliding, running a few steps, catching at branches to slow his descent then turning to see her progress. She followed, lifting her skirts a few inches with one hand and reaching for the bushes with the other.

The last few feet were still steeper. Sir Tristram bounded down to the lower path and turned to steady her. She let go of her skirts to grasp a branch on the wrong side, missed her footing, and slid helplessly down the muddy slope to an inevitable collision.

She knocked his feet from under him. He landed full-length on top of her, breaking his fall with his arms just enough to let her breathe.

For a long moment he gazed deep into her eyes, then he bent his head and very gently kissed her lips.

At once he rolled aside and stood up. A deep flush staining his cheekbones, he helped her up. Too astounded to speak, she brushed ineffectually at her skirts.

"Miss Gray, I most humbly beg your pardon," he said, not looking at her. "That was inexcusable of me."

"Oh, no!" Her breathing was uneven. "It was only a brotherly—no—a *cousinly* kiss."

"The devil it was," he said sombrely, then recollected himself. "You are not hurt? I must have been crazy to let you use that path."

She looked straight at him. "I enjoyed it," she said.

They walked on, not touching, she puzzling over his "devil" and he wondering just what it was she had enjoyed.

The mill stream was right beside them now, and very soon they came to the wooden bridge over it. On the other bank was a lush green meadow, with scabious, purple knapweed and oxeye daisies growing amid the long grass. At the far end stood several stone buildings.

A donkey grazed near the stream. When it saw them it ambled over to investigate and stood still while Octavia stroked its velvety neck.

"Perhaps I could learn to ride on a donkey," she said. "It is not so far to fall."

"An excellent idea." Sir Tristram had recovered his countenance sufficiently to smile at her. "The ears are big enough to catch hold of if you lose your seat. This fellow will be busy as soon as the cider apples ripen, but we may easily find another."

As they approached the mill buildings a medley of

sounds reached them: a deep rumble, hammering, clanging, a rhythmic rasp and, now and then, a peculiar hiss.

The wheelwright and blacksmith between them proved responsible for the hiss. They were shrinking tyres of red-hot iron onto wooden wheels by pouring cold water over them. Steam rose in clouds, hiding the red, sweating faces of the craftsmen.

The sight of the hot metal brought back memories of Captain Day's agony, and Octavia was glad to move on to the saw-pit. The bottom sawyer was invisible in a cloud of sawdust as he and his mate above pulled the long saw rhythmically up and down, turning logs into planks.

The workshops of saddler, carpenter, and mason followed, and then they went into the ciderhouse, where the little donkey would soon be walking round and round, turning a wheel to crush the apples. A door at the back opened onto the huge mill wheel; its steady rumble sent a constant vibration through the building.

In the mill itself, next door, Sir Tristram explained the working of the wheels and cogs and shafts that turned the great millstones to grind grain into flour.

Octavia was fascinated by everything, and full of questions. The baronet answered as best he could, referring often to the way things were done in Gloucestershire. At last he laughingly confessed that she had wrung him dry of knowledge.

"Besides," he said, pulling out his watch, "watching all this labour has made me amazingly hungry. I sent a message to the miller's wife first thing this morning to ask her if she could provide bread and cheese at midday, and it is nearly two, so let us see whether she has complied."

The miller's cottage stood close by. Its garden was gay with sweet William, love-in-a-mist and candytuft, and a yellow climbing rose ran riot above the front door, blossoms nodding in the gusty wind. Inside they found a cosy kitchen and a table set with bread and cheese, not to mention Cornish pasties and blackcurrants with clotted cream and a tall earthen pitcher of cider.

Octavia looked at the latter mistrustfully, and was happy to accept a glass of primrose wine instead.

While they ate, Sir Tristram talked about Dean Park, about his staff and tenants and neighbours. Octavia ventured to ask about his family, and found out at last why he had spent so much of his youth with the Edgcumbes.

His father had been a diplomat and spent little time in England. His mother had died young, of yellow fever, in some foreign port, and he and his sister had lived with their respective godparents, there being no suitable relatives. He scarcely knew his sister, who was several years older and had married her godmother's son.

Octavia's eavesdropping in the chapel had taught her his opinion of his brother-in-law. It had been the reason for his sudden decision to marry. That, she felt, was a delicate subject, and fearful of mentioning something she ought not to know, she turned the subject to her own family.

Seven brothers and sisters with families of their own provided plenty of material for amusing anecdotes. Sir Tristram was soon helpless with laughter at the exploits of her nieces and nephews.

"You always make me laugh," he said, wiping his eyes.

Octavia realised with surprise that it was true. She could not recall ever having made anyone at home laugh. In fact, in spite of boasting to Julia that she was used to take part in political discussions, she never said very much of anything at home. She was becoming a shocking chatterbox.

Not unnaturally, this thought made her fall silent. Sir Tristram looked at her questioningly, puzzled at the effect of his words, but said nothing. Overcoming their hospitable hostess's reluctance to be paid, he settled with her and they went out into the meadow.

"Shall we walk farther along the valley?" he suggested. "There is plenty of time before we need return."

She agreed. They went back over the little bridge and

followed the path beside the stream. Octavia averted her eyes when they passed the spot where she had fallen, and he did not comment. They walked for the most part in silence, though he did point out a mossy tree trunk lying across the stream from which he and Lord William had frequently fallen into the water.

They came to an elaborate stone dam, where the stream was divided into two branches. The upper branch ran in a conduit to the mill wheel, which it turned by falling on it from above. Sir Tristram had explained the system back at the mill and now passed the dam and pond lost in thought. Reaching the hamlet of Newhouses, he turned back without consulting Octavia, then came to himself with a start.

"I beg your pardon! I have so often walked to this point and no farther that I do it without thought. Do you care to go on?"

She smiled and shook her head, and he soon returned to his reverie. Walking beside him, for even in his concentration he never outpaced her, she took pleasure in his company, the exercise, the woods and rushing stream. She resolutely refused to think of anything else.

As they passed the mill and went on down the valley, the stream grew wider and slower and began to meander between reedbeds. A double-arched stone bridge crossed it, but they turned the other way, going towards the Tamar and Cotehele Quay.

"I must go away," announced Sir Tristram abruptly as the buildings by the quay came into sight. "Ten days, a fortnight, I cannot be sure. You must do something for me while I am gone: do not let Julia elope with Wynn."

"If I can," said Octavia, heavyhearted.

== 20 ==

THE TAMAR WAS shrinking as the tide ebbed. A flock of tiny sandpipers dashed back and forth across the newly exposed mudflats, stopping as one to poke busily then darting away again, their legs moving too fast to see.

The only vessels at the wharves were a fishing dory and another rowboat. Three salmon fishers sat outside the Edgcumbe Arms, mending their nets. One of the three hailed Sir Tristram.

"Ahoy, zir!" He was a wrinkled, bent old man who looked as if the river damp had got into his bones long since. He hobbled up to Sir Tristram and Octavia. "Oy be afeard oy zees trouble acomin', zir," he announced, hooking his thumb over his shoulder.

Following the gesture, Octavia saw he was pointing up the path through the woods towards Sir Richard's chapel.

The other men were nodding solemnly, and a dock-worker, coming out of the tavern, joined them.

"What is it, Ned Poldhu?" asked the baronet. "Are the dragoons returned?"

"Nay, zir," he cackled. "T'other way about. 'Tis Cap'n Day's men acome to zee how he do go on. Stopped fer a mug o' zider, they did, an' zum vool did tell 'em as there be a 'Ziseman livin' in the chapel."

Sir Tristram looked at the rest of the men.

"Aye, zir, 'tis true," confirmed one, " 'zeptin' it were rum as they did drink."

" 'Twere owld Barney," said another, tapping his forehead significantly. "Telled 'em 'bout the Customs lieutenant acomin' upriver all the time, beggin' your pardon, miss."

Octavia blushed fiery red and hoped he did not mean what she thought he meant.

"Waren't nowt we could zay," shrugged the wharfman. "Them bein' rarin' to go after the gentleman."

"When did they leave?" asked Sir Tristram sharply.

"Vive, ten minute agone. Armed, they was, and right cantankersome."

"They know me. I do not fear them. Octavia, I hope you will come for your cousin's sake, but stay behind me."

She had little choice, since he set off up the track at a pace she could not match. The path was straight for some distance so she could see him, and soon spotted the sailors from the *Seamew*.

Sir Tristram called to them but they ignored him, or did not hear. Their rolling, unhurried gait carried them round a curve and out of sight.

Octavia picked up her skirts and ran until she was breathless. Her legs felt like lead. She walked a few steps, trotted, then walked again. Sir Tristram disappeared round the curve. The way was uphill now and she could run no more, but she was close enough to hear the men shouting.

Julia screamed.

At last she reached the clearing by the chapel. Julia was standing against the door, her arms spread as if to defend it against all comers. Sir Tristram was nearly at her side, his mouth open, his voice indistinguishable from those of the four smugglers, who were all still shouting. They had drawn pistols and cutlasses and were advancing in a semicircle on the chapel. Octavia recognised the piratical face of the one-eyed Yorkshireman, and hook-handed Dan Small.

Julia's high voice cut through the clamour.

"James, jump!"

Everyone fell silent. There was a rustling in the bushes.

"Good-bye, my love!" called James.

The sailors rushed towards the sound. Sir Tristram and Julia ran after them. Octavia followed slowly, still breathless, a grin dawning.

By the time she joined the others at the top of the cliff, the smugglers and Sir Tristram were all in whoops. Julia alternated between scolding them and calling words of encouragement towards the river.

Octavia looked down. James Wynn sprawled on his back in the mud, his legs buried above the knees. As she watched, he attempted to lever himself up. His arm sank in to the shoulder and he pulled it free with a great deal of difficulty and a horribly glutinous noise.

"Help him!" wailed Julia.

Biting her lip to stop herself joining the laughter, Octavia hurried to her cousin's side and put an arm about her shoulders.

"We'll rescue him, never fear," she promised. "The tide is still ebbing so there is no immediate danger. Oh dear, whatever possessed him to jump over?"

"Sir Richard Edgcumbe escaped that way," said Julia with injured dignity. "I shall never believe another romantic legend as long as I live."

"I was afraid you had misinterpreted the story. Sir Richard only threw his cap over, and even then he must have known it was high tide for his enemies would never have been misled by a cap lying on the mud!"

"James said they are Bow Street runners come to arrest him for the article he wrote, so I told him he must swim across the river and find somewhere to hide." Julia burst into tears. "And I was so afraid he would drown and now everyone is laughing at him and they will catch him and take him away to prison."

"No, Ju, they are smugglers! They think he is a spy for the Customs and Excise. Sir Tristram will tell them he is not, as soon as he stops guffawing." She glared at the baronet.

"But why should they think he is a spy? And why should they believe Sir Tristram that he is not?"

"He has been seen talking to Lieutenant Cardin. It seems everyone at Cotehele knows James is here, and probably why, but the smugglers misunderstood what some old man said. I daresay he was jesting about our suitors."

"How odious! Tavy, do not stand here talking, we must save poor James! What shall we do?"

Except for occasional chuckles, the men had stopped laughing. The smugglers were listening to Sir Tristram's assurance of Mr Wynn's innocence, at least as far as their suspicions were concerned. He was being as tactful as possible about the real reason for James's presence in the chapel, but inevitably they guessed the truth. Dan Small winked at Julia, to her fury.

"Pay un no mind, missy," advised the Yorkshireman kindly, enveloping the girls in a cloud of rum fumes. "Us'll fish thy lover out, never fear." He turned to Octavia. "Us be right good rescuers, bain't we, missy?"

"We plumb fergot as the lieutenant 'ad other good reasons for comin' 'ere, miss," added Dan Small, with an apologetic wave of his hook.

Octavia flushed at Julia's astonished look. She had never mentioned that the sailors who had rescued her from the waters of the Plymouth Sound had been smugglers, and she had forgotten that they had witnessed Mr Cardin's impassioned promise to wait for her.

"They seem to be acquainted with you as well as with Sir Tristram," Julia said acidly.

One of the respectable-looking seamen reminded Dan Small that they had come to see the captain.

"Us brung un some clo's," he added.

Sir Tristram persuaded them that it was not safe to approach his hiding place in daylight, but as the tide would not turn till after midnight, they might come back after dark.

"Jack is much improved," he assured them, "but one arm is very weak. I doubt he'll go to sea again."

"Captain Day would be dead," Octavia interrupted, "if Mr Wynn, who is stuck down there in the mud, had not doctored him. Do let us go to his aid."

Julia, who had been listening in mounting astonishment and indignation, snorted in a sadly unladylike manner.

"I do not care to know about your havey-cavey goings-on," she said coldly, "but since you are all too busy discussing Captain Day's health, I shall doubtless find someone at the quay to assist me." She turned on her heel and set off down the path, then spoiled the effect by running back to call down to James a promise of prompt rescue.

Sir Tristram glanced down the cliff, and such an expression of unholy glee entered his eyes that Octavia was afraid he would start laughing again. She pinched him.

"Come on!" she hissed. "We cannot let her go alone."

They all headed back down the path towards the quay. Fortunately Julia's notion of a rapid walk was much more ladylike than her snort, since Octavia was unable to manage more than a strolling pace. Sir Tristram strode ahead; the four sailors ambled behind, in no great hurry to deliver their victim from his predicament.

When Julia and Octavia reached the quay, Sir Tristram was explaining the situation to the fishermen, and to a crowd of amused wharf and farm labourers who had come out of the alehouse.

The salmon fishers shook their heads. It was nearly low tide; the boats, shallow-draughted as they were, could not be launched for an hour or two, and if they could, it would be impossible to row in close enough to the gentleman to pull him out.

The seamen refused to allow that a mere river could stop them. As soon as rivalry entered the picture, they were full of zeal for the rescue. Their boat, the *Seamew*'s gig, was resting on mud but there was water still at the end of one dock, which had recently been dredged. Enlisting a couple of the sturdiest wharfmen, they pulled it bodily from the riverbed and lowered it again in a couple of feet of water.

The fishermen, meanwhile, not to be outdone, had put on their thigh-boots and waded ankle-deep into the mud to push their dory riverward. Julia ran along the quay, insisting that she must go too, and Octavia, with a tired shrug, followed her. She would have preferred to sit and watch the whole affair, but thought it best not to let her cousin go alone.

Three of the smugglers had climbed into the gig, and its keel was touching bottom. Nonetheless, the Yorkshireman swung the girls into it, followed them, and pushed off hard with a boathook. They slithered into deeper water. The fishing dory came after them, with Sir Tristram, resigned, sitting in the bow.

The tide was slack. Rowing against the Tamar's current, the gig with four oarsmen soon outdistanced the dory. They swung round the grassy curve and the cliff came in sight. At its foot, helpless as a fly in a spider's web, James Wynn lay patiently in his sticky trap some twenty feet from the water's edge.

"He does not seen interested in escaping," observed Octavia. "I expect he is rehearsing his next article in his head."

"James!" cried Julia.

At the sound of her voice, he raised his head a little, then lifted his arm to wave. This gesture pushed his upper body downwards, so he quickly lowered it again.

The fishermen came up beside the smugglers, oarsmen sculling gently to keep their place.

"Un be too var to reach wi' the boathook," confirmed one of the fishers with gloomy satisfaction. "Be a tidy while afore tide'll be up enow."

"Can none of you throw a rope's end accurately enough to reach him?" Sir Tristram demanded irritably of the smugglers. "Fine sailors you are! Jack Day would be ashamed of you."

Octavia thought this somewhat unfair to the Yorkshireman and Dan Small. The missing eye of the one must impair his aim and the missing hand of the other make it difficult to throw at all. However, one of the others found a small coil of rope in the bilge and stood up, preparing to toss one end.

"Wynn, we shall throw a rope to you," called Sir Tristram. "You had best cover your face, but be ready to seize it."

It took four attempts, and James's antics had sunk him several inches deeper before he had a secure hold on his lifeline. The fishermen were shaking their heads and hiding grins, but they said nothing as the smugglers began to haul on the rope.

With a gurgling swish he came free. He slid smoothly across the mud towards the gig, and the gig slid smoothly towards him through the water until the keel slid smoothly into the mud and stopped.

Dan Small cursed and tried to push off with the boathook. It sank into bottomless ooze. He had to stick his hook hand into one of the benches and pull with all the strength of his overdeveloped right arm to retrieve it. The others philosophically ignored the chortles of the river boatmen. They dragged James up to the side of their stranded craft and lifted him in.

Julia embraced him, filth and all.

He was shivering in the blustery wind, but apparently quite unaware of the ridiculous spectacle he had made of himself. He had an innate dignity, or perhaps, thought Octavia, an innate lack of dignity, which protected him from self-consciousness. He thanked the smugglers for rescuing him, without the least suggestion that they had been responsible for his problem in the first place.

"Now we shall pull them off," said Sir Tristram to his crew.

The old man took up his oars. The other two looked doubtful and shook their heads.

"Tide'll float 'em in a while," one of them pointed out.

"There is still half an hour till low tide!" The baronet was clearly growing impatient with the whole business. "Go in closer and take their rope, then row downstream. They cannot possibly pull you onto the mud with them."

"Pray do bring us off!" pleaded Octavia. "Mr Wynn is chilled to the bone and must not wait for the tide."

"Fer missy's zake," urged old Ned Poldhu.

The two younger fishermen gave in and soon both boats were heading back to the quay.

The Edgcumbe Arms, being only an alehouse as the landlady apologetically explained, could not provide better than an attic chamber for Mr Wynn. To this she promised to bear her own tin bathtub and plenty of hot water. Octavia with difficulty persuaded Julia to leave her beloved to the landlady's ministrations. It was past time to change for dinner and Julia herself was sadly in need of a bath.

They left Sir Tristram talking to the smugglers and walked wearily up the drive.

They all arrived at the dinner table several minutes after the gong had sounded. Lady Langston accepted their apologies and excuses with unruffled calm.

"You will not make a habit of it, I know," she said. "I have received a communication from Lord Edgcumbe. He brings a party here again the day after tomorrow and it will not do to be late for dinner while he is here. Fortunately Mrs Pengarth returned this afternoon, in time to make all the arrangements."

Julia looked as if Mrs Pengarth's return brought her no comfort. With their host and his guests about the place it would be difficult or impossible to continue her meetings with James.

Octavis saw her distress and squeezed her hand. "Do not worry," she whispered, "I have an idea. I will tell you after dinner."

"There is a great deal you must tell me!" Julia whispered back.

Miss Crosby frowning her disapproval of this furtive exchange, they both sat up straight and applied themselves to their plates.

Sir Tristram was distrait. He several times answered Lady Langston at random and ate what he was offered without his usual wholehearted enjoyment. When the ladies withdrew he did not go with them as was his custom, but asked Raeburn to bring the brandy.

The girls went to the spinet, where under cover of Julia's idle strumming Octavia explained her idea.

"James shall come the day after tomorrow to stay here!" she declared. "Only think, Lord Edgcumbe will suppose him a guest of my aunt, and she will believe he is a member of that party! I am certain she does not recall his name, for she told me so weeks ago and I made sure not to mention it."

"Tavy! Do you really think it is possible? I am so afraid he is going to be ill after what happened today, but if he was here I could nurse him."

"You will have to be careful. You must pretend to be strangers."

"At least he will be better off here than at that tavern or in the chapel. But when I asked you to post that letter in Plymouth you were unwilling to help us. Why have you changed your mind?"

Octavia pictured James lying on his back in the mud. Julia had not seen him as either ridiculous or pitiable, though he could scarcely have appeared to his beloved in less gallant guise.

"I have come to the conclusion that you will suit very well," she said. "We shall endeavour to convince your mama that he is an eligible gentleman, and then we shall go to work on your papa. After all, he cannot keep you here forever, and when you are back in London you may discover to him that James is to inherit land. Do you suppose you might persuade James to give up the excesses of rhetoric? Sir Tristram said that his views are actually perfectly acceptable when stripped of flowery verbiage."

"I shall try!" Julia assured her grimly. "When we are married he may go back to his sonorous periods. But I fear Papa will never accept him as long as Sir Tristram continues to seek my hand."

Octavia did not want to think about Sir Tristram. "Let me tell you about Captain Day," she proposed.

"Yes, do! What is all this mystery that has been going on under my nose? It is monstrous provoking in you not to have let me into the secret!"

"It was not our secret. Captain Day's life was at stake! But now the worst danger seems to have passed, so there is little risk from a slip of the tongue."

Julia was offended at the suggestion that she could not govern her tongue, but the story fascinated her.

"And he is related to Lord Edgcumbe!" she marvelled. "Well, if the earl is to introduce the captain to the company without arousing suspicion, he will scarce quibble if we do the same for James!"

Sir Tristram lingered long over his brandy, and came into the drawing room only to take his leave. He told Lady Langston that he was called away on business, and begged her leave to return to Cotehele when it was finished. This she granted, though she wondered at his not proposing again to Julia before he went. Not, she thought dolefully, that she had any reason to suppose her daughter now looked on his suit with favour.

Sir Tristram next stopped by the spinet.

"I am going to London for a week or two, as I told you," he said to Octavia. "Our friends will take me to Plymouth on the midnight tide. You will remember what you promised to do for me?"

Her gaze on her clenched hands, Octavia nodded, unable

to speak. She would do her best to stop Julia and James eloping, for their own sakes as much as his.

"Another mystery?" asked Julia in disgust. "What a pair of odious wretches you are, I vow!"

=== 21 ===

"WE OUGHT TO have told Sir Tristram!" wailed Julia, bursting into Octavia's bedchamber at an excessively early hour the next morning. "How shall we smuggle James into the house? There will be no chamber prepared for him and all the guests will know he did not come with them and someone is bound to say something to Mama about him which will give everything away. We do not even know at what time Lord Edgcumbe will arrive!"

Yawning, Octavia tackled the last question first.

"They must arrive no later than the hour of high tide, so all we need to do is find out when that will be."

"The tide! I declare I have no patience with these tides! Why cannot they be the same every day?"

"It is something to do with the moon. Never mind, we shall simply ask Mrs Pengarth, and about the chamber too. She is not like to demur after what James has done for her Jack."

"Oh, yes, I had forgot. Is not James prodigious talented? It is beyond anything! But how shall we bring him into the house?"

"Hush, Ju. Let me think. And wrap yourself in my counterpane, you are shivering."

Julia obeyed, and curled up at the foot of the bed, watching hopefully her cousin's thoughtful frown.

Octavia sighed. "I cannot think of any way to smuggle him in at the moment of Lord Edgcumbe's arrival."

"We had best consult your Captain Day. He is a smuggler, after all!"

"I shall come up with something, only I must find out exactly when they will arrive. What time is it?"

"Just after six, I think."

"Six! Heavens, Ju, even the maids will scarce have risen! I expect Mrs Pengarth will not be up for at least an hour. No wonder I cannot think straight. Go away and let me sleep!"

After breakfast, they found Mrs Pengarth in the housekeeper's room, directing the preparations for the houseparty. She was explaining her orders to Doris, the upper housemaid, in anticipation, Octavia guessed, of her move to Picklecombe Cottage. The prospect of marrying at last the man she had loved for twenty years made her look ten years younger.

Julia announced that they wished to speak to her privately, so she sent Doris off to supervise the other maids and closed the door. Octavia explained the problem.

"My Jack's to be in the Great Hall when they arrive, miss," she said. "Sir Tristram brought instructions from his lordship. They'll be taking luncheon on the river, and they'll get to Cotehele about two o'clock."

"Perfect!" exclaimed Octavia. "I have a plan. Listen!"

She arranged everything with Martha Pengarth, and explained to Ada and Raeburn their part as reserve troops. Then the girls walked down to the Edgcumbe Arms.

A sea mist had blown up the river and enveloped the world in dripping greyness, in Octavia's eyes a perfect day for curling up with a book. If James had been at the chapel still she would not have stirred, but she could not let Julia visit a common tavern on her own.

The shifting mist half hid the bustle of the quayside, and muted the sounds. Farm carts appeared out of nowhere with baskets and sacks of fruit and vegetables. Wharf labourers unloaded them, ready for the barges which would soon arrive on the tide. Kiln workers refilled them with lime for the fields, and they disappeared again into no-where.

Julia tripped into the taproom as if she owned it. A few elderly men drowsed over their pints of cider or ale in the comfortable warmth of a smouldering coal fire. The land-lady bustled forward, all smiles and curtseys.

"Ye'll be come to zee the gentleman, miss? He's in my own zitting room, miss, for there ben't no private parlour. 'Tis not fitting, but there, beggars can't be choosers as the zaying goes."

"Is he well?" asked Julia anxiously.

"Bit of a cough but nowt to worrit over. Land sakes, what a shocking business! Them free-traders is getting too big for their boots, as the zaying goes, but there, there's not a man on the water don't have a hand in it, zaving only them as works for the 'Zise." She ushered them into a tiny closet of a room, where James sat by a glowing fire with his nose in a book.

He looked up at once at the sound of Julia's voice, his face brightening. Octavia turned from their enthusiastic meeting to request a pot of tea. When she turned back decorum was restored and he was explaining that Sir Tristram had brought all his possessions from the chapel last night.

Julia unfolded the plot to smuggle him into the house. He accepted it with a placidity that suddenly reminded Octavia of Lady Langston.

They went back to the house at noon, Octavia insisting that even her aunt would not believe they had taken a picnic on such a day. After luncheon, her ladyship retired as usual to the drawing room for her forty winks, taking Matilda Crosby with her. Miss Crosby had formed the habit of taking a few stitches in my lady's embroidery in the afternoon, leaving my lady with the pleasant impression that she had been industriously engaged in sewing and not sleeping at all. It even looked as if the roses might one day be finished.

The girls returned to the tavern, where Octavia spent the longest and most miserably insipid afternoon she could remember. She tried to concentrate on Julia and James's conversation, so as not to dwell on Sir Tristram's absence.

Had he gone to inform Lord Langston of James's inheritance, thus exposing his rival's whereabouts to the incensed father? Or had he intended his departure to warn her that she must not refine upon a casual kiss? She ought not to have as good as told him she had enjoyed it! But what had he meant with his "devil"?

"Do you think Mama has sent for Mrs Pengarth yet?" Julia interrupted her unhappy thoughts. "Suppose she does not!"

"Then Mrs Pengarth will ask to see her. Do not worry so, goose."

At that very moment, the housekeeper was mendaciously assuring her ladyship that the earl had made a particular point in his instructions of not wishing to disturb her by his arrival.

"You'll not be wanting to sit about in that draughty Great Hall, my lady, specially if it's a mizzly day like today. His lordship will come up to the drawing room to pay his respects."

Lady Langston said serenely that it was very thoughtful of his lordship.

"I shall go down, of course," put in Miss Crosby, "to wait upon Lady Emma."

"Lady Emma's not coming, miss," said Martha Pengarth, not without satisfaction. "So there'll be no cause for you to desert her ladyship."

She left Matilda Crosby looking disconcerted, and went to tell Ada and Raeburn that she thought she had spiked the old maid's guns.

"We'll be ready to head her off if so be 'tis needful," promised Ada.

The next morning, Julia and Octavia fetched James up from the tavern to the cave. Julia was fascinated by the hiding place, and inclined to be highly indignant that she had not been shown it long ago. She also thought it a great adventure to meet Red Jack again now that she knew him to be a master smuggler, though she scolded him for the behaviour of his men. He grinned at her and agreed that it was a poor return for Mr Wynn's medical assistance.

Shortly before two o'clock, all four repaired to the Great Hall. Jack Day, no longer "Red" nor "Captain" since he was turning respectable, walked slowly, his injured arm hanging limp at his side. His clothes hung loose on his haggard frame and his face was pale from his confinement, but he professed to feel very well and there was nothing lacking in the hearty embrace with which he greeted Martha.

Lord Edgcumbe arrived in due course. With him he brought a bluff, good-natured admiral and his wife; his lawyer from London, with wife and daughter; his chaplain, a pompous young man given to quoting Greek and Latin; and Lieutenant Cardin.

Octavia had to admire his choice of guests. Within minutes the admiral was swapping tales of the sea with Jack. The lawyer would take his part if there were any problems with the Excisemen. The chaplain could quietly marry him to Martha in the chapel in the house. For a moment the lieutenant's invitation puzzled her, then she realised that he could hardly arrest a fellow guest of his benefactor, and his presence might serve to deter his colleagues.

His lordship accepted Mr Wynn's presence without a blink. By the time the company met in the drawing room before dinner, the time for formal introductions was over and there was nothing to suggest to Lady Langston that he had not arrived with the rest of the party. Octavia breathed a sigh of relief and hoped that he and Julia would remember to act with circumspection.

Mr Cardin was clearly delighted at the opportunity of being with her daily. At Lord Edgcumbe's request he had been given a week's leave, and he meant to make the most of it. Octavia found herself treating him much as Julia had treated Sir Tristram when she first arrived at Cotehele. She tried to be kind though distant, but it irritated her almost beyond bearing when he always gravitated straight to her side.

The August days were sunny and warm, and the six young people often walked out together. After two days of being ignored or snapped at by Octavia, Mr Cardin turned to the lawyer's daughter. She was a plain young lady, just turned twenty-one, with shy, gentle manners and fifteen thousand pounds. Octavia thought they suited admirably.

The chaplain became her usual escort. She soon discovered that he was perfectly happy with the sound of his own voice. Provided she murmured appreciation when he translated his quotations for her, he left her to her own thoughts.

He would have been excessively shocked had he known how often they ran on the word "devil!"

The author of that "devil" had made record time to London, his spirits in a ferment of wonder at his own blindness and of hopes for the future. After a few hours' sleep in Plymouth he left in the late morning, and spending freely to obtain the best post-horses, he arrived in town at noon on the third day.

Still in his travelling clothes, Sir Tristram went to see his lawyer. That worthy received instructions to set about two tasks: to set his client's affairs in order in preparation for making marriage settlements; and to find out the address of a certain Surrey squire.

Sir Tristram repaired to his hotel, where he scribbled a brief note and sent it round to Bedford House. By the time he had bathed and dressed in clothing more suitable to an evening in London, a reply arrived. Lord John Russell, third son of the Duke of Bedford and Member of Parliament for Tavistock, was in town, happy to hear from his friend, and begged the honour of his presence at dinner that very day.

Lord John's guests were all gentlemen and all politicians of liberal sympathies. Sir Tristram was interested in only two of them, Henry Brougham, one of the founders of the *Edinburgh Review*, and an MP by the name of Gray. To the former he mentioned his recent acquaintance with James Wynn, and heard in response a paean of praise of his genius at writing speeches.

To the latter he mentioned his recent acquaintance with Miss Octavia Gray, and requested permission to call on her parents with news of her.

After dinner he had a brief but highly satisfactory private interview with Lord John, a young man of delicate health and strong reformist principles. They shook hands on their agreement and returned to the rest of the company, where Sir Tristram retired to a corner and fell asleep.

The next morning, upon receipt of a communication from his lawyer, he rode out of town. He spent a pleasant day inspecting a neat small estate of about three thousand pounds per annum, escorted by its master, Mr Thomas Wynn, Esquire, of Surrey. On his ride back to London he pondered the unworldliness that would fail to utilise such a weapon, and shook his head.

On the fifth day since leaving Cotehele, Sir Tristram called in Chapel Street. Lord Langston was pleased to see him, sorry that he had not come to announce his betrothal, distressed at his withdrawal of his suit, astonished to hear him plead his rival's cause, and bewildered at the news that that rival was no penniless scribbler but secretary to Lord John Russell at a goodly salary and heir to a comfortable estate.

The viscount's emotional journey did not end there. He was saddened by his much-loved daughter's misery on first arriving in Cornwall, angered by Mr Wynn's appearance there, disturbed at their mutual joy and devotion, and greatly diverted by the story of the river jump. Finally, wearying of Sir Tristram's insistence, he grew resigned to the unequal match.

"They need not think to have my blessing!" he growled, "but I am too fond of the silly chit to disown her."

Sir Tristram chose to interpret this as permission. With a clear conscience he headed for Doctor's Commons where, for a price, he obtained a Special License from a representative of the Archbishop of Canterbury. He was taking no chances of his lordship changing his mind.

His singing heart sustained him through a day spent with his lawyer. All his property was in excellent order, his tenants satisfied and satisfactory, his investments safe in the Funds. The lawyer ventured to enquire what marriage portion his chosen bride might be expected to bring.

"Nothing!" said Sir Tristram with a grin. "Or at least, she may have something but her parents are undoubtedly more in need of it than she will be."

The lawyer tut-tutted, but added in a fatherly way that it was a pleasure to have a client who had no need to consider dowry when choosing a wife.

The next day was spent in a tall, narrow house in Holborn. Mr and Mrs Gray's civility soon turned to rapture, and they agreed eagerly to his every proposal. Due to the constant coming and going of family, friends, colleagues, and acquaintances, the consultations were barely completed by dinnertime. Though pressed to stay, Sir Tristram pleaded a prior engagement and escaped to his hotel, where he dined alone and retired early to bed, exhausted.

Rising betimes, he was on the road by eight the next morning. As stage after stage passed, bringing him ever nearer to Cornwall, he began to wonder whether he was taking too much for granted.

He had been so stunned to discover it was Octavia he loved that he had thought only of how to free himself as quickly as possible from his obligation to Julia. He had considered it dishonourable to declare his new love while

Lord Langston still laboured under the illusion that he wanted to marry his daughter.

Octavia had no more reason to suppose that he adored her than he had to suppose that she adored him.

Did she care for him? He searched back over the weeks, looking for clues, and saw nothing but friendship. The adventures they had been through together had brought them close, but how zealously she had tried to forward his pursuit of her cousin!

At least he could take her away from that depressing house in Holborn. Even if she did not love him, that must be a point in his favour. He would persuade her that that and friendship were a firm foundation for marriage, for he was very sure he could not live without her. The only insurmountable obstacle he could imagine was if she had given her heart to another.

Unbidden, a vision of Lieutenant Cardin rose before him. The demon jealousy awoke.

He leaned out of the window of the chaise and shouted to the postilion to whip up the horses.

The chaise pulled into the Golden Hind Inn at Plymouth shortly after nine in the evening of the following day. Enquiring after the tides, Sir Tristram learned that he must embark by four in the morning to catch the flood upriver. He gave orders that he should be roused at three.

He woke to brilliant sunshine. Someone had not been told, or had forgotten, or had fallen asleep, or even had not liked to wake the gentleman when he looked so tired. He heard all these excuses in the next hour but since there was nothing to be done about it, he did not trouble to investigate the true reason for his oversleeping.

Since he had slept the clock round, he had only a few hours to wait for the next tide. He spent them searching the jewellers' shops of Plymouth for a ring, but found nothing he considered good enough for Octavia. He boarded a private boat at two, and all the way up the Tamar he sat gnawing his knuckles and trying to compose a speech to do justice to his passion.

He arrived at Cotehele just in time to change for dinner. Impatiently throwing on his clothes, he hurried to the drawing room. He managed to conceal his surprise at the sight of Mr Wynn, apparently perfectly at home there, while he was introduced to those few guests he did not know. The gong sounded as he turned away from the lawyer's daughter with a polite murmur. He found himself taking her down to the Great Hall for an interminable banquet during which Octavia studiously avoided his eye.

At last the ladies withdrew. Sir Tristram beckoned to Raeburn, who was setting out port and brandy.

"Ask Miss Gray to meet me in the chapel in a quarter of an hour," he whispered. "I must talk to her."

A few minutes later, he excused himself and made his way through the empty dining room to the chapel. Octavia came in a moment later, cast one apprehensive glance at his face, and lowered her gaze to her twisting hands.

"You wished to speak to me, sir?" she faltered.

He forgot all his speeches. Falling on one knee, he took her hands in his.

"Will you marry me, Octavia?" he asked simply.

She looked at him aghast.

"I am betrothed to Mr Cardin!" she wailed, burst into tears, and fled.

=== 22 ===

As THE DAYS passed with no word from Sir Tristram, Octavia had become convinced that he had left to escape her. She quickly grew tired of the company of the chaplain and her own miserable thoughts.

Mr Cardin showed no disposition to resent her temporary defection, and she was soon on her old footing with him. She felt guilty at displacing the lawyer's daughter from his side, until that damsel confessed that the lieutenant had constantly sung her praises.

"He admires you excessively," she said. "How lucky you are! I believe he is the kindest gentleman I have ever met."

Octavia began to consider the advantages of marrying the Customs officer. They would be poor, but she was used to that and had no desire to cut a figure in the world. With her thousand pounds and his pay and prize money, they might live comfortably if modestly.

She did not love him, but she was fond of him and felt sure he would be a considerate husband. There was nothing about him she positively disliked.

And the alternative was to return to London, to the dark, noisy house in Holborn that was rapidly becoming a cheerless prison in her memory.

On the day before his return to his duties, he proposed and she accepted.

"I ought to have spoken to your father first," he said anxiously, after his first delight had calmed somewhat. "I won't be able to get leave to go to London. I'll have to write a letter." He sounded daunted at the prospect.

Feeling utterly depressed and deceitful, she uttered a few words of encouragement.

"We'd best not tell anyone else till we have his blessing," the lieutenant continued. "Will he give it, d'you suppose? He won't refuse his permission?"

"I do not believe so. He let my sisters marry where they would. Your profession is respectable and you are bound to rise in it, with Papa's influence as Member of Parliament added to Lord Edgcumbe's support and your own abilities."

"If I do not prosper, it will not be for want of effort," he promised, as pleased with her words as at the most fulsome compliment.

He went back to Plymouth the next day. She missed his cheerful presence, which made her feel happier about what she had done until, two days later, Sir Tristram arrived.

She was furious with him. If he had given her a hint, only a hint, of his feelings before he left, she would never have led on Mr Cardin to the point of making an offer, let alone have accepted it. How could she turn around now and disappoint that frank, good-hearted young man?

But how could she marry him, when she loved Sir Tristram and he, it seemed, loved her?

A rush of joy flooded through her. He loved her! She must think of a way to extricate herself from the bumble-bath she had fallen into, without hurting the poor lieutenant.

Until she had done that, Sir Tristram would have to suffer in suspense, as she had for the past ten days.

Too agitated to return to the drawing room, she retired to her chamber, where she fell asleep fully clothed.

In the chapel, Sir Tristram rose to his feet and sank heavily onto the nearest pew. He was too late: she loved Cardin.

And he had once thought how admirably those two would suit each other!

Unable to face the rest of the company, he retired to bed, where he lay staring blankly into the dark, picturing all the dreadful things he would like to do to the unfortunate lieutenant.

After a restless night, he rose late and went down to breakfast. Only Julia and James Wynn were there, huddled over a newspaper. Julia was in tears.

"Must you really go?" she cried as Sir Tristram entered the dining room.

"I must, my beloved. Sir!" He jumped up. "Have you heard of this shocking business at Manchester? Peterloo, they are calling it."

"Manchester? There was some mention of the city the other day when I was at the Grays', but I fear I did not listen for details. What has happened?"

"A massacre!" Julia told him. "And James says he must go to London at once."

"It was a meeting in St. Peter's Fields. Tens of thousands come to hear Orator Hunt speaking, and the cavalry charged them. Women and children trampled down and sabred, dozens dead, hundreds wounded. Hunt himself was arrested and badly beaten. You see, I must go immediately."

"Ye gods! Let me see the paper." Sir Tristram scanned it rapidly. "Yes, I believe Lord John will need you, but do not act precipitately."

"Lord John?" asked Julia. "Who is he?"

Sir Tristram nonchalantly explained that he had obtained employment for Mr Wynn with one of the foremost Reformist parliamentarians of the age.

"Of course there are scores of younger sons seeking a position with him," he told the astounded young man. "He knew you by reputation, but what swung the balance was your medical training. His constitution is delicate, but he hates to be reminded of it. He dislikes having a doctor always in the house almost as much as having to send out for one. As his secretary and speech writer, you will be able to care for him unobtrusively. I hope you do not dislike the scheme?"

"Oh, no!" stammered James. "I have a great admiration for Lord John Russell and it will be an honour to work with him. But how can I thank you?"

"Hold your thanks until you hear the rest of my meddling! I went to see your father, Miss Langston."

He described the result of that interview, and produced the Special License. Julia seized it, hugged him, and became suddenly very practical.

"Captain Day and Mrs Pengarth are to be married this afternoon in the chapel," she said, "and the earl will take them with the rest of his guests to Mount Edgcumbe this evening. We shall be wed at the same time, James, and go with them. Then tomorrow we shall cross over to Plymouth, hire a post-chaise and leave for town. Do you go and explain to Lord Edgcumbe while I tell Ada to start packing, and oh dear! how am I to break the news to Mama? Does Octavia know, sir?"

"I have not told her," he said with heightened colour.

"She went down to the valley garden. I shall need her support when I tell Mama. Would you be so kind, Sir Tristram, as to send a footman to find her for me? I never thought to be married in such a rush, I vow, but it is vastly exciting! James, my love, I shall see you in the chapel at half past two!"

She danced out, leaving the gentlemen breathless.

"I daresay you would like my support when you tell Edgcumbe," suggested Sir Tristram, seeing James's bewilderment. "If you do not mind waiting, I believe I had best go and find Miss Gray first. Excuse me."

She was sitting in the arbour by the pond. The wren and its family had long since abandoned their nest in the thatch, water lilies had replaced the faded iris, but white pigeons still cooed on the roof of the dovecote and huge carp swam lazily in the still water. He watched her watching them, wondering what her dreamy smile meant.

She saw him. He bowed, and said the only words that came into his head.

"Your cousin has urgent need of you, Miss Gray, and begs you to go to her at once."

Alarmed, she jumped up and started up the path.

"Tell her you will go with her to Mount Edgcumbe tonight," he said urgently as they hurried towards the house.

"To Mount Edgcumbe?"

"Please!"

"If you wish." She glanced at him in puzzlement.

Ada ran round the corner of the house to meet them.

"I'm that flurried, miss!" she gasped. "Miss Julia sent me to fetch you. She's all of a twitter how to tell my lady and there's the packing to be done, and it don't seem right with no bride clothes somehow. I'm to go to London with her."

"Bride clothes? To London! Whatever is Ju up to now?" Octavia quickened her steps.

Julia poured the story into her astonished ears. It was difficult not to reciprocate with the news that she was engaged to Mr Cardin and that Sir Tristram wanted to marry her too. Today was Julia's day, though, and she allowed her cousin to drag her to the White Bedroom, where Lady Langston was still abed. She was not certain she understood the details herself, but she did her best to explain to her aunt calmly and reasonably.

Not unnaturally, even that somnolent lady was roused to agitation by the news that her only daughter was to be married in a few hours' time, with her father's permission, to a gentleman she had thought a stranger. Or perhaps an assassin, she was not sure which. And then to dash off to London because there had been a massacre in Manchester! It was all highly irregular, and her ladyship collapsed in a most uncharacteristic Spasm.

Waving Julia away, Octavia set herslf to soothing her

aunt's overwhelmed sensibilities. In this she succeeded so well, that at a quarter past two she settled Lady Langston in a front pew in the chapel, dressed in finery to suit the occasion.

"But I will not rush off to Mount Edgcumbe on such short notice!" her ladyship whispered, detaining her. "Let alone to London!"

"Of course not, ma'am. Miss Crosby will stay with you. I shall come back tomorrow and we will make plans to return at leisure." She slipped away to attend the bride.

With all due ceremony, the Earl of Mount Edgcumbe gave away two brides that afternoon, the daughter of his friend Viscount Langston to a political scribbler of radical views, and his housekeeper to his relative, the free-trader. Known for his acting ability, he let nothing of what he was thinking appear on his face.

A magnificent wedding banquet followed, cut short only by the necessity of sailing with the tide. It was a merry group that floated down the Tamar by the light of flaring flambeaux and arrived at Mount Edgcumbe late that night.

Chambers were hastily made up for the unexpected guests. As the party dispersed to their rest, Sir Tristram pressed Octavia's hand.

"We shall escort Mr and Mrs Wynn to Plymouth tomorrow," he said in a voice that brooked no argument. "I must talk to you, and I have business there." If he could not persuade her to marry him, to tell Mr Cardin that she was mistaken in her sentiments, he would set off for Gloucestershire at once. The prospect of returning to his peaceful, solitary life at Dean Park now seemed odious.

She looked up at him enigmatically. "Yes," she said, "I must see my cousin safe on her way. Good night."

He kissed her hand, and she went away to sleep with it pressed to her cheek.

In spite of Mr Wynn's hurry to leave for London, he and his rosy-cheeked bride did not come down until nearly noon, when they appeared with their arms entwined about each other in a total disregard for propriety.

Sir Tristram looked dispassionately at Julia's glowing face. She was beautiful, certainly, but he had not the least desire to spend the rest of his life with her. Even when he had thought himself in love with her, he had had difficulty imagining her settled quietly at Dean Park. She was destined to become a brilliant political hostess, like Lady Holland or Lady Melbourne. He envied neither her nor James for anything but their obvious happiness together.

Octavia had been chatting intimately with the lawyer's daughter all morning, ignoring his discreet attempts to attract her attention. The fear that she truly loved the lieutenant grew till it seemed to choke him.

It was mid-afternoon before Mr and Mrs Wynn and Ada and a large quantity of baggage were safely packed up inside and outside a hired chaise at the Golden Hind. Last good-byes were exchanged, the postilion urged the horses on, and the carriage rumbled out of the yard with Julia hanging out of the window waving happily.

Octavia looked up at a nearby church clock.

"We must hurry!" she exlaimed. "The tide turned half an hour ago and I promised my aunt to return today."

"I must talk to you!"

"Not now. There will be time later."

He followed at her heels down the busy street to the harbour, unwilling to embark upon a private conversation in the midst of a crowd but determined not to go back to Cotehele while she was engaged to the lieutenant.

When they reached the quayside, she turned to him.

"Will you hire a boat?" she requested breathlessly. "I sent a note to Mr Cardin this morning and he will be waiting for me, I hope."

Not waiting for an answer, she dashed off towards the Customs House. She was excessively eager to see her betrothed, he thought.

He found a boat willing to sail upriver and hired it, with

a sinking feeling that Octavia would sail alone on it. When he turned back towards the Customs House, Mr Cardin had come out. Her hand tucked into his arm, Octavia was walking up and down with him, talking earnestly.

Utterly dejected, he sat down on a bollard and watched them.

After a few minutes, they came towards him. As he stood up, he tried to read the lieutenant's face. It displayed none of the hoped for misery that would have signalled a disappointed suitor, looking more perplexed than anything else.

"I daresay I ought to call you out, sir," said Mr Cardin hesitantly.

Sir Tristram's heart leapt.

"I beg you will not," he responded with forced calmness. "I've no desire either to hurt you or to be forced to flee the country."

"I should lose my place in the Service if I fought a duel."

"Then you may consider the challenge issued, I shall beg your forgiveness, and the matter may be forgotten. Indeed, I am sorry to have caused you pain, but it is a female's prerogative to change her mind, you know."

"And a male's to blame his misdeeds on female inconstancy," said Octavia tartly. "If you had only *told* me . . . !"

"You will excuse us, Mr Cardin," said Sir Tristram, grinning. "I prefer to quarrel with Octavia privately."

The lieutenant saluted and went off with a tolerably unafflicted air.

"How very unflattering," said Octavia with a sigh, as he helped her down the stone steps to the waiting boat. "Instead of being cast into the dismals he was anxious to learn how long Miss Newell is to stay at Mount Edgcumbe. I should never have told him that she admires him prodigiously. Female inconstancy is nothing to it!"

He lifted her aboard and they sat down. The sailors cast

off. As they pulled away from the quay, he took her hand and held it tight.

"Alas," he confessed, "I cannot claim to be a paragon in that respect."

"No, and you are quite as unflattering as he! Would you not have fought a duel for me?"

"Of course I would, my darling, but it seemed wasteful to risk depriving you of two prospective husbands at once." He laughed joyously.

She leaned her head against his shoulder and they sat in companionable silence watching the sailors run about raising sails.

After a while, she asked shyly, "It is not because you cannot have Julia that you want to marry me? Just to keep your brother-in-law from Dean Park?"

"I think I fell in love with you when you fell in the water," he said contemplatively as they sailed between Cremyll and Devil's Point. "The splash made my heart stand still. But I did not realise until I kissed you that there was a great deal more warmth in my cousinly affection for you than in my supposed adoration of your cousin. In the well-worn phrase, it struck me like a thunderbolt." He turned his head as if to kiss her for the second time.

She shook her head, with heightened colour, and quickly asked, "Why did you not tell me then, instead of making ambiguous remarks about the devil?"

"About the devil? Did I really? Was that before or after you told me you had enjoyed my kiss?"

"I did not!" Her cheeks grew still rosier. "I said I had enjoyed *it*. I meant you to think I referred to the scramble down the shortcut."

"Now who is ambiguous! My love, my love, you were so ambiguous I had no idea whether you cared for me in the least or not!"

"I do," she assured him earnestly, "very much! Ever since you called me 'sweetheart' to deceive the dragoons."

He laughed and hugged her.

"The sailors!" she hissed, disengaging herself reluctantly.

A thought struck him. "My brother-in-law! What do you know of my brother-in-law?"

She was forced to confess to her eavesdropping in the chapel, which made him laugh and hug her again.

When they passed Halton Quay, Octavia at once noticed the scarlet petticoat hanging prominently on the washing line.

"Red Jack left just in time," she said. "Look, the Excisemen are back. I hope the Riding Officer and his dragoons have not scared my aunt half to death."

"If they have, I shall scare them half to death," said Sir Tristram grimly. "However, I expect they are merely searching the cargo of your friend Captain Pilway."

The light was fading when they reached Cotehele Quay, but they could see that all the wharves were occupied. On the quay a swarm of dragoons inspected the contents of every basket as it was swung ashore. The hired boat pulled up to the reed-grown bank just south of the little harbour.

Sir Tristram swung Octavia ashore safely and made to follow her. He lost his footing, slipped, and landed knee-deep in mud.

Standing there, hands on hips, he shook his head in rueful disgust.

"It serves you right for laughing so heartily at poor Mr Wynn when he jumped off the cliff," said Octavia severely. "But all the same, I shall help you out. Take my hand."

He looked at her, suddenly serious. "Don't offer me your hand unless you really mean it," he said. "If I take it, I shall never let you go for the rest of my life."

She held out both hands.

Squelching, he pulled himself out onto the bank and took her in his arms.

"How could I have been such a clunch as to have spent all that time chasing that wretched cousin of yours," he marvelled.

"And how could I have been such a featherhead as to have done my best to persuade her to have you?"

They looked at each other, half laughing, then he bent his head and kissed her long and hard.

A cheer arose from the smugglers, from the Customs men, and from the wharf labourers. Octavia blushed furiously as Sir Tristram looked up and waved.

Then he kissed her again.

NOTE

Cotehele now belongs to the National Trust, Mount Edgcumbe to the City of Plymouth and the Cornwall County Council. Both are open to the public and well worth a visit.